THE SPANISH WITCH

She was a Spaniard – and beyond his reach...

When Doña Magdalene d'Ortega was summoned to take her place next to Nicholas Treggaron, Queen Elizabeth's envoy, at dinner with the King Philip of Spain, little did she guess that her days of innocence were numbered. Soon she would be caught up in the nightmare of the Inquisition, and accused of witchcraft and heresy. Treggaron was prepared to disobey his Queen to save her, but what would he demand in return? When Doña Magdalene learnt the true nature of his mission, would she turn from him in hatred?

THE SPANISH WITCH

The Spanish Witch

by

Anne Herries

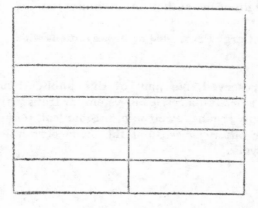

Magna Large Print Books
Long Preston, North Yorkshire,
BD23 4ND, England.

British Library Cataloguing in Publication Data.

Herrie, Anne
    The Spanish witch.

    A catalogue record of this book is
    available from the British Library

    ISBN   0-7505-2274-7

First published in Great Britain 1987 by Mills & Boon Ltd.

Copyright © Anne Herries 1987

Cover illustration © Len Thurston by arrangement with
P.W.A. International Ltd.

The moral right of the author has been asserted

Published in Large Print 2004 by arrangement with
Linda Sole

Magna Large Print is an imprint of Library Magna Books Ltd.

Printed and bound in Great Britain by
T.J. (International) Ltd., Cornwall, PL28 8RW

CHAPTER ONE

'You are a liar, sir, and I demand that you retract the accusations made here against me!' A shocked hush fell across the assembled company as Lord Chevron's words rang out.

All eyes turned towards the man who had caused Chevron's outburst. Taller than most of the richly-garbed courtiers strolling in the sunlit gardens of Whitehall, his hair was as black as the mood which gripped him. At this moment his blue eyes were diamond hard, his chiselled features set like granite as he regarded the man he had come to kill.

'I repeat the charge,' Nicholas Treggaron said, each word clipped and cold. 'You are a seducer of innocent maidens and a murderer.'

An excited buzz ran through the watchers who had gathered round, fascinated by the drama. It was obvious that Treggaron meant to provoke a duel if he could. It was an audacious act, here in the grounds of Her Majesty's palace, and could cause the hot-tempered Cornishman to be banished from Court if it came to Elizabeth's ears.

Fear flickered over Lord Chevron's

handsome but weak face, and he cursed the ill-luck which had brought him into direct contact with Treggaron. He knew, as those watching did not, that the Cornishman had been trying to bring about a public confrontation for several days, now he had achieved his aim and there was no escape. He must challenge his accuser or stand convicted of cowardice, as well as of the baser crimes of rape and murder.

Gripping an embroidered leather glove in hands he could hardly keep from shaking, Chevron took three steps towards the taller man. He paused for a moment, forcing his lips to a scornful sneer, knowing that everyone was watching and judging his performance. He was not a popular man at Court, though his family was an old and respected one – not like this upstart Cornishman who had come to favour merely because his bold manners pleased the Queen! A surge of indignation gave him the courage to slap Treggaron's face with his glove.

'You will be good enough to name your seconds, sir?'

'Certainly.' A chilling smile curved Treggaron's lips. A smile so confident that it struck terror into the heart of his victim. 'Sir Ralph Goodchild and Anton Barchester have offered to support me, sir.'

The two seconds named were both from

the same stable, Chevron realised, all hope of an attempt at peacemaking by the Cornishman's friends fading. Like Treggaron they had achieved their positions at Court because they were young, bold-eyed, and daring rogues. It was rumoured that all three sailed under letters of marque from Elizabeth, attacking any Spanish vessel unlucky enough to cross their paths. They hunted like a pack of dogs – and this time he was their quarry! Chevron paled as he looked from Treggaron to the equally determined faces of the men standing a few paces behind him. He had received a death sentence, and he knew it.

Controlling his fear as best he could, Chevron named his own seconds, bowed and walked on, trying not to hear the titters of amused bystanders, most of whom were not deceived by his show of bravado.

'By God, you've done it, Nick!' Anton Barchester exclaimed, clapping his friend on the shoulder. 'I never thought you'd bring the cowardly dog up to scratch, but you've pulled it off.'

The blue eyes glinted with an icy amusement as Nick turned to his friend. 'He had no choice, if he wishes to show his face at Court again. He may be a swine, but he has some pride. Besides, if he had not challenged me to a duel I would have taken a horsewhip to him. For what he did to

11

Catherine and Jack, he deserves to die.'

The other men murmured their agreement. Returning to England ten days previously from a successful voyage, they had all been stunned by the news that awaited them. Treggaron's lovely young cousin Catherine had been married to her childhood sweetheart Jack Harston for a year this spring. A young man of gentle manners and modest means, Jack had set up home with his new wife in a house provided for them by Nick, a few miles from Treggaron Manor. Having lived most of her life at the manor, Catherine had assumed the duties of chatelaine, and she continued to cast an eye over her cousin's household while he was away at sea. It was when she was walking home one summer evening that she was set upon by a party of drunken bucks out on a spree. She had put up a courageous fight, but was knocked almost senseless and raped by at least three of the brutes. When her husband found her stumbling through the woods hours later, she was able to name only one of her attackers before collapsing in his arms. She had died that night of her injuries, and in the morning her gentle young husband set out with vengeance in his heart. He had not stood a chance against Chevron, having scarcely touched a sword before that day. He had been cut down without mercy and was buried beside his beloved wife in the ground of the little church where his wedding vows had been taken such a short time before.

Almost a year had passed since then, and no doubt Chevron had believed himself safe from retribution. Now he knew that he was mistaken! Recalling the fear he had witnessed in the other man's eyes, Nick's mouth thinned with scorn. At least one of Catherine's murderers would pay the penalty for his crime, but there were still two others.

'Ralph, I want you to attend on Chevron at his lodgings. Tell him you may be able to persuade me to spare him if he gives you the names of his accomplices that day...'

'You won't spare that swine?' Anton exclaimed. 'If you haven't the stomach for it, I'll do it myself.'

'Patience, my hot-headed friend.' Nick's eyes gleamed with sudden laughter. 'Do you not want all three of them dead? Ralph will promise only to try to persuade me – he will not succeed.' He glanced at Sir Ralph. 'I am sorry to ask it of you, my friend, but I fear Chevron's secret will die with him unless you can prise it from him.'

Ralph nodded, looking thoughtful. He was a large, slow-speaking man, less inclined to acts of rashness than his companions; but he too had sworn that Catherine's murderers should pay for their foul deeds with their lives.

'I must do it,' he said at last, 'for you cannot, and Anton would give the game away with those fierce looks of his. No man in his right man would believe him a peacemaker.'

'Nor you if they knew you!' Anton retorted with a grin.

'Fortunately, Chevron does not know him,' Nick said, his eyes going cold. 'I don't believe his lordship was the leader of those brutes – he hasn't the guts for it unless spurred on by another. The other two must have been strangers, or Cathy would have known them... My God, I wish I'd been there when she needed me.' His face creased with pain. 'She was only a child.'

Ralph's large, sun-browned hand clasped his shoulder. 'No one could have known it would happen, Nick. Don't blame yourself. Catherine wouldn't want that.'

'No, but she does want vengeance. I hear her voice in my dreams. She cries out to me to avenge her.'

'And you will,' Sir Ralph said. 'Chevron is as good as dead.'

'But two more escape unpunished,' Nick replied bitterly. 'I swear that I shall not rest until they are...' His words trailed away as he saw a man striding purposefully towards them. 'Damn! Here comes someone I would rather not meet just now.' He turned away, but was stopped by the commanding voice which rang out clearly.

'Treggaron, hold! I must speak with you.'

'Sir, I have pressing business elsewhere.'

'Ay, so I've heard.' Sir Francis Drake glared at him. 'Damn you for a fool, man! Do you not know what you have done? Her Majesty is incensed. She hates quarrels at Court, and Chevron has his friends. Surely you could have chosen a less public place to provoke him?'

'Possibly – but I wanted to be sure of him, so...'

'So you chose to endanger our work? You know we need Elizabeth's goodwill if we are to continue harassing the Spanish treasure-ships. Although Spain's ambassador Mendoza was expelled for plotting against the throne, he continued to work with the Guises on Mary Queen of Scots' behalf – and they will seek revenge for her death in whatever way they can. Through the French ambassador the devious work goes on, and the Queen is always being pressed to do something about "those accursed pirates", as they call us.'

'Her Majesty should tell Philip of Spain to send his armada against us: we'll sweep it from the seas!'

'Bold words, Treggaron!' Sir Francis frowned. 'You had best repeat them to the Queen. She requests your attendance on her at once.'

'Could you not tell her you were too late to stop me leaving?'

'And pay for it with a sojourn in the Tower? I have more respect for Her Majesty than you, sir. Come with me now – or must I arrest you?'

Nick laughed suddenly. 'No, for I have no love of the Tower either, my friend. I shall come with you and win Her Majesty's consent to the duel when she learns the truth.'

'Ay, perhaps you will.' Sir Francis allowed his stern features to relax slightly. 'You're a bold rogue – and Elizabeth always had a fondness for those with the courage to ride out her storms!'

'As you yourself know full well,' Nick retorted. 'Lead on, sir, we must not keep Her Majesty waiting...'

'Are you ready, Magdalene?' The dark-haired girl's face stiffened as she saw her cousin in the white satin gown she herself had chosen. The gown was as plain as it was possible to make it without disgracing them all, and there was only a thick rope of pearls with a heavy silver cross around Magdalene's slender throat; but she looked magnificent, needing no other ornament but the raven dark gleam of her abundant hair. 'Father is waiting. Surely you must be ready by now!'

16

'I have been ready for some time, Isabella. I was waiting for you. I could not go down without you, could I?'

Isabella d'Ortega's eyes flickered with annoyance. She knew her cousin had behaved correctly, but she was feeling nervous, and Magdalene's beauty had disturbed her. Supposing Don Rodrigo Cortijo was attracted to Magdalene instead of to her? Tonight she would meet her betrothed for the first time, and though she knew that nothing could break the marriage contract Rodrigo had signed without ever setting eyes on his future bride, she was uneasy when she looked at the other girl. Remembering that Magdalene would soon be betrothed to Don Sebastian de Valermo gave her scant reason to rejoice. The Don was old enough to be Magdalene's father, and Isabella had expected her cousin to refuse the match stubbornly. That she had not done so was a surprise to both the Ortegas, and father and daughter were suspicious of her docility.

It was not usual for Magdalene to be so meek. Despite the modesty of her gown and jewellery this evening, chosen purposely so that she should not outshine her plainer cousin, Magdalene was a considerable heiress. Although her fortune was in her uncle's control until her marriage, the girl was aware of her power. She could have demanded a younger, more exciting bridegroom, but seemingly she was content with the match. Isabella could not understand why. Rodrigo was both young and handsome; she had fallen in love with his likeness when she first saw the miniature he had sent her as a betrothal gift, and she was terrified that something would happen to prevent the marriage she longed for.

Seeing the jealousy in her cousin's eyes, Magdalene sighed. She had allowed Isabella to choose her gown this evening, hoping to reassure her that she had no wish to steal Don Rodrigo from her, but it was useless. Isabella had always been jealous, and nothing would change that. Sometimes Magdalene wished that she had been born ugly and penniless; perhaps then she and Isabella could have been friends. It would of course have been easier for them both if fate had not forced them to live beneath the same roof. If only her father, Don Manuel d'Ortega, had no insisted on taking that last trip to the New World...

Tears pricked Magdalene's eyes as she remembered her mother's face the day the news of his death had arrived. She had slipped to the floor unconscious, lingering on in a twilight world until she, too, was gone, leaving Magdalene to live on as her uncle's ward. A widower himself, Don José had welcomed her kindly enough to his home, but she knew he would have been less generous had it not been for the huge fortune that was now hers. Like Isabella, he was jealous of the wealth that Don Manuel had brought back. Time and again Don Manuel had braved the long sea journey, returning with his ships loaded down with silver. His fleet had been waylaid by pirates on several occasions, but he had beaten off the attacks until that last fatal encounter.

There was no point in sighing for the past; Magdalene had realised that long ago. She was sorry that her uncle and cousin resented her wealth, but pride prevented her from despairing. And she was proud of the father she had adored and her gentle mother, despite the fact that Doña Maria had been born in England. It was from Mary Fisher, the daughter of an English merchant, that Magdalene had inherited her exquisite complexion. Although her skin was not as white as her mother's had been, the girl was careful to protect it from the sun's destroying glare. She never walked in the garden without a lace mantilla to protect her skin, and spent long hours sitting in a shaded room when often she would have preferred to stroll in the olive groves behind her uncle's country house. It was expected of her that she should behave in a restrained, ladylike manner, however, for she was the daughter of an important man, and she would marry into one of the best families in Spain.

It was because she had been reared to accept her destiny that Magdalene was prepared to marry Don Sebastian de Valermo. Although he was several years her senior, he was exactly the type of man her father would have chosen for her. His breeding was impeccable, he was wealthy in his own right, and his manners were always correct. He was also a kind, considerate man who would be a god husband to her and she was content with the prospect of being his wife. The Don would make few demands on her and she would be free to continue in her own way... It was at his house that the banquet was to be held this evening. The house that was soon to be her home.

'Are you coming? Father will be impatient. We have some distance to travel.'

Isabella's petulant voice interrupted the girl's thoughts. She nodded, holding back the angry retort she might have made. It was Isabella who had caused the delay by changing her mind about her gown at the last minute. The heavy crimson velvet she had finally chosen did little to flatter her olive-toned colouring, Magdalene thought, wondering why her cousin had discarded the pale peach silk which had been specially made for this evening. Could it be because she had admired it earlier? Surely not! Could even Isabella be as foolish as that?

Magdalene's face was sober as she followed her cousin from the room and along the dark passage. If Isabella disliked her so much, it would be best if her marriage were to take place as soon as possible. There would then be no reason for the cousins to meet, except on the rare occasions when the two families came together at Court gatherings.

Watching as Isabella ran down the last few steps of a wide stone stairway, Magdalene felt a stab of envy. Don José was fond of his daughter and it showed in his smile of welcome. It was a long time since anyone had smiled at herself in just that way, and she realised how much she missed the warmth of her parents' love. For a moment the pain was unbearable, but she hastily shut it out.

Lifting her head a fraction higher, Magdalene schooled her features to a calmness she was far from feeling. It did not matter that the smile left her uncle's eyes as he looked at her. Soon she would be Don Sebastian's wife, and then she would be free to spend her time sewing or dreaming in her quiet little room, safe from the outside world and the spite of her cousin. Then no one would ever be able to hurt her again. She had suffered enough grief to last her a lifetime, but she would never feel the pain of losing a loved one again. Her husband would be kind, but he would not love her and she would not love him… It was the only arrangement acceptable to Magdalene, and she was thankful that it had been pressed on her by her uncle. It was easy to accept his demands when they suited her own wishes so exactly.

'If you do not hurry we shall be late, Magdalene,' Don José said sharply. 'Should we arrive after His Majesty, we could not take our places at the banquet, and it would be a grievous insult to the King. He is giving this entertainment in honour of the English envoys, and you have been invited because you speak their language fluently. You may well be called upon to translate. I hope you are aware of the honour?'

'I do not believe I shall be needed, uncle. His Majesty was married to Mary Tudor – he must be as capable of understanding the English ambassadors as I, and so must several of his ministers.'

'Indeed, that may be so, but these men must be shown every courtesy while they are here. You will be seated next to one of them and you must endeavour to entertain him. King Philip is anxious to create a favourable impression this evening.'

'Don Sebastian told me that His Majesty is preparing for war against England…'

'Precisely.' Don Ortega's clipped tones silenced her. 'But we are not yet ready to invade England. It will be many months –

perhaps years – before we have sufficient ships to form an armada. Even now there are quarrels over who should be given command of the fleet – and all the while these accursed English dogs attack us and sink our vessels!'

'And you expect me to be pleasant to one of these men?' Magdalene asked, her tone dangerously quiet. A terrible anger was beating in her brain and she had to fight very hard to control it. 'Have you forgotten that my father died because of such a man?'

A rusty colour swept up Don José's neck and into his plump cheeks. 'No, I have not forgotten, but you must do your duty. His Majesty commands it, and you will obey. Besides, these men are courtiers, not pirates; you can be sure that none of those devils would dare to set foot on Spanish soil – they know they would never leave it alive. They would be arrested, condemned as heretics by the Inquisition, and burned at the stake.'

Magdalene regarded him thoughtfully. She could not hate all the English as many of her countrymen did, because her own mother had come from that land, but she could and did hate all those who were little better than murderers, roaming the seas like a pack of wolves in search of prey. One of them had sent her father to a watery grave, and though she would never know his

23

name, she hated him – hated him and all his kind with a fierceness that sometimes made her want to strike out in revenge. It was at those moments that the pain of her loss became unbearable and then she would retreat to her own little world. Only when she knelt in prayer in the coolness of the chapel could she forget her grief.

'You are right, uncle,' she said at last. 'Such a man would be a fool to risk his life by coming to Spain. Besides, the English Queen would not dare to insult His Majesty by sending a pirate as her envoy. Very well, I shall obey your wishes and do as the King requests.'

'Good. I knew you would accept your duty.' Don José gave her an approving nod. He had suggested that his niece's unfortunate connection with England might come in useful, and he was hoping for some recognition for his services to the crown. 'Now, the carriage awaits, and we must delay no longer.'

'This place is like a tomb!' Sir Ralph shivered, eyeing his companion with quiet amusement. Nicholas Treggaron was dressed as richly as any Spanish don in his gleaming gold and white satin, a large diamond drop dangling from one ear. 'It puzzles me why they shut out the sunlight all the time; you'd think they'd be used to it.'

24

'You would be the first to complain of the heat if the shutters were open all day! But I know what you mean, I've felt it myself.'

Nick let his eyes wander round the spacious apartment he had been given for the duration of his visit. The stone walls were covered with blue-green tiles to shoulder height, and the furniture was heavy, carved, dark wood. The windows were small and barred with intricate ironwork, the floors of grey marble. The result was a cool, quiet atmosphere that reminded him of a church, and he found himself longing for the mellow softness of English oak and the smell of lavender scented beeswax. He shrugged, a wry smile twisting his mouth.

'We're not here for our own pleasure, Ralph, so stop complaining. The sooner our mission is completed, the sooner we can go home.'

'I'd as lief have taken the Tower as this mission,' Sir Ralph said gloomily.

'And the Tower it would have been had I refused,' Nick mocked him. 'Her Majesty forbade the duel and arrested Chevron. She has promised that he will be forced to disclose the names of his accomplices before he faces a trial.'

'The poor devil would have been better off if he'd died at the point of your blade!'

'Ay, I believe you.' Nick's carved features were grim, as he pictured the methods the questioners would use if Chevron proved stubborn. 'There's little difference between a Spanish torture chamber and an English one, I'll wager.'

Sir Ralph saw the flicker of pain in his friend's eyes and frowned. 'Your father – it still hurts you after all these years?'

'He was a broken man when the Inquisition had finished with him, Ralph. I sometimes think it would have been better if they had killed him. I watched him die slowly, little by little. By heaven! If I ever get my hands on any of those devils…'

'Hush, my friend, remember where you are. Even though these walls are thick, they may have ears pressed against them.'

'Ay, and we're here to promote peace. Peace!' Nick laughed harshly. 'Elizabeth has a wicked sense of humour, has she not? I wonder what she would have done if we'd refused the mission?'

'Hung us as pirates and sent our heads to the Spanish King as a gift, I dare say.'

There was a gleam of humour in Sir Ralph's dark eyes, and Nick smiled. 'At least she was wise enough not to send Anton with us! He could not have contained his temper long enough to greet our host, let alone get through his accursed banquet tonight.'

'Given in our honour,' Sir Ralph reminded him. 'We should leave now, if we don't wish to be late.'

'I could wish myself a thousand leagues away,' Nick replied honestly. 'But Her Majesty's commands must be obeyed, even though it chokes me to mouth pleasantries when I'd rather stick a blade...' Ralph shook his head and Nick grinned, the hot anger dying as swiftly as it had flared into being. 'Ay, there'll be plenty of that another time – when this farce is over. Come on then, man, why do you tarry?'

'I'm lost in wonder at your sartorial splendour,' Sir Ralph quipped. 'Is this truly the same Nicholas Treggaron who can strike terror into the heart of any laggard sea-dog?' He choked with laughter at the indignation on Nick's face. 'Peace, my friend! I could not resist the jest.'

'You would not have me shame Her Majesty by appearing in leather trunks and a salt-stained jerkin?' Nick's brows went up. 'Are you afraid I shall outshine you?'

As Sir Ralph's clothes were of a sombre hue, though fashioned of the finest materials, the question brought only a wry twist of his lips. The two men were like brothers in their devotion to one another; the ties between them forged in the heat of many a battle, when only their skill and daring stood between them and certain death. Yet this mission was perhaps the most dangerous they had ever undertaken. Both knew that if their true identity were even suspected they would be arrested and handed over to the Inquisition. It was sheer madness to have accepted the Queen's challenge, but neither man would have considered refusing once it was offered.

Elizabeth's eyes had gleamed when her proposal was so promptly accepted. She knew what these men risked, and their boldness delighted her.

'I know Philip of Spain is my enemy,' she had said. 'He would have me believe otherwise, but he has always coveted my crown. Since I will not share it with him, mayhap he thinks to wrest it from me. Go to him with gifts and smiles, my brave friends. Talk of peace, but use your eyes and those keen wits that have kept you safe from these men before. I know that I can trust you to bring me back the truth. You are not fools, like some who serve me! You will not be taken in by false smiles and honeyed words.'

There was no refusing the request which was in reality a command. Robbed of his revenge by the Queen's intervention, Nick could only accept that Chevron would be punished according to the laws of England, which meant that he would hang and his body be left for the crows to eat as it rotted on the gibbet. Having no choice in the matter, Nick and his companion rode to Portsmouth that same night, where they provisioned *Treggaron Rose* and set sail on the morning tide. An uneventful voyage had brought them to Cadiz, whence they rode to Jerez, where they were the guests of a wealthy merchant who had established trading links with England for his fine wines, and was therefore concerned that peace should be established between the two countries. The man was honest enough in his own way, but neither Nick nor Ralph trusted him completely. A Spaniard was a Spaniard, and hatred of the race ran deep in both of them.

They managed to control their feelings, however, as all three left to attend the banquet being held in the house of a nobleman who had offered his house as neutral ground for the talks which were to take place in the days following this evening's entertainment. Don Sebastian de Valermo had a reputation, even in England, as a man of honour, and it was because he had personally guaranteed their safety that the two Englishmen had been prepared to venture so far from their ship.

They were met in the courtyard by the Don himself, elegantly dressed in black velvet, which complemented the silver of his hair and beard.

'Welcome to my house, señores. I am honoured by your presence in my home,' he said, making a courtly bow. 'His Majesty will join us shortly. Please will you come with me now?' He turned to lead the way inside.

The house was really a small palace, Nick thought, as he saw the size of it. A Moorish influence was evident in the arches and domed roofs of the pavilions that enclosed several secret gardens where fountains played into tiny pools and little streams meandered among orange and lemon trees heavy with unripened fruit. The house itself was shaded and cool, with tiled walls and small windows, but the Don was a cultured man who had filled his home with beautiful things from every corner of the world. Precious silks from the east softened the coldness of marbled arches; Persian carpets covered tables and were even scattered on the floors as if to proclaim the man's wealth, while the gleam of silver was evident in candelabra, huge urns and platters bearing the de Valermo arms.

'Impressive,' Ralph murmured. 'A pity we cannot touch it...'

Nick scarcely heard his friend's jest. They had entered a large chamber where several people had gathered, obviously waiting to greet the guests of honour. A woman was standing by a window; a little apart from the others, she seemed withdrawn, her eyes staring into a secret world that only she could see. The Englishman was struck by her beauty and by the terrible sadness in those lovely eyes, and then she turned to look at him...

Magdalene gazed out of the window. The gardens were so lovely, she thought, so peaceful, on this warm, still evening. She could smell the perfume of flowers and hear the sweet song of tiny birds as they fluttered in the trees, their jewel-bright colours delighting her. How pleasant it would be if she could walk in the gardens alone, she mused, away from all these people she did not wish to meet.

She had withdrawn from the others after greeting Isabella's betrothed. Rodrigo was very handsome, with his bronzed skin, dark, flashing eyes and curly black hair. She had noticed a spark of interest in those eyes as he looked at her, more interest than was seemly for a man to show when he was betrothed to another woman. Magdalene had seen that look in men's eyes before, and she knew that Rodrigo desired her, so she moved away to the window. Beauty such as hers was a curse – she felt it instinctively, and tried to hide it as much as she could.

She did not want men to look at her in that way, and did everything she could to avoid arousing that part of a man's nature she felt to be distasteful. A good woman was a fragile ornament, to be cherished and adored, but not stared at in that way. There

31

were other women to satisfy men's baser instincts. Doña Maria had taught her that it was so, and her own sheltered life had given her no reason to believe otherwise.

She turned from the window at last, sighing as she heard the sound of footsteps. Don Sebastian had returned with the English envoys, and it was time for her to do her duty. Her eyes moved over the refined, cultured features of her betrothed to the tall man beside him, and for one terrible moment her heart stopped beating. She had never seen such a man! He had arrogance and pride, but these qualities were not new to her; it was something intangible – a masculine vitality, an inner awareness, that she had never before sensed. It was almost as if those bright blue eyes possessed the power to see into her soul, as if she had no defences from him, and it terrified her. She wanted to turn and run from the room before it was too late, but of course that was impossible. She was Don Sebastian's intended bride; she must behave in the manner expected of her. Already they were coming towards her, and Don Sebastian was smiling. A little of her panic receded as she saw that smile. The Don would protect her. She was safe while he was near.

'Doña Magdalene, it is pleasant to see you here this evening. You visit us too seldom.'

Magdalene was vaguely aware of the

black-robed figure at her side. Father Ludovic was the Don's personal confessor; she had always disliked him, feeling oddly uncomfortable in his company, but at this moment he might not have been there for all the attention she could spare him. It was as if her whole being had been possessed, as if she were burning in the fires of hell, and yet she was cold at the same time. She shivered, feeling as if she would faint if those blue eyes did not turn away from her.

Don Sebastian stopped a few paces in front of her, turning to indicate his guests with a wave of his arm. 'Magdalene, may I present Sir Ralph Goodchild and Señor Nicholas Treggaron.'

The Don's soft, carefully polite tones eased her fright, though her heart was beating so wildly that she felt breathless as she sank into a graceful curtsey. The large man smiled kindly at her, merely touching the tips of her fingers and bowing, but the other – the other held her hand, raising it to his lips. She felt a searing pain run through her entire body at the contact and she almost cried out, managing to control herself only because of her years of strict training.

'Doña Magdalene, I am delighted to make your acquaintance. I had thought this would be along evening, but now I fear it will be all too short.'

Sir Ralph had paid her a charming

compliment. She knew she must make the effort to reply, but the other one would not release her hand. He was staring at her so intently that she could feel the colour rushing to her cheeks. Her fingers fluttered in his grasp, and he seemed to realise her difficulty.

'Forgive me,' he murmured, and she found herself released.

'You are welcome, Sir Ralph,' she said, and smiled a little as she saw surprise register in their faces at her perfect English. 'Mr T – Treggaron, I believe we are to be dinner partners?'

'I thought that colouring must be English,' Nick exclaimed. 'I have been staring rudely – you remind me of someone I once knew.'

'My mother was English,' Magdalene said, her fear of him ebbing away as she saw a flicker of pain in his eyes. It was not really herself that he was so interested in, only her likeness to someone he knew – no, someone he had loved. She felt instinctively that he had loved that other girl very much and that something had happened to hurt him badly. She knew it inside her, as she knew so many things that were unspoken. It was a gift she had – or perhaps a curse. There were times when she would rather not know these things. Even before the news of her father's death had reached them, she had sensed that something bad was about to happen –

just as she had felt it when the Englishman looked at her!

Magdalene's thoughts were rapidly recalled to the present as horns sounded and a hush fell over the guests: His Majesty had arrived. Sinking into a deep curtsey, the girl kept her head bowed until the King and his ministers reached them. He greeted Don Sebastian and the English visitors, turning at last as she rose.

'Doña Magdalene, your presence enchants me. Don Sebastian is greatly to be envied. How soon may I expect to be invited to your wedding?'

The King was resplendent in blue brocade embroidered with diamonds and pearls: silver lace frothed beneath his neatly-trimmed beard and a huge ruby flashed from the index finger of his right hand. But he was smiling kindly, and she felt no fear of him.

'You must ask Don Sebastian, sire. For myself, I await the happiness of being his wife most eagerly.'

He nodded approvingly. The girl had beauty, breeding and modesty. Don Sebastian had chosen well. He offered his arm to her and there was a general movement towards the banqueting hall, where the long tables were weighed down with silver plate and decorated with dishes of the choicest fruits and comfits.

Cool and confident once more, Magdalene was unconscious of the eyes which turned in her direction. She felt safe and secure, unaware of the undercurrents of jealousy, suspicion and hot, burning lust she had so unwittingly aroused. She could not guess, as she took her place of honour between the King and the English envoy, that the days of her innocence were numbered and that she was soon to be caught up in a terrifying destiny that would cast her into a nightmare such as she had never known...

Nick watched the girl walk away on the arm of the Spanish King. For a moment, when he had first looked into those wonderful green eyes, he had been reminded of Cathy, but the likeness had been only fleeting and dispelled as soon as the girl spoke. Cathy had been a child, but full of life and the joy of living – there was a coldness in this girl, and fear. He did not understand why she should be afraid of him; Cathy had known no fear – but she was dead, and the grinding ache inside him showed no sign of abating.

'She is very beautiful,' Ralph said softly at his side. 'Did you see those eyes?'

'Too beautiful,' Nick muttered. 'It's as well these Spanish hidalgos lock up their women so securely.'

'What do you mean?' Ralph asked, but then he too saw the looks certain men had directed after the girl, and he nodded. 'Lust is an ugly thing, my friend, especially from such a one.'

Nick's face was grim as he saw that Ralph had seen and felt as he had. 'The young one is smitten, I believe he means her no harm – but that other...'

Ralph frowned as he heard the growl issue from his companion's throat. 'He probably wears a hair shirt for his sins, Nick. Besides, the girl is no concern of yours – and the man's vows will prevent him from giving way to his desires.'

'I hate those canting hypocrites that hide behind a priest's robes. He would burn us for our faith, yet he lusts after a child!'

Nick's face was white with anger, his hands moving at his sides as if in search of his sword. Hatred for the Inquisition and the black-robed brethren that served such masters churned in his guts, making him want to strike out. The girl's faint likeness to Cathy had disturbed him badly, and he wanted to kill the man who dared to look at her with naked lust. She was not his sweet little cousin, but she was innocent and lovely – and he felt that she was in need of protection.

'Steady, my friend!' Ralph's calming influence checked the rush of blood to his heated brain. 'Remember why we're here.'

Nick drew a deep breath. He could not kill

every man who looked at a girl with lust in his eyes! Damn it! he'd bedded his share of women in his time; but they had all been willing partners who came to his bed of their own free will. There was something about that black-robed creature, who stood so silently to one side as the guests took their seats at the tables, that stuck in his throat. Outwardly, he appeared a meek, reverent man of the church, but for a few brief seconds his eyes had revealed the serpent that lived within the man. Somehow, Treggaron felt that Doña Magdalene was in danger from him; but as Ralph had said, it was not his concern... Despite her English mother, the girl was Spanish to the core. She was cold, proud and about to marry a man old enough to be her grandfather. She would not thank him for his warning if he were fool enough to offer one. Besides, in a few days he would be on his way home to England...

Magdalene got to her feet, refreshed from her devotions. She had spent a restless night, and she felt better for having opened her heart to the only person she could confess to. She felt that God was always ready to listen to her prayers, even though she could not bring herself to confess to Father Ludovic. That he would expect her to do so once she was the Don's wife was a little disturbing. She could not see why she was obliged to share her thoughts with a confessor, when God was there to hear her prayers. She had tried to explain her feelings to Father Ludovic once, but he had been horrified.

'These are the ways of heretics,' he had cried, his eyes burning into her. 'They come from the Devil. Put them from your mind before Satan puts his mark on you.'

The priest was always warning her of the perils of sin. She was too proud for her own good, too free with her thoughts and stubborn in refusing his guidance. Seeing him waiting for her at the entrance to the chapel, Magdalene sighed. She had wanted to return to her uncle's house after the banquet, but Don Sebastian had insisted that his guests all stay on for a few days. Rodrigo was a distant cousin of his, and it was he who had arranged for Isabella to meet her betrothed under his roof. If would have upset everyone if Magdalene had insisted on leaving, and so she had slept in the beautiful apartments that would soon be her own. The chapel connected her rooms with the gardens, and she must pass through it to join the others who would be waiting for her.

'You have been praying, Doña Magdalene.' The priest's words were almost an accusation. 'I had hoped that you might send for me.'

'I have nothing to confess,' Magdalene replied coldly. Why did this man make her feel so uneasy? 'I shall send for you if I feel the need.'

Father Ludovic's eyes narrowed. 'You must not neglect your confession, lady. Absolution can be given only by a priest.'

'Why?' Anger flickered in her eyes. How dared he intrude into her private world? 'I feel closer to God when I pray to him – why must I confess my thoughts to you? Only God can judge my sins...'

The priest crossed himself. 'You do not know how deep in sin you are, Doña Magdalene. Your words are blasphemy and...'

'Because I do not bow to your bigoted ideas? Who made you God's arbiter? I believe he will listen to me as willingly as he will hear your intercession on my behalf.' She lifted her head proudly. 'Excuse me; I am expected. I must not keep my friends waiting.'

She swept past him, her long, heavy skirts brushing over the tiled floor. Outside in the sunshine, she saw Rodrigo standing by a fountain and hurried to greet him, uncaring of the angry stare that followed her.

'I was delayed,' she explained, relieved to be away from the priest's malevolent gaze. 'Have you been waiting long?'

Rodrigo's eyes glowed as he saw her. He came and took her hands in his, kissing her cheek. 'Magdalene,' he said. 'You had my note. You came...'

'Your note?' Magdalene frowned. 'No. I thought Isabella, my uncle... Are we not to take refreshments together in the rose garden this morning?'

'You did not get my letter, then.' Disappointment showed briefly in his face. 'But no matter, you are here. I am rewarded for my vigil. I have longed to be alone with you since I first saw you last night. I must speak with you, Magdalene, before it is too late.'

'I don't understand,' she faltered, a sinking feeling inside. 'We have nothing of importance to say to one another, Don Rodrigo. You are betrothed to my cousin, and I am to marry your kinsman.'

'But neither of us is married yet,' Rodrigo said, a note of desperation in his voice. 'I know I have no right to speak to you thus – but how can I marry Isabella when I love you?'

Magdalene realised he was still gripping her hands and tried to wrest them from his grasp, but he held on tightly. 'Please release me,' she said quietly. 'You are behaving very foolishly. You hardly know me, and...'

'It took only a moment to know you,' he interrupted her impetuously. 'You are the loveliest woman I have ever seen. Your beauty has bewitched me. I hardly know what I am doing...'

41

Magdalene became aware of the priest standing near by. He was watching them closely, and as she turned her head to glance at him, she was shocked by the expression of hatred on his face.

'Take care, Don Rodrigo,' she warned. 'We are watched, and Don Sebastian will hear of this. Remember that you are guest in his house.'

'You are as honourable as you are lovely,' Rodrigo said, 'and I am a fool for exposing you to Don Sebastian's displeasure. I was carried away by my love for you ... I was unable to sleep last night. I know not what I do or say.'

'Don Sebastian will listen to me when I explain you meant no harm.' Magdalene smiled. 'We shall forget...'

'No, never!' The young man's face twitched with emotion. 'I shall not give up hope that you will look upon me kindly, but even if you turn from me in disgust it makes no difference. I cannot – I will not! – marry Isabella when I love only you. I shall find her and tell her so at once.'

'No, please do not. You cannot break your promise to her...' Magdalene begged, horrified by his impulsive words, but her plea was useless. Already he was striding away. 'Oh, poor Isabella,' she whispered. 'He will break her heart. How could he be so cruel ... so cruel?' Men were always cruel, even those who professed to love their womenfolk. It was their way: Doña Maria had told her it was so.

Tears were pricking behind her eyes as she watched Rodrigo disappear through one of the gates into the next garden. Then she became aware of the black shadow hovering behind her. She turned to look at the priest, impatience making her voice rise sharply. 'I suppose you will run to Don Sebastian with your tales? Do not bother; I shall tell him everything myself.'

The priest was staring at her with horror in his eyes. He crossed himself swiftly, his face twitching as if he were suffering some kind of a fit. 'Why did I not see it before?' he whispered hoarsely. 'You are a witch and a heretic. You have bewitched Don Rodrigo – as you have bewitched us all…'

'What nonsense are you mouthing now?' Magdalene cried angrily. 'I have no magical powers, nor am I a heretic. You should be careful, Father Ludovic, or I shall see that you are dismissed when I am mistress here!'

With that, she turned and walked away, leaving him staring after her with a fierce hatred in his expression. It was all so clear to him now, he thought: those nights of agony when he had wrestled with his desire for her, scourging himself until the blood ran in his efforts to rid his mind of the evil thoughts she had aroused had all been in

43

vain. He was bewitched, and he would never be free of the burning in his loins while she lived to torment him, tempting him to sin with her beauty. She was a witch, a handmaiden of the Devil – and only her death could set him free!

CHAPTER TWO

Magdalene knew that she must find Don Sebastian and speak with him before the priest could poison his mind with lies. Rodrigo had behaved badly in approaching her when he knew she was promised to his host. It was an insult, and one that could deeply offend Don Sebastian if it was not explained to him in the right way; such insults often led to duels between men, and she wanted no quarrels over her. It was bad enough that the young man had spoken so rashly before Father Ludovic! She could only hope that Rodrigo had not meant it when he said he would break his promise to Isabella.

'Doña Magdalene, may I speak with you a moment, please?'

Absorbed by her thoughts, Magdalene had not seen the tall Englishman until he spoke. Her heart jerked and raced for one moment, then she was in control once more. She had nothing to fear from this man. Indeed, he had proved a pleasant companion at the banquet last night, making her smile at his stories about his childhood in Cornwall, though she had secretly been a little shocked when he told her how the young girls and their sweethearts went a-maying together in the fields; but she liked hearing how the prettiest girl was crowned Queen of the May and fêted by her friends while everyone danced round the maypole and sang. Doña Maria had never talked about England much, and Magdalene had found herself asking many questions, which Mr Treggaron had seemed happy to answer. So when she stopped walking and smiled at him, there was no trace of the coldness Nick had seen the previous evening.

'Mr Treggaron,' she said, 'how may I help you?'

'For a moment Nick was lost for a reply. He did not know why he had indulged his sudden impulse to stop her, or why her smile of welcome was so pleasing. Why had he thought her cold, he wondered. She was not cold, merely unawakened... But it was madness to let his thoughts stray in that direction. It would be another man who brought her to a gradual awareness of her womanhood, another man who watched the fires of desire begin to burn in those wondrous eyes, and that was as it should be. She was a Spaniard and beyond his reach... He became conscious of the silence stretching between them, and smiled oddly.

'I seem to have lost my way! I came out for a stroll in the gardens, and I cannot find the 'right entrance.' It was a lie, but he thought it an acceptable one.

Her laughter was so light and joyous that it surprised him. He had never suspected that the serious Doña Magdalene he had admired last night could look like this. When she laughed, it was as if a light came on inside her, revealing an entirely different woman – a woman who made his pulses throb.

'Why do you laugh?' he asked, knowing that he was merely seeking an excuse to keep her from walking on. 'If I am late, it could cause terrible havoc, you know.'

'Oh, I do not think so,' Magdalene murmured. 'We are all civilised, reasonable people, are we not? I believe if you look behind you, Mr Treggaron, you will see your friend. I think he is waiting for you. But in case you are both lost, the entrance you seek is just round the corner.' She pointed in the direction from which he must have come. 'Now, if you will forgive me, I must speak with Don Sebastian.'

'He is with the King. We are all waiting for the audience to begin. His Majesty has delayed it for some reason.'

'Oh...' Magdalene frowned. 'Then I must not disturb them. It does not matter; I shall see him later.'

Nick wondered at the faint anxiety he saw in her face. 'Perhaps I could give Don

47

Sebastian a message?'

'No...' She blushed, a pale rose colour highlighting her cheeks. 'Perhaps you and Sir Ralph would care to join my cousin, some others and myself for some refreshments in the gardens while you wait?'

'That is kind of you, but...' Nick saw his friend's signal. 'I believe we have been called. Perhaps another day?'

'Of course.' She flicked open her fan of painted chicken skin, using it to cool her cheeks. 'I hope – I hope the audience goes well for you, Mr Treggaron.'

'Thank you.' Nick watched as she walked away, admiring the proud carriage of her head and the graceful movement of her body. He found himself wondering what she might look like without the heavy, wide-skirted gown that Spanish ladies favoured. And her hair would suit her better if left softly flowing on her shoulders, instead of being wired into those fashionable ringlets...

A movement at his side brought his wandering thoughts to a safer channel. He saw Ralph's grin and scowled, knowing that the other man had read his mind.

'Don Sebastian is a fortunate man, is he not?' Ralph said. 'I wonder if he realises what lies beneath that docile mask she wears?'

'So you sensed it too?' Nick frowned, and his friend laughed.

'Ay, but I doubt her future husband has – or perhaps he does not care to see. It's the way they keep their womenfolk shut up, mentally as well as physically. She has not rebelled against it as yet – maybe she never will.'

'I think she has been hurt, Ralph. Sometimes there's such sadness in her eyes...'

'Forget her, Nick.' Ralph's tone was so harsh that it made the other man stare at him. 'She could bring you only trouble. Even if she were free, you are worlds apart – and she is not free.'

'I'm no fool!' An irrational anger made Nick's voice sharp. He turned aside from his friend and strode off towards the house, leaving Ralph to shake his head and follow in his wake.

Don José, Isabella and Rodrigo were seated on stools beneath the shade of a silken awning, sipping glasses of cool fruit juice and eating iced sherbet. The ice had been brought from the Sierra de Ronda in close-packed wagons at great expense by Don Sebastian, and was a luxury much appreciated by his guests on such a hot day.

Joining the others, Magdalene looked anxiously at their faces. It was immediately apparent to her that Rodrigo had not yet spoken of his desire to break the marriage contract, and she drew a sigh of relief.

Obviously, he had thought better of his rash declaration, or perhaps his courage had failed him at the last moment. It did not matter. For the moment Isabella was happy, her dark eyes shining as they dwelt on the handsome face of her beloved.

'You are late, Magdalene,' Don José said. 'I had begun to wonder where you were.'

'I was delayed,' she replied, and saw a flicker of what might have been apprehension in Rodrigo's eyes. Did he imagine she would tell her uncle about his foolishness? 'Señor Treggaron had lost his way in the gardens, and I stopped to show him which way to turn.'

'He approached you – when you were alone?' Don José looked horrified. 'Tell me at once, Magdalene, did he offer you any disrespect?'

'No, Uncle, he merely asked the way. He meant no harm – he does not understand our customs. Beside, Father Ludovic was in the garden.'

'Heaven be praised! Only an Englishman would behave so badly. Any Spaniard would have better manners than to approach a lady of good family when she was alone.' He frowned. 'Perhaps it would have been better if we had gone home – with these men free to come and go as they please...'

Rodrigo was trying to look unconcerned, but his colour had heightened and

Magdalene felt sorry for him. He was young and thoughtless, and he must be regretting his hasty words by now. She gave him a warm smile, to show that she was not angry with him. Almost immediately she realised it was the wrong thing to have done. A flame of adoration leapt into his eyes and the look of longing he sent towards her was noticed by Isabella. Her face froze and she began to tap her foot irritably.

'The way you were flirting with the Englishman last night, I am not surprised he approached you! He probably thought you were infatuated with him.'

Isabella's spiteful outburst startled everyone, including her father. He frowned at her, looking annoyed. 'Magdalene has more sense than to encourage the attentions of such men. She was merely polite, and at my request. Perhaps you would like to apologise, daughter?'

Isabella's face was bright pink and tears sparkled in her eyes. It was clear that she had no desire to apologise, but she dared not disobey her father. She mumbled something, miserably aware of Rodrigo's dark eyes watching her, knowing that she had shown herself in an unfavourable light.

Magdalene helped herself to a tiny cake made of almonds, exclaiming over the delicious taste and offering the dish to Rodrigo and then her uncle. Everyone tried not to look at Isabella until she had recovered herself and was able to join in the conversation, which was mostly concerned with the coming wine harvest. Both men had large vineyards, though their estates were in widely differing areas; soon they were deep in a discussion of the merits of their own wines.

Wandering away to examine a dark red, scented rose, Magdalene bent her head to inhale the perfume. She glanced up as her cousin came to join her, sighing as she saw the look of dislike in Isabella's eyes.

'You are satisfied now that you have turned everyone against me, I suppose?' she hissed, her voice deliberately low so that the men should not hear.

'What do you mean?'

'I saw the way you smiled at Rodrigo. I know you want to take him from me. You want him for yourself!'

'No, Isabella. Please listen to me. I am quite happy to marry Don Sebastian.'

Isabella stared at her uncertainly, her mouth quivering. 'I would not want to marry such an old man.'

'Don Sebastian is kind and gentle, Isabella. Please believe me, I do not want to steal your betrothed from you.'

Doubt was visible in Isabella's eyes as she regarded her cousin. She could not bring herself to believe Magdalene. Besides, she had seen that smile – and Rodrigo's response to it! He had not looked at her like that, despite all her efforts to please him.

'Magdalene, I...' The rest of her words were lost as she saw Don Sebastian approaching.

'I see you are admiring my new rose, ladies.'

He smiled benevolently. He was a collector of beautiful things; his garden boasted unusual plants from as far away as the New World. Magdalene, he thought complacently, would be the most beautiful of his possessions; the perfect addition to his home. He took the hand she offered and kissed it reverently.

'Is the Englishmen's audience with His Majesty over?' Magdalene asked.

'For the moment,' Don Sebastian nodded. 'It goes well, I think. At the King's request they are to accompany him to Don Antonio Cosano's estate for a few days of hunting the boar. His Majesty begs your pardon, Magdalene; he asked me to give you his good wishes before he left.'

So the Englishman with the piercing blue eyes had gone. She would not see him again, for when he returned from the hunting trip she would be at her uncle's house. It was perhaps fortunate, since he had such an odd effect on her, and yet Magdalene could not explain her sudden sense of loss...

It was a warm night, far too warm for comfort. Magdalene was restless; she had been unable to sleep and had sat by her window looking out at the gardens for hours. How much cooler it would be outside, she thought, feeling the walls of her apartments somehow imprisoning. It was no good! She could bear this stifling heat no longer.

She knew she would find it impossible to change into one of her cumbersome gowns without the help of a maid, so she pulled on an embroidered silk robe over her thin night-chemise. Her soft slippers made hardly any sound as she walked unhurriedly through her apartments and the shadowed stillness of the chapel, to the gardens beyond.

The night air was cool and perfumed with the scent of flowers. A full moon had turned the sky almost white as Magdalene moved silently towards her favourite spot in the garden. The pale rose marble of a Moorish pavilion gave access to a small courtyard with a fountain and a tiled pool, surrounded by stone urns filled with a profusion of tumbling blooms.

Kneeling by the pool, Magdalene dipped her hands in the cool water, letting the sparkling droplets run through her fingers before splashing its refreshing coolness on to her face and throat. She thought how pleasant it would be if she could remove all her clothes and bathe in the pool, but her thoughts were slightly shocking and she resolutely shut them out. It was bad enough that she had left her apartments at this hour and wearing only her night apparel! Yet how good it felt to be alone and free of all restrictions for once... Her thoughts were interrupted as she heard a slight scraping sound, and she glanced over her shoulder, startled to find that she was not alone.

Getting to her feet at once, she felt a shiver of fear as the man took a few steps towards her. Then she saw that it was Rodrigo, and her fear turned to anger. How dared he spy on her?

'Why did you follow me?' she demanded, knowing that he must have done so, because his own apartments were on the other side of the house.

'I was outside the chapel,' he replied, not bothering to deny the charge. 'I could not sleep. I I wanted to be near you, so I kept a vigil outside your chambers, and then I saw you. I had to follow you. You do not know how much I adore you...'

'You must not say such things to me!' Magdalene cut across the tempestuous flow of words. 'You have no right...'

'Only the right of my love for you,' Rodrigo cried, his face tight with passion. 'You cannot marry that old man – it is obscene. You belong to me! I shall make you see that it is true!'

Before the girl realised what he meant to do, he covered the distance between them and seized her, his arms imprisoning her as his mouth sought possession of hers. She fought desperately, twisting her face aside to avoid his kisses and beating at his chest with her fists.

'No!' she cried. 'How dare you! Oh, let me go, señor, I beg you! You must not do this.'

'I cannot let you go,' he groaned. 'You have robbed me of my senses. I am on fire for you – mad with desire...' His lips pressed against her throat, making her struggle violently as a shudder of revulsion went through her. Suddenly she lashed out at him with her nails, scoring his cheek. 'You – you witch!' he cried, staring at her in surprise as he felt the sting of torn flesh. 'Mark me with your talons, my beloved she-cat, it does not matter. I still adore you.'

His greedy mouth was devouring her lips, her cheeks, her eyelids – whichever way she turned, she could not escape the hot rain of his passionate kisses. Now one of his legs was behind hers, holding her so that she was pressed against him while his hand moved down to caress her breast. She gave a despairing cry, knowing that in his moon-madness Rodrigo was beyond reason. Then there was a muffled shout from somewhere near by, and she saw a large shadow fall across the grass. Rodrigo gave a yell of pain as a hand clutched his hair and a hard, muscled arm encircled his throat. He was jerked backwards, gasping for breath, and hurled to the ground with such fury that he lay stunned and winded, staring up at his attacker in bewilderment.

'It is polite to take notice when a lady says No, señor.'

The harsh growl that accompanied Nicholas Treggaron's warning was sufficient for the Spaniard. He got to his feet, his expression a mixture of surprise, dismay and fear. It was clear that he was confused; he had been carried away by the sight of Magdalene in the moonlight. He was a hot-blooded man by nature and his sexual appetite had led him into trouble before. Memories of another night and another place crowded into his mind, making him sweat with remembered fear. He had been drunk that night, following blindly as others led the way. He had never meant to harm that girl, only to have some fun. But she had been a stranger, and Magdalene was the daughter of a Spaniard he respected. He must have been mad! He had not meant to press Magdalene so forcefully, but once she was in his arms he had lost his head. Before the cold, accusing eyes of the Englishman, he felt stripped of his pride, and foolish. For a long moment he stood in silence, then he bowed stiffly and walked away. When he was out of Magdalene's sight he began to run, as if shame – or conscience – snapped at his heels.

Magdalene held her silk wrap tighter, covering the tear where Rodrigo had ripped the fine material of her nightgown. She was shivering, still a little distressed by the unpleasant attack on her by Isabella's betrothed. For a moment he had acted more like a wild beast than a man.

'Are you hurt?'

Nick's voice was gentle, but it sent a tingle down her spine. She could scarcely bear to look at him as she shook her head. 'No. He did not harm me, Mr Treggaron. Don Rodrigo was...'

'Carried away by his feelings,' Nick supplied with a wry twist of his lips. 'It happens with young men sometimes, when they meet a lovely woman in circumstances such as these. If I had thought it more than foolishness, he would not have escaped so easily, believe me. Next time you arrange a secret tryst with your lover, be more careful.'

'He is not my lover!' Magdalene exclaimed. 'He followed me. I did not invite him to join me.'

'You invited his attentions by walking here alone at this hour – and in such attire.' Nick frowned, not understanding why he felt so angry with her. 'Don Rodrigo should not have forced himself on you, but you must have known how he felt about you. You should not have given him the opportunity to make love to you.'

The accusation in his tone angered her. He was blaming her for what had happened! Like most men, he believed that if a woman was molested she must have done something to encourage the attack.

'I came out here because I wished to be alone. I thank you for your help, Mr Treggaron, but I should be grateful if you would leave now. This garden is usually reserved for members of Don Sebastian's family.'

'And I am trespassing? Perhaps you did not wish for my help, after all?' Nick's eyes glinted in the moonlight. 'Forgive me, Doña Magdalene.' He turned abruptly as if to leave.

She blinked at the sudden sting of tears. 'No – don't go,' she choked. 'I – I am grateful for what you did, Mr Treggaron. Please believe me, Don Rodrigo is not my lover, but – but you are right, I was foolish to come here alone at this hour. I – I wanted to be free for a little while; but you will laugh at me…' She blushed as his eyes fixed on her face, suddenly conscious of how she must look to him with her hair streaming down her back and only a clinging robe to hide her slender form from his piercing eyes. 'Of course I should not have left my rooms…'

The irrational anger that had gripped him at the thought of her arranging to meet the young Spaniard secretly faded as he looked into her misted eyes. Why should she not be able to walk alone without fear of being molested? It was easy to condemn her for tempting the man, but Rodrigo should have had more control over his desires. A man could not just reach out and snatch what he wanted greedily, no matter how much he might want that tantalising prize which glittered just out of reach. For if he did, it might turn to ashes in his grasp.

'Forgive me,' Nick said softly. 'I had no right to accuse you.'

'It does not matter.' Her smile took his breath away, and he understood why Rodrigo had lost his head. God! she was lovely! There was something about her that might make any man believe the world well lost for love. 'But how came you to be here, Mr Treggaron? I thought you were hunting with the King?'

Nick took a firm grip on his spiralling thoughts. 'My horse went lame, and I decided to lead him back here, since I could not borrow another. I do not care much for hunting boar. It was an acceptable excuse, though I must join the others tomorrow. Señor Cosano sent his servant with me.'

'Yes, you must go back, or His Majesty will be offended, and your mission will fail...' Magdalene's words died away. It was no good! She could not lie to him, nor could she tell him that his mission was doomed to failure, that war was inevitable between their countries whatever he did or said. He was not her enemy but his people were the enemy of hers, and she should not be here alone with him like this. 'I must go, Mr Treggaron. Thank you for helping me.'

She walked quickly away, knowing her sudden change of mood had surprised him, but not daring to stay a moment longer. She must not begin to like this man! That would indeed be foolish...

The maid had just finished dressing Magdalene's hair when Isabella burst into the bedchamber. One glance at her cousin's face told her all she needed to know, and she waved the maidservant away.

'I shall not need you again this morning, Juana. Don Sebastian and I are to visit his aunt...'

Magdalene got to her feet, gripping a lace kerchief. She felt a sinking sensation inside as she saw the other girl's red eyes. Isabella had been crying, and now she was ready for a quarrel.

'Is something wrong?'

The words had scarcely left her lips before

Isabella flew at her. She jerked her head away as she felt the sting of her cousin's hand on her cheek.

'How dare you pretend you don't know?' Isabella screamed. 'You are a lying, scheming...'

'Isabella, don't,' Magdalene begged. 'Please tell me what I've done to upset you like this?'

'You swore to me that you did not want Rodrigo...'

'I do not.'

'Then why did you let him make love to you?' Isabella asked, her eyes angry and scornful. 'He told me he must wed you because he has dishonoured you, and would be forever shamed if he did not take you for his wife. You led him on! You flaunted yourself before him in your night clothes. It was all your fault!'

'It is not true, Isabella! You must believe me.'

'Are you saying that you did not meet him in the gardens last night?' Isabella demanded. 'Can you swear to me that he has never kissed you, never held you in his arms?'

Magdalene was silent, unable to decide what to do. If she lied to her cousin, Isabella would know it, and then she would believe the worst.

'He – Rodrigo did kiss me, but...' The words froze on her lips as she looked beyond

Isabella at the man who stood on the threshold of her chamber, his face wearing an expression of disgust. 'Don Sebastian, I – I did not know you were there.'

'Or you would have lied to spare me?' His eyes were cold as he looked at her. Her beauty was marred for him, now that he knew she had been defiled by another. 'Doña Isabella, will you be good enough to leave us, please?'

Isabella's face was triumphant as she meekly obeyed. Now her cousin would be punished as she deserved. Don Sebastian would cast her aside, and the world would know of the harlot's shame!

Don Sebastian closed the door behind her. Turning he let his eyes move slowly over Magdalene's lovely face, waiting for her to speak. When she did not begin a frantic denial, he frowned.

'Have you nothing to say to me – no word of apology or explanation?'

'I am sorry that you have been hurt, Sebastian.'

'Then you do not deny that this – this man made love to you?'

'He kissed me,' Magdalene sighed. 'It was not by my wish, but perhaps I was to blame. I should not have been in the gardens at that hour.'

'A kiss? Was that all? Rodrigo claims it was more.'

'Believe him, if you will,' Magdalene said quietly, her face proud. 'Why should he lie?'

'Perhaps because he wishes to force a duel on me?' The Don's brows rose. 'I am not a fool, Magdalene. I have observed the way he looks at you. He is sick with love for you, but I thought it a young man's foolishness.'

'That is all it need have been, Sebastian, had he not told these lies to you and Isabella.'

He came towards her, studying her face intently. 'You swear to me that he did not ... has not...?'

'I swear it. I am a maiden still, Sebastian. I swear it on the graves of my father and mother. He was carried away by the moonlight. I beg you to believe me. It was wrong, and I accept my share of the blame. I promise you that I shall never allow it to happen again.'

Some of the coldness left his eyes. 'You have given me your word, and I shall forgive you. I believe it was only a kiss, but one kiss is too much. When we return from my aunt's, I shall tell Rodrigo he must leave – your uncle and Isabella, too. You will stay here in the care of a duenna I shall arrange for you. I want no hint of scandal attached to my bride; your relations will not speak of this again...' Don Sebastian held out his hand to her imperiously. 'Come, Magdalene, my Aunt Leonora is very old nearly a hundred years. She is looking forward to your visit; we must not disappoint her.'

Magdalene felt a stab of surprise. She could hardly believe her ears as he dismissed the subject so abruptly. There was to be no scandal, no duel – Rodrigo was simply to be sent away. Don Sebastian did not even want to know if she cared for the young man. It did not matter to him: all that interested him was his bride's innocence. Why should it suddenly distress her that he did not care if her heart was aching?

Looking at her future husband, Magdalene experienced a surge of rebellion. Was this really what she wanted of life – to be wed to a man old enough to be her grandfather? A man who thought of her only as a beautiful object to add to his collection? She wondered what he would do if she told him that she had changed her mind – that she no longer wished to be his wife. And, yet, what else could she do? It would be impossible to go on living beneath Don José's roof for much longer, and it would cause a terrible scandal if she were to live alone. No, she had gone over it all so many times in her mind; this was the best way...

Smiling a little stiffly, she took the Don's hand. 'I am ready,' she said. 'We must not keep your aunt waiting.'

Isabella stared at herself in the little silver

hand-glass, hating the reflection she saw there. Her eyes were red and she knew her skin was blotchy from crying. She was ugly, and she could not deny it even to herself. When she gazed at her own image she realised there was no reason for Rodrigo to come back to her and say that it was all a mistake, that he really loved her and not Magdalene after all. If he had come she knew that she would have forgiven him, because she still loved him in spite of his cruel rejection of her. But he would not come. Don Sebastian was sending him away; she might never see him again, and she could not bear it. It was so unfair! It was all Magdalene's fault, but of course, she was not to be punished.

'Oh, how I hate her!' Isabella cried. 'I wish... Oh, how I wish that she were dead.'

The words horrified her once they had left her mouth. She was not a wicked girl, only a rather silly, unhappy one. Crossing herself, Isabella knew that she must go to confession at once. It was a terrible sin to wish for another's death – and yet if Magdalene were dead, perhaps Rodrigo would turn to her for comfort...

'Will you hear my confession, Father Ludovic?' Isabella asked, an expression of fear in her dark eyes. 'I have a terrible sin on my conscience and I need your help.'

The priest nodded, his eyes approving as he looked at her. This was as it should be: it gave him a feeling of power when sinners came to him begging for absolution – especially when they were young women. It was a pity that the other one could not be brought to realise her need of him...

'Father, will you hear me?'

Isabella's plea interrupted his thoughts. He motioned for her to kneel on a little cushion, remaining in a standing position so that he could place his hand on her bowed head. She was not pretty, but there was something appealing about her, particularly when she begged him for help.

'Speak then, my child,' he said. 'I am listening, and through me God will absolve you of your sins.'

'Father, I am guilty of a most terrible sin. 'I – I desire...' Isabella's voice faltered, and the priest's eyes gleamed with sudden interest.

'Tell me what you desire,' he commanded. 'I shall not be angry with you even if you have committed sins of the flesh.'

'No, Father, it is even more terrible. I – I desire my cousin's death...' She felt his hand jerk on her head, and caught her breath in a sob of fear. 'I know it is a great wickedness in me, but – but I hate her so much that I cannot stop wishing she were dead.'

'Why– Why do you hate Doña Magdalene

so much, child? Come, you must tell me the truth.'

Isabella was struck by the urgency in his tone, and she glanced up. To her surprise there was no sign of the disgust she had believed he would feel at her confession: instead, he seemed eager to hear what she had to say. Forgetting Don Sebastian's insistence that she must not tell her stories to anyone, she began to pour out her unhappiness to the priest, repeating every word that Rodrigo had said to her.

'He will not marry me,' she ended breathlessly. 'He intends to break the contract between us, even though Magdalene will not have him.'

'Don Rodrigo is bewitched by her,' the priest said. 'I heard him confess it myself, and it must be so. He would never behave thus if he were in his right senses. She has cast her spell on him and he knows not what he does.'

'That is exactly what Rodrigo said,' Isabella exclaimed. 'He cannot sleep or rest. He does not know what he is doing.'

'She is a witch,' the priest muttered, his eyes glittering. 'She has bewitched us all.'

'Yes, it is true,' Isabella agreed. 'I thought Don Sebastian would cast her aside when he knew she had let Rodrigo make love to her. He was angry with her when he sent me away, but then he said it was all nonsense

68

and he ordered Rodrigo to leave his house tomorrow morning.'

'She cast a spell over him. She has him in her power...' He frowned, his eyes narrowing in thought. 'She is an enchantress – a sorceress – and she should be brought to justice for her crimes.'

'Oh yes,' Isabella cried, shivering in sudden excitement. 'She should be punished for her wickedness.'

'This is a matter for the Inquisition. I shall bring it to the attention of those best qualified to make a judgment in the case. You, Doña Isabella – you would be prepared to testify that your cousin is a witch?'

'I – I don't know...' the girl faltered, frightened now by the wild look in his eyes. She got to her feet uncertainly, half wishing she had told him nothing.

The priest's fingers curled round her wrist, bruising her flesh. 'You have not been lying to me?'

'No– No, I swear all I have said was true.'

'You must know more. You have lived with her – seen her ways. Has she a familiar?'

'She– She has a singing bird that feeds from her hand...' Isabella frowned, remembering something. 'Sometimes– Sometimes she sees things – things that haven't yet happened.'

'She can foretell the future.' Father Ludovic's eyes gleamed with triumph. 'I knew it!

69

She is a witch.'

Isabella stared at him. 'So she really has cast a spell over Rodrigo? If she were dead, he would come back to me.'

'Once he was free of her spell he would come to his senses, I am sure of it. He is an honourable young man and would not lightly break such a binding contract.'

'Then I shall testify,' Isabella declared. 'She likes to walk in the gardens at night alone. Surely that is very strange, is it not?'

The priest nodded. 'It is then that she works her evil magic. I shall report my suspicions to the Inquisition this very hour. Do not fear, child, from today she will be watched. Everything she does will be noted, and when we have the proof...' He smiled coldly. 'When we have the proof, Doña Magdalene will be arrested.'

A little tremor ran through Isabella. Much as she hated Magdalene, the thought of her cousin being arrested by the Inquisition filled her with horror. She began to wish she had not confessed her sin to Father Ludovic, but it was too late now. If she tried to stop him reporting her cousin to his masters, she might be the one who was arrested...

'The hunt was exciting, was it not?' Ralph glanced at the man riding beside him curiously. 'You are very quiet, my friend. You should be well pleased with yourself.

That fool of a servant was only too eager to tell us everything he had overheard once you plied him with wine and gold. The news we shall take home is what we expected – no?'

Nick nodded, his eyes squinting against the fierce heat of the sun. The road they had been following for some time was little more than a narrow track between hills covered in brownish boulders, gorse bushes and coarse grass. They had seen no sign of any habitation for miles, except for one peasant's isolated cottage an hour since.

'Yes, the news is good. The Spanish mean war, but their ships have not yet reached sufficient numbers...' Nick broke off and shaded his eyes as he surveyed the empty countryside. 'Are you sure this is the way we took when you rode with Cosano and the King? I'm sure we should have reached that little village before this. I had hoped to reach Don Sebastian's house before dusk.'

'We may have taken the wrong road, Nick,' Ralph agreed. 'We should have let Cosano send his servant with us.'

'Well, we'd best continue as we are for now. Maybe we'll find some shelter for the night, or someone to direct us.'

Nick frowned, wondering why he had a strange feeling that it was necessary for him to reach the Don's house tonight. It was stupid, and yet it had been nagging at him for some time.

'If your knowledge of Spanish is good enough to make these peasants understand us – or allow us to understand them?' Ralph grinned. I've never needed to understand them before.' He made a cutting gesture with his hand across his throat, and Nick nodded. 'We must be vaguely in the right direction. It can only make a difference of half a day's journey at most – what can happen in a few hours?'

'You tempt the fates, my friend,' Nick laughed. 'We could be set upon by brigands or murdered as we sleep, but it is more than likely that we shall chance across a village soon. As you say, it makes very little difference whether we reach the Casa de Valermo tonight or in the morning...'

But why did he feel that it might make a great deal of difference to Doña Magdalene? Why did he feel that she was in danger?

Magdalene was lying on her bed with her eyes closed. The window had been shuttered against the heat, and she was wearing only a thin robe. In a little while she knew she must make an effort to dress for dinner, but her head was aching so badly. Tomorrow Isabella and her father would be leaving, and she would remain here in the charge of the duenna Don Sebastian had sent for. The woman was a relative of his who would be happy to remain until the wedding, which was now to take place in two weeks' time. Magdalene knew she should be happy that she would not have to return to her uncle's house, but strangely, her heart was heavy. She did not understand why the thought of her wedding no longer pleased her. Why was she so reluctant…?

Her thoughts were suddenly interrupted as the door of her room burst open, and several unknown men appeared on the threshold. She screamed, clutching at the bedcovers and holding them to her breasts in an attempt to cover herself.

'Who are you?' she cried. 'How dare you enter my room?'

'There she is!' The priest's voice rang out as he pushed his way through to the front of the little group. 'Take her! Take the witch!'

Magdalene stared at him in horror. 'You have lost your mind, Father Ludovic!' she said. 'When Don Sebastian hears what you have done, he will punish you severely for this intrusion.'

'The Don is dead, as you know full well, witch.' The priest's eyes glowed with triumph. 'You have robbed him of life with your evil spells.' He held up a handkerchief with her initials embroidered on it. 'This lay by his side, and there are strange herbs tied inside it – feathers and the leg of a lizard, too. Proof of witchcraft!'

'Don Sebastian is dead?' Magdalene caught the sob as it rose in her throat. 'Oh, no, no! I cannot believe it. He was well when I left him but an hour or two ago...'

'And now he is dead. You convict yourself with your own words, witch! You were the last person to see him alive, and now he lies cold on his bed.' The priest turned to his companions, who Magdalene suddenly realised were wearing the colours of the Inquisition. Her face turned pale as she understood that she was being arrested. 'Take her, I say! She is my prisoner until I hand her over to the Inquisitors.'

Trembling, Magdalene slipped from the bed, reaching for a loose silk robe. She put it on hastily, her chin going up as the guards made a move towards her.

'You will give me a few minutes to dress, señores?'

They hesitated, looking at each other uncertainly, but the priest pushed his way through their ranks. Seizing Magdalene's arm, he thrust her into their midst.

'Bring her as she is – I do not trust her! If we leave her for one moment, she may change into a bird and fly away.'

Magdalene looked at him scornfully. 'If I had the power to change my form, do you imagine your presence would stop me? You know I am not a witch. You have made up these lies to punish me because I would not listen to you.'

'I am not the only one who calls you a witch. Your cousin Doña Isabella d'Ortega will give evidence against you, and Don Rodrigo is living proof of your wickedness. You have bewitched that unfortunate young man...'

'He is merely in love with me.' Magdalene laughed mockingly. 'Even the Inquisitors will not listen to charges such as these!'

'There is still Don Sebastian's murder,' the priest reminded her, 'and you are a self-confessed heretic.' He smiled nastily. 'I think you will find that a serious charge, Magdalene d'Ortega.'

Magdalene shivered as she heard the note of menace in his tone. It was the first time that he had ever dared to drop the courtesy title of Doña when he addressed her, and it told her more surely than anything else that her situation was desperate. His lack of respect towards her was proof of the confidence he felt in his ability to have her condemned as a witch and a heretic.

She was suddenly very afraid. He saw it in her eyes and laughed, sensing his triumph. Leaning towards her, he looked into her face and she recoiled from the sour smell of his breath.

'So, you are beginning to fear me,' he muttered, grinning. 'You will learn your lesson well, witch.' Turning to the guards, he flung out his arm dramatically. 'Take her to the cart, and make sure she cannot escape. Bind her if she struggles.'

'Lifting her head, Magdalene looked at him, her pride returning as the fear ebbed. 'I shall not struggle,' she said disdainfully. 'You think me friendless, but I still have my uncle and Don Rodrigo – they will help me.'

'Perhaps.' The priest met her proud look with anger. 'Yet I doubt either would risk being questioned by the Inquisitors.'

Magdalene was silent as her captors led her outside. The priest was right, she thought bitterly; her uncle would not try to save her. If she were dead he would most likely inherit her fortune – but not if he angered the Inquisition. No, there was only Rodrigo to whom she could appeal for help. Perhaps, if he knew she was being arrested, but who could she send to him...?

A little crowd was gathered in the courtyard. Don Sebastian's servants, her uncle – and Don Rodrigo! At the sight of him, a faint hope sparked in her eyes.

'Help me,' she cried, twisting her head to look into his face. 'Tell them it isn't true! Tell them I did not bewitch you. You know I am not a witch. You know it!'

'Say nothing, Don Rodrigo,' the priest warned. 'Speak in her defence, and you may be questioned about Don Sebastian's murder. It may be thought that you conspired against him together ... that you, too, are contaminated by her evil.'

Rodrigo's face paled. He stared at Magdalene, torn by the desperate appeal in her eyes and his fear of the Inquisitors. Then he shook his head, taking a step backwards. 'No,' he whispered. 'I know nothing of the Don's death. I have been with Doña Isabella all afternoon... I have been with my betrothed, planning our wedding. Ask her. She will swear it was so. She will swear it, I say!'

For a moment Magdalene swayed as the faintness swept over her. She was alone, deserted by all those who had been her friends. Even Rodrigo had turned from her in her time of need; his passionate love forgotten as he felt fear prick him – fear of pain and a terrible death.

Someone spat at her as she passed, and there were angry cries all around her. The Don had been a good master, and his servants wanted to vent their fury on the woman who had killed him – the woman who should have been his wife! They all believed her guilty of his murder, these people she had known, who had been so willing to smile at her and serve her. If they could turn on her so swiftly, what chance had she of being found innocent by the fanatical Inquisitors?

Magdalene's face was pale as her guards forced her through the crowd, which was growing both in numbers and hostility. Men from the village had joined the estate workers, and some of them shook their fists at her as she was pushed up the steps into the cart. She, who had always travelled in her family's coach with the d'Ortega crest emblazoned on the side, was now to be driven through the town in a common cart! She felt the sting of shame, holding her silk robe tighter around her body defensively. If the mood of the villagers was anything to go by, she might never reach the stronghold of the Inquisition. They were hurling insults at her now, and one man threw a stone that struck her cheek. She gave him a haughty look, daring him to throw another. He gazed into her eyes, hesitating as if suddenly uncertain; then his arm dropped to his side and he fell back through the crowd and walked away.

The priest held up his hand, demanding silence. 'You are good, honest people,' he said as a hush fell over them. 'I know you want this evil woman punished but you must leave her to those who understand these things. The Inquisition will give her a fair hearing, and she will pay for her wickedness. Believe me, my friends, she will not die too easily.'

A burst of hoarse cheering greeted his words. Magdalene sank into the corner of the cart, half fainting as she heard the hatred in their voices and saw the menace in every face. Not one of them showed any sign of sympathy for her. How could these people believe the priest's lies about her? It was all so confusing and frightening and yet she knew that her ordeal had hardly begun. She had still to face the Inquisition...

'Don Sebastian dead?' Nicholas Treggaron stared at Don José in disbelief. 'Magdalene taken as a witch? I don't believe it! Before God, man, why did you let them take her? You must know what the Inquisitors will do to her?'

'They will put her to the question, but if she is innocent...' Don José's eyes slid away from the burning accusation in the Englishman's gaze. 'There was nothing I could do to save her. Proof was found of her witchcraft, and Don Sebastian had such a look of horror on his face...'

'Proof? A kerchief with some feathers in it? Anyone could have laid it beside the body. I doubt not that the Don was murdered, but not by Magdalene. You must know that she is not a witch!'

'Steady, Nick,' Ralph warned, seeing his friend's clenched fist on the hilt of his sword. 'From the sound of it, you could have done little to help her if you had been here yourself...'

'They would not have taken her while I lived,' Nick growled. 'You know what evil thoughts that black-robed snake has in mind, Ralph. I'll wager he is behind this somehow.'

'Ay, I've no doubt of that, but what can you do? If the Inquisition have her they'll not give her up. You would not dare to try to save her. You would burn right merrily beside her.'

'Would you have me stand aside and leave her to her fate?' Nick demanded, his eyes bright with anger. 'I was too late to help Cathy, but I'll not let it happen again, Ralph. Not if it means my life is forfeit!'

'Then you mean to go after her?'

'Yes.' Nick frowned. 'You must go back to the ship. Wait for me for two days, and if I do not come...'

'...skulk back to England like a frightened rabbit, I suppose? If you were not my friend, I'd have your hide for that, Nick. If you intend to risk your neck for this wench, I'll stand by you.'

'Then we must lose no time,' Nick said, his eyes bleak. 'I thank God for that peasant who brought us here for the promise of a few silver coins. Had it not been for him, we should undoubtedly have arrived too late.'

'Then perhaps it is God's will that we shall save the girl.' Ralph smiled as he kicked his horse's flanks. 'Lead on, my friend. I am sick of this place and ready for some action!'

CHAPTER THREE

How long had they been travelling, Magdalene wondered as she stared round at the unfamiliar countryside. She had lain in a daze while the fierce heat of the sun beat down on her, hardly aware of the discomfort as the cart rattled over ruts and holes in the road. Roads that had been hardened by weeks of dry weather so that clouds of fine white dust rose in the air as the wheels churned. Now at last the sun was dipping behind the distant hills, and the night brought a welcome coolness.

Magdalene sat up cautiously, looking at the guards walking beside the cart, and at the back of the man who had condemned her to this shameful arrest. He rode beside the driver, and at this moment was seemingly asleep with his head nodding forward on his chest. Two guards were plodding in the rear and a third trailed far behind them, but where were the others? There had been nearer a dozen when they took her prisoner, and she surmised that they must have gone on ahead to warn of her coming. The remaining few looked weary, as if the heat and the dust had taken its toll of their strength. They seemed to be looking at the ground, concentrating on putting one foot before the other.

It occurred to her that, if she were to have any chance of escape at all, this must be the moment, before they reached the castle of the Inquisitors; for that was surely where she was being taken. The Inquisition had many strongholds, but there was a castle on the hill overlooking the sea some way further up the coast, past Cadiz, and it must be there that she was bound. It was a terrible place, she had heard, and one from which no one had ever been known to escape.

A sudden surge of desperation drove her to action. She sprang to her feet, clambering over the side of the cart and throwing herself to the ground, landing on her hands and knees. The fall winded her for a moment, stinging her flesh with the impact; then she was on her feet and running, even as the shout of warning went up.

She did not dare to glance back, but she could hear the cries of the pursuing guards. Sobbing with fear and gasping, she began to scramble up the steep incline at the side of the road. She had no idea where she was going, but she knew she had to get away from her captors now! The sound of heavy breathing was close behind her. They were gaining on her! With a cry of desperation, the girl redoubled her efforts and missed her footing. She felt herself slipping and made a wild grab at a gorse bush; but as she pulled herself to her feet again, they were on her. She screamed wildly, clawing and kicking as the rough hands reached out for her, dragging her downwards. She slithered over the dry earth and rock, feeling the sting of grit against her hands and face. Now one of them had his fingers in her long hair. Tears stung her eyes as he jerked hard, forcing her to cease fighting.

'Be still, witch, or it will be the worse for you!' The priest had caught up with them. His face twisted with hatred as he looked at her. 'Bind her wrists and ankles; we'll not risk another escape attempt.'

Magdalene was silent as they obeyed him, wincing as the ropes cut into her soft flesh, but biting back the cry of pain she knew her tormentor wanted to hear. She raised her eyes proudly to his, refusing to let him see her fear.

'So the witch is still defiant?' He smiled coldly. 'Good! It would be a pity if the entertainment were over too soon.'

A shiver of pure terror ran through Magdalene as she looked into his face and saw the cruelty there. He was enjoying his moment of triumph! He wanted to see her begging for mercy! How long would she be able to stand the pain the torturers would inflict on her? How long before she screamed for mercy and crawled at the feet of this vile creature, weeping for an end to the agony?

She saw that he had read her mind, and his lips curved into a horrible grin. 'Ah, I see that you begin to understand, witch,' he murmured. 'Before I have done with you, your pride will be humbled a hundred times.'

He turned away as two of the guards bundled her into the cart, and she lay where she fell, too shocked to move as she felt the jolting motion begin again. Closing her eyes, she began to pray silently, her body tense with fear. Soon she would be at the castle, and then... Then she could pray only for a swift death.

'I had hoped to see some sign of them before now.' Nick reined in at the brow of a hill, his eyes straining in the gathering dusk as he searched the long, twisting road below. 'We were some hours behind them, but they cannot travel swiftly with that cart. Surely we must catch up with them soon!'

Ralph nodded, his face grim as he heard the note of desperation in his companion's voice. He had known from the first that Nick had been struck by the Spanish girl's faint resemblance to Cathy, and he understood what was driving him now. Cathy's death had been tormenting the man for weeks, and somehow this girl's plight had assumed a terrible significance in Nick's mind. He had blamed himself for his cousin's tragic death, and this was his chance of atonement. Ralph knew he would rather die than abandon the girl, and he could only hope that by some miracle they would be able to rescue her before it was too late.

'You know they can't reach the castle before nightfall,' he said. 'If Don José is right, they will probably sleep on the road for a few hours and continue their journey at daybreak.'

'Then we must come across them soon; and if fortune smiles on us, they'll be taken unawares.'

'Ay, for they'll not be expecting an attack.' Ralph grinned at him. 'Besides, Don José said there were no more than a dozen at most. It will be light work for our swords, my friend.'

Nick laughed, the shadows fading from his eyes for a moment, only to return as the haunting fear swept into his mind. 'By heaven! If that serpent has harmed her, I'll see he pays for it a thousand times over!'

'Surely he will not dare?' Ralph raised his brows. 'Even he fears his masters. He cannot touch her until she has been examined by the Inquisitors.'

'I pray that you are right,' Nick replied, his

voice harsh with anguish. 'I know you think me a fool, Ralph, but if I should fail her too...'

'I understand more than you realise. She is beautiful – and Cathy was dear to me, too, remember?'

'Yes, I remember.' A curt nod of the head. 'Then we'd best waste no more time in talk.'

Nick urged his horse on down, guiding it gently but firmly as its hooves slipped and faltered on the uncertain footing. This was the shortest route, and he was in a hurry! Ralph might be right about the priest's fear of his masters, but Nick had seen the hunger in his eyes when he looked at Magdalene, and there was always a chance that his lust might overcome the fear...

'We'll rest here until dawn.' The priest's words reached Magdalene through the haze of apathy that had held her mind. 'Build a fire by that stream, and bring the girl to me. I want to question her.'

Magdalene stifled the cry of pain that reached her lips as she was dragged roughly from the cart. She tried to stand but collapsed on the ground, shaking her head as the guards ordered her to her feet.

'You have bound me too tightly,' she said. 'My limbs are numb. I cannot feel them.'

'Untie her ankles, but leave her wrists bound,' the priest ordered, and was obeyed.

She almost cried out at the agony as her blood began to circulate again, hobbling unsteadily towards her tormentor, who was kneeling by the stream. She stood watching him while he cupped the clear water in his hand and drank, her tongue moving over her dry lips as she realised how thirsty she was. It must be six or seven hours since her arrest, and for several of them she had lain beneath a burning sun.

The man glanced up and saw her watching him. Her thin lips twisted with mockery and he cupped his hands in the water once more, letting it run through his open fingers, deliberately taunting her.

'Are you thirsty, witch?'

'Yes.' Magdalene knew she was a fool to confess it, but the sight of the water was tantalising. 'Are you planning to let me die of thirst? That won't please your masters.'

'You wrong me, Magdalene,' he said, his voice suddenly soft and full of cunning. 'I will give you water – if you ask me for it in a properly humble manner.' He cupped his hands in the stream and stood up, coming to stand in front of her. 'Ask me, you proud bitch. Ask me!'

Magdalene shook her head. Her thirst was making her tongue seem too big for her mouth, but she would not beg. She knew that he would not let her drink even if she pleaded with him. As if to prove her suspicion, he opened his fingers and let the water run away.

'Still the haughty bitch disdains my help,' he muttered, his eyes glinting with anger. 'Always she turned from me as if I were beneath contempt – but no more. I'll teach you better manners, witch!'

He suddenly sprang at her with a snarl, one podgy hand tangling in her hair as he forced her head back. As his wet, slobbering mouth fastened over hers, Magdalene experienced such a surge of revulsion that she acted without thinking, bringing her knee upwards in a sharp jerking motion that caught him in the groin. When he recoiled, yelling with pain, she twisted away from him, dodging out of reach and tripping over the hem of her nightrobe as she tried to avoid his grasping hands. He shouted for the guards, but even as he did so, there were more shouts and the sharp crack of a pistol, followed by the clash of steel against steel.

Surprise and then fear registered in the priest's face as he turned and saw the furious fighting a short distance from where he stood. A cry of agony from one of the guards made the colour leave his cheeks; he backed away as a wounded man stumbled past him, clutching at his belly while the blood trickled through his sprawled fingers. And then his stunned gaze was drawn to the face of the tall, wild-eyed avenger who had just dispatched a second victim to the fires of hell. What he saw there terrified him so much that he turned and ran, hitching up his black robes to reveal the thin legs beneath – legs that could scarcely support him as he fled in panic.

'The scurvy swine!' Ralph cried, laughing as he watched the priest's undignified flight. 'See how the rabbit runs!'

But Nick's eyes were elsewhere. Throwing down his sword, he moved swiftly towards the white-faced girl, catching her in his arms as she swooned. For a moment her eyelids fluttered as she gazed into his face, and then she went limp in his embrace, as if her strength had suddenly drained away. Nick held her gently against his chest, cradling her like a child.

'Be at peace now, my little one,' he murmured softly. 'You are safe, my sweet Magdalene, and no one shall ever hurt you again. I swear it.'

Whether his words had reached through the darkness that clouded her mind, he could not tell. She lay limp and still in his hands as he carried her towards his friend.

'Her wrists are bound,' he said. 'Cut her free quickly. See the scratches on her cheeks! The brutes have treated her ill, Ralph, but at least she is alive.'

'Then we came in time. God be praised!' Ralph used his sword to sever her bonds, scowling as he saw the red weals on her flesh.

'She lives. But for the rest, only time will tell.' Nick's face was grim. 'Who can say what harm had been done here today? Her whole world has been destroyed, for she can never go home – torture and certain death would follow if she attempted it.'

'No, she cannot return to her family.' Ralph frowned, his eyes watchful as he studied the other man's face. 'So what do we do with her now?'

'I shall take her to England.'

'And then?' Ralph arched his brow. 'She is a Spaniard and a Catholic, Nick, had you forgotten that?'

Anger flashed momentarily in Nick's eyes. 'I know it. Yet if she were in truth the witch they named her, I could not leave her here knowing what they would do to her. She goes with us, Ralph. With or without your approval.'

'By heaven! I believe you mean that...' Suddenly he understood, and the laughter rattled in his throat. 'If that's the way of it, my friend, I'll say no more. Come, we must hurry to catch the wind, for unless I'm mistaken, that rabbit will run straight to his warren and there'll be a reckoning to pay for this night's work.'

Magdalene's sigh brought both men's attention swiftly to her. As her eyes flickered open, she gave a faint cry and jerked in Nick's arms.

'You are safe now, Doña Magdalene,' he said, gently lowering her so that her feet touched the ground, but holding her still as she swayed and clung to his arm for support. 'In a moment I shall put you on my horse. We cannot take the cart.'

'I shall not get in that shameful cart again,' she retorted indignantly, bringing a faint smile to his lips. 'I can ride with your help, Mr Treggaron. I am better now. It was foolish of me to faint, just when you had saved me. Have you any water, please?'

Ralph handed her his water-bottle, and his soft chuckle brought her eyes to his face. He smiled reassuringly at her. 'You cannot stay here now, Doña Magdalene. Will you come to England with us?'

She frowned, looking at him thoughtfully between sips of water as she tried to gather her wits. 'I must,' she said at last. 'There is nothing for me here. But I do not wish to be a burden to you, sir. When we reach England, I shall seek out my mother's relatives, and ask them to give me a home until...' The words died in her throat as she realised for the first time how desperate her situation really was. She had no money, no possessions – not even a gown to clothe herself in.

'There will be time enough to worry about the future when we reach England,' Nick interrupted harshly. 'Are you able to ride now?'

Magdalene stared at him in surprise. He had been so gentle with her, but now he seemed angry. Why? What had she done to displease him? She could see no reason for his change of mood, unless it was because Sir Ralph had offered to take her to England. Yes, of course, that must be it. The Englishman had felt obliged to help her when he saw her struggling in Father Ludovic's loathsome embrace, but she was an embarrassment to him – a burden he had shouldered but did not want! Well, she would be as little trouble to him as possible, she decided, jutting her chin as she gazed up into the cool blue eyes.

'Certainly I can ride, and thank you for the water,' she said, her face proud. 'Why do we wait, Mr Treggaron?'

'Why, indeed?'

There was a suspicion of laughter about his mouth, and she wondered if he was mocking her. Then two strong hands encircled her waist and she was swung up into the saddle of the great black horse he rode; another moment and he was behind her, his arms firmly holding her closely pressed against him as he took up the reins. For one second she felt dizzy and feared she would faint again, but then the warmth of his body flowed into her and his strength restored her. Within the circle of his arms she felt safe and protected, sheltered from the terrible memories she was trying so desperately to shut out of her mind.

Leaning against him as he urged his horse to a gentle canter, she closed her eyes, allowing herself to relax. For a little while she would not think about the future or what had happened to her. She would pretend that this was all a dream and that she would wake up in her own little room. Except that she was not sure that she wanted to wake up. Ever...

Magdalene stirred, throwing one arm across the bed as the dream made her begin to toss restlessly. Suddenly she gave a cry and sat up, her eyes flying open. For a moment she stared about her wildly, wondering where she was. Then she felt the gentle rocking motion of the ship, and memory returned. She was on board *Treggaron Rose*, and had been for several days now. For the first three days she had been sick all the time, her head constantly aching.

Putting her feet gingerly to the floor, she was relieved to find that her limbs no longer felt unsteady beneath her. Her eyes moved round the cabin, which was adequately furnished but in a spartan, masculine manner befitting the man to whom it belonged. There were no luxuries here, nothing but the basic essentials necessary for the minimum of comfort. Captain Treggaron was quite obviously not a man to pamper himself; she had seen that when he showed her to the cabin the first night on board, apologising gruffly for his poor hospitality.

'It is not fit for you, Doña Magdalene,' he had said. 'But it's all I can offer for the moment.'

She had been surprised to discover that she was to sail on Nicholas Treggaron's own ship; though, when she thought about it, she realised that the signs had all been there if she had cared to look for them. His skin was lightly tanned as if he spent most of his life outdoors, and there was that inner vitality which she had noticed when they first met. It should have been obvious to her then that he was not simply a courtier, despite the fine clothes he had worn to greet the Spanish King. Now that she had seen him in the leather trunks and jerkin he wore at sea, she knew that this was the real man – a man who walked alone.

It was a strange phrase to describe the captain of a ship and all its crew, but Magdalene had seen enough these past days, in spite of her sickness, to believe that it was true. There was something in him that kept him apart from other men. She had watched him at the wheel when he thought himself unobserved, and sometimes she had seen such loneliness in his eyes that it touched something deep within her, making her want to reach out to him. Yet, when he was with his friend, those eyes were warm and full of laughter, and she wondered if she had imagined that haunted look. If she had dared, she would have liked to stand by his side as he stood, feet apart, on the poop, surveying his ship and the ocean so coolly, and she would have liked to see if she could bring a smile to his lips, but she was afraid to approach him. He would not have been angry if she had, she knew that, for he was always pleasant and considerate of her, but he might feel it an intrusion into his private world. So she could only watch from a distance, and wait for him to remember that she was there.

Sighing, Magdalene began to dress herself, struggling with the ties of her petticoats and those of her bodice. She had always been used to the services of a maid, but she was learning to manage alone, mainly because she knew that she must. The future was uncertain, but it would be very different from the sheltered life she had known, of that much she was sure. The clothes she was wearing had all been given to her by Mr Treggaron – no, she must remember to call him Captain now or he might be offended! – and they were a little large for her, but she was pleased to have them. They were pretty and fashioned of the softest silk, in a shade of blue she had always liked. There had, however, been an odd look in the Captain's eyes when he gave them to her.

'These may fit you,' he had muttered harshly as the big, leather-bound chest had been brought in by one of the crew. 'They were purchased as a gift for someone else, but she has no use for them now. You are welcome to wear what you choose until new gowns can be commissioned in England.'

'You are very kind,' Magdalene had replied, peeping at his face beneath lowered lashes and wondering at his stern expression. 'But are you sure your friend won't mind my wearing her clothes?'

A flicker of raw pain passed across his face. 'Cathy would have given them to you herself if she'd been here,' he said, his voice grating with emotion. 'Excuse me; I have work to do on deck.'

'Cathy...' Magdalene whispered as the cabin door closed behind him. His pain had touched her, making her throat feel tight and hot. Cathy must be the woman to whom she bore some resemblance – and she was certainly the reason for that haunted look in his eyes. But who was she?

For three days Magdalene had felt too ill to care who Cathy was but this morning, wearing her clothes, she was determined to solve the mystery. She knew she dare not ask Captain Treggaron – it was obviously too painful for him to discuss – but Sir Ralph was far more approachable. He had been kind to her since she came on board, helping her to find her way about the ship and sympathising when she was forced to rush to the rails and vomit over the side. He would tell her who Cathy was, and why Nicholas Treggaron looked so agonised whenever her name mentioned. He clearly cared very much for Cathy, whoever she was, but why was she no longer in need of her clothes?

There was no mirror in the cabin, so Magdalene was forced simply to drag a comb through her hair and leave it falling on her shoulders. She believed it made her appear untidy, but there was nothing she could do about it; the elaborate hairstyles she had been used to wearing took much skill and time to achieve. Besides, Sir Ralph had told her it suited her that way. Naturally, he was only trying to make her feel comfortable, but she was grateful for his thoughtfulness. Although she knew that she was safe enough now that the shores of Spain were left far behind, the future loomed uncertainly before her, and it was good to know that she had at least one friend. She hoped that Sir Ralph might help her to find her mother's relatives once they reached England, which could surely not be long now...

A queer, booming sound startled her as she made her way between decks. It sounded like the roar of a cannon! Reaching the hatch, she put her head out and gasped at the sight that met her eyes. Men were working with feverish haste in response to the attack on them by … two Spanish galleons! Rushing to the ship's rails, Magdalene stared in disbelief at the flag flying from the mizzen-mast of the nearest vessel. It was her own flag! Her own ships were firing on them!

'Oh no!' she cried. 'They don't know what they're doing. Someone must tell the captain to stop…'

'You must go below, Magdalene.' Nick's voice surprised her and she spun round, staring at him wildly. 'I cannot be responsible for your safety if you remain on deck while we are under fire.'

'But they're my ships,' she said, grasping at his arm in her desperation. 'How can the commanders attack us? They cannot know I'm on board.' Her face turned pale as she saw the strange expression on his face. 'You think they do know … that it's the reason for the attack? No… No! My uncle would never…'

'Don José is on board the ship that fired on us. The only reason I let them get near enough to attack us was because I thought your uncle might have come in friendship.

He is in command, Magdalene.' Nick frowned, knowing how deeply his words must wound her. 'He gave the order to fire on us as soon as he was close enough. There was no warning, no request to come aboard. It's my opinion that he means to sink us if he can – which he won't, if you go below and let me be about my business!'

She gasped at the cold brutality of his words, staring at him ashen-faced for one brief moment before she turned and ran below.

'Damn!' Nick muttered, wishing he had handled the situation better, but knowing there was no time to waste if he was to save his ship – and her life! 'Damn. Damn. Damn!'

Back in her cabin, Magdalene leant against the door, trembling as she fought for breath. It was no wonder Captain Treggaron was furious with her; she had brought on this attack merely by being on his ship. He had risked his life for her once already, and now he was being forced into a battle he could not want. He might well lose his ship – and his life! – and it was her fault. How he must be regretting the impulse that had caused him to come to her rescue. She was a curse on him, just as she had been on Don Sebastian, and it would be better for everyone if she were dead.

Covering her face with her hands, Magdalene let the hot tears slip between her fingers. She had not cried once since her ordeal at the priest's hands, but now all the fear and misery returned to sweep over her in a great wave and she was seized by violent shudders that shook her whole body.

Above her head were the sounds of a fierce battle, and every now and then she could feel the shock as *Treggaron Rose* loosed her own guns. The noise was tremendous, but through it all she could hear one man's voice, directing, commanding … and somehow it comforted her. She had an inner sureness that somehow Nick would win despite the terrible odds against him. She ought to have been frightened, but she wasn't.

Gradually the shudders coursing through her body lessened, becoming tiny shivers, and then she was quiet again, the storm of grief leaving her as suddenly as it had overtaken her. She realised that she felt much better, that she had been holding her emotions in check all this time, afraid to give way to the nightmare that hovered at the back of her mind, threatening to destroy her. Now at last she had faced it and it no longer had the power to frighten her. Don Sebastian was dead and she had been condemned as a witch, but the Englishman had saved her. He had told her that she was safe with him, that no one would ever hurt her again. When had he said that? She could not remember, but it seemed that he had done so. Perhaps it was in her dreams... Dreams that troubled her strangely...

Magdalene became aware of the sudden silence. What was happening? It must be some time since the battle had begun, so why had the guns stopped firing? She went to the window to look out. What was that cloud of smoke on the horizon? A loud burst of cheering from the deck above her set her pulses racing. Had they beaten off the attack? Unlikely as it seemed, they must have done so. Yes, something told her it was so. The Englishman had saved her again, as she had instinctively known he would. Her heart pounded with excitement. What a brave, bold man he was!

Hearing the sound of booted footsteps outside her door, she looked up, her heart jerking as the door opened and she saw Nicholas Treggaron standing on the threshold. She rose hastily to her feet, smiling at him tremulously as she witnessed the elation of victory in his face.

'You have won,' she said, hiding her shaking hands from his view. 'I knew you would! Don José is not used to commanding a ship. The fleet was my father's, and mine before...'

'I'm not sure if you mean that as a

compliment?' Nick grinned, seeing her fiery blush when she realised how her words had sounded, almost as if she was implying that he had won only because her uncle was not a skilled captain. It was definitely not what she had meant! The Englishman's smile of amusement widened as he saw her confusion. 'I shall believe that you meant well. No, don't apologise! It is I who should beg your pardon for shouting at you when we came under fire. I was concerned for your safety...' He broke off, frowning at the tear-stains on her cheeks. 'You have been crying. Was that my fault?'

'In part,' Magdalene admitted with a faint sigh. 'But I have not cried since ... since I was accused of Don Sebastian's murder.' She lifted her clear eyes to his, pride making them sparkle like jewels. 'You have not asked, Captain Treggaron, but I am innocent of that charge. I am neither a witch nor a murderess.'

'I know.' He smiled at her and she felt a peculiar warmth spreading through her entire body. It was almost as if he had caressed her even though he had not touched her. 'You are as innocent as you are beautiful, Doña Magdalene. I need no proof, nor shall I ever speak of this again ... unless you wish it?'

'No.' She shook her head, wishing she understood this man. He was like no other she had ever met. He made no demands on her, and yet she felt the strength of his personality binding her to him. It frightened her a little, for she did not know what he wanted from her, but he must want something. No man gave as much as he without demanding a reward. 'There will be no need to speak of it again. I shall simply forget it happened, and make a new life for myself with my mother's family, if I can find them...' Her voice faltered, and Nick saw the anxiety in her.

'If you wish to find your relatives, I shall of course do all I can to help you, but in the meantime you will live at Treggaron Manor.'

'At– At your house?' She stared at him, feeling breathless. Was he about to demand his reward at last?

'It is a large house,' he said, a little smile playing about his lips, 'and I am very seldom in it. You need not fear that I shall intrude upon your privacy – or that I shall ask anything of you that you would rather not give.'

'Oh, I did not mean...' She could find no words to explain her feelings, for she did not understand them herself. The man frightened her at times, but now that he had made his own intentions clear, her main reaction was disappointment – disappointment that she would not often see him.

And yet why should that matter to her?

Had she not always longed for peace, to be left alone in her own little world to dream and pray? Somehow, ever since she had first looked into those blue eyes that were surveying her so thoughtfully now, her world had never been the same; nor did she want to turn back time, she realised now. If she could return to her life as it had been before that night, she would not do so. She had changed, was changing even at this moment. She was becoming another person: a person she had always known was there inside her, waiting... The knowledge scared her, yet she found it exciting, too, especially when Nicholas Treggaron was near her. As he was at this moment. So near that she was afraid he would hear the wild beating of her heart. Why did he make her feel as if she had been asleep all of her life, as if she had never really lived at all until the moment she first saw him?

The answer when it came was so terrifying that she drew away from him instinctively, afraid to believe the prompting of her own heart. Looking out of the cabin window, she kept her face averted, not wanting him to read what was in her eyes. She was nothing to this man, nothing more than a burden that had been forced upon him. He had made no demands on her – and she must make none on him. She must not ask for more than he was willing to give.

'You are very generous, Captain Treggaron,' she said, marvelling that she could sound so calm when her whole body was on fire. 'I shall accept your invitation – for the moment.'

'I'm glad,' he said, and the gentleness in his voice was once more like the silken stroking of a lover's hand. It caused her to tremble, and her knees felt so weak that she almost swayed with the strange longing he aroused in her. 'Believe me, Magdalene, I would rather die than hurt you...'

She felt a rush of emotion in her throat. No one – no one! – had ever spoken to her with such tenderness before. It sent her senses swimming, bringing tears to her eyes. Surely it must mean that he cared for her a little! She turned round, a smile lighting her eyes and found herself staring at an empty room. He had gone so softly and swiftly that she had not heard him leave.

'But you are hurting me,' she whispered. 'I – I do not want to love you...'

From the moment it came into view, Magdalene was surprised by Treggaron Manor. Somehow she had not expected it to look so grand. It was really a castle, she decided, but in recent times a more modern wing had been built for comfort, the red-brick walls panelled with English oak and the windows fitted with thick, bubbled glass instead of merely being shuttered. A luxury that must have cost its owner a small fortune!

It was to the new wing that Captain Treggaron's housekeeper showed Magdalene a short time later. The woman was stout, grey-haired and frankly curious as she looked at her master's guest.

'These rooms have not been used since ... for quite a time now,' she said with a little sniff that seemed to indicate disapproval. 'If I'd known Captain Treggaron was bringing a guest home, I could have had them ready for you.'

'I'm sure they will be quite comfortable, Mrs Penrith – I have your name right?'

'Ay, that's near enough.' The housekeeper sniffed again. 'Would you be from London then, miss?'

Magdalene smiled to herself, hearing the prejudice in the older woman's voice. She would be a foreigner if she came from the next town, let alone another country. It was always so with village folk who scarcely ever left their homes, and she had heard her own peasants talk in just such a way about workers from a neighbouring estate.

'I come from Spain,' she replied, knowing that it would be foolish to lie. 'But my mother was born in Devon. Is that far from here?'

'A Devon woman, was she?' Mrs Penrith

106

eyed her consideringly. 'I was meself until I married. Well, you'll find it a bit strange hereabouts after them foreign parts, but I expect you'll settle after a while. I took my time, but you get used to it.'

Magdalene realised that the woman had not understood she came from so far away. To her Spain was just another place, like London or Edinburgh, and Mrs Penrith had no idea where any of them were. Nor did she wish to, for in her mind they were all wicked, sinful parts, and she clearly believed in staying at home. However, Magdalene's mother had been a Devon woman, and some of the suspicion left the housekeeper's eyes.

'And what was your mother's name afore she married then, miss?'

'Mary Fisher. I think her father was a chandler. She met my father when he came into the shop to provision his ship. She fell in love with him, and when he went, she went with him.'

'Mary Fisher! Her that went off with that foreign nobleman?' Mrs Penrith exclaimed, her eyes gleaming with excitement. 'I recall the talk that caused, right enough. You'll be Will Fisher's granddaughter then. An honest man, Will Fisher. Well, bless my soul!'

'Do you know my grandfather?' Magdalene asked, feeling a tingle at the base of her spine.

'Oh, I knew him well afore I was wed. The

poor soul passed away a good many years back now.'

'Oh...' Magdalene sighed, disappointed. So she had no English relatives, after all.

There was a distinct look of approval in Mrs Penrith's eyes now. She stopped walking and took a key from the bunch at her waist, inserting it into the lock of a door. 'We'll soon have things nice and comfy for you, miss. I'll send Susan up to light a fire, and we'll make up the bed while you take supper with the master.'

Magdalene looked round her, feeling a little surprised. She was in the first of what was obviously a well furnished set of rooms. It was not a large chamber, but it had a pleasant atmosphere. Light pink velvet curtains hung at the window, and there were cushions of the same colour on the oak settle by the fireplace. A virginal lay on the floor near by and there was a small, brightly-patterned rug in front of the hearth – obviously made by the same hands that had sewn the cushions and curtains. A frame for embroidery was standing by the window, and a viol was hanging by its ribbons from a hook on the wall. It was clearly the chamber of a talented and lively woman – a woman who had never known an idle moment in her life.

'Well, miss, shall you be comfortable here?'

Burning with curiosity, Magdalene turned to the housekeeper, who was observing her reactions with bright, watchful eyes. 'Who had these rooms before me?' she asked. 'Whoever it was must have been someone special, I think?'

'Why, it was Miss Cathy, of course. She always meant to fetch these things away, but she never seemed to make up her mind to it ... poor lass.'

'Miss Cathy?' A little shiver ran down Magdalene's spine. She was wearing Cathy's clothes, and these were Cathy's things, but who was this mystery woman? And where was she?

'She never will now, of course.' Mrs Penrith went on as if Magdalene had not spoken. 'Dead and buried she is – and the master in such a state when he came home! I've never seen a man look like he did. Half out of his mind with grief, he was, and who's to wonder at it?'

'Was–Was she his wife?' Magdalene asked, her mouth going suddenly dry.

'No, though we all thought she would marry the master when the time came.' Mrs Penrith sighed and shook her head. 'I was never more surprised in me life when she up and wed Jack Harston.' The housekeeper suddenly seemed to realise she was talking too much. 'Miss Cathy was the master's cousin, you see. Now, if you'll excuse me,

I've work to do, miss. Susan will be up shortly, and she'll show you the way to the dining-hall.'

'Thank you...'

The door had hardly closed behind the housekeeper before Magdalene realised she had not told her how Cathy had died. Yet it did not really matter, she thought sadly. Captain Treggaron's cousin had married someone else, and then died a short time later. It was not surprising that he sometimes had a haunted look in his eyes. He had lost the woman he loved. And Cathy had been deeply loved – you could tell that simply by looking round her room. She had been happy here, and because she had been happy, she had left her possessions where they were, as though she wanted to keep her memories intact.

Suddenly Magdalene felt as if she were intruding. She did not belong here in this room, amongst these things which still retained so much of Cathy's personality.

It was then the suspicion entered her mind. Was that why Captain Treggaron had brought her here and given her his cousin's apartments? He had said she reminded him of Cathy; was he trying to bring a ghost back to life?

'Oh no...' she choked. 'No! I'm not Cathy. I cannot give you back the love you have lost.'

Tears had begun to cloud her eyes, but she checked them as someone knocked at the door, calling out so that whoever it was might enter. A burly manservant came in, carrying the trunk which contained her clothes – no, Cathy's clothes! He took them through into the next chamber, nodded his head and went out again without speaking.

The incident had given Magdalene time to recover herself, however. She had no right to be upset; she knew it and accepted it. Captain Treggaron had not asked her to come into his life; he had simply been there when she needed him. She had nothing of her own and no family, if Mrs Penrith were speaking the truth, and there was no reason for her to lie. So Magdalene must simply take what had been given her, though her heart cried out against it. She was Magdalene d'Ortega, not Cathy's pale image. A woman in her own right – and she wanted to be loved for herself!

No, she must not look for love here, a tiny voice in her head warned her. To love was to become vulnerable. She had seen the pain in Doña Maria's eyes when her husband ignored her, heard the anguish in her mother's voice when she begged for understanding. Poor Mary Fisher had given up her home and family for the man she loved, but though he had married her, he had soon tired of her, finding his pleasures elsewhere. It was the way of men. Magdalene knew how much it hurt to lose the people you loved, for she had adored both her parents. Don Manuel had always been kind to her, seeming proud of his only child, but often he had been deliberately cruel to his wife. Yet Doña Maria had gone on loving him, so much that she could not face life without him. What fools women could be! Magdalene thought.

As she changed into the second of the two gowns Captain Treggaron had given her – an evening creation, softly styled in the French way Magdalene summoned up all the reserves of strength her strict training had instilled in her. Nicholas Treggaron had saved her life and given her a home, therefore she must be properly grateful. She must try to do whatever she could to make his home a place of comfort, and already she had noticed little signs of neglect – the kind of neglect that occurred when the master was too often from home. If her guardian, for she must think of Captain Treggaron as such, wanted music, she could play for him; she would work in the still-room beside Mrs Penrith, and assume all the duties of a chatelaine. It was small recompense for what he had done for her, but she would not – must not! – fall in love with him. For that could lead only to heartbreak...

'I'm sorry, miss I've no training as a lady's

maid.' Susan Watts stared at the beautiful Spanish girl in dismay. 'I'd like to dress your hair for you, but I don't know how. Nice if my sister Hanna were here, she could do it in a trice.'

'It doesn't matter.' Magdalene smiled at her. 'I am grateful for your help with the laces at the back of my gown. Now, I am ready. Will you show me the way to the dining-hall, please?'

'Yes, miss, I can do that.'

Magdalene looked at a dainty fan lying on the polished top of an oak coffer. She would have liked to carry it, for she was accustomed to do so, but she could not bring herself to use yet another of Cathy's possessions. She sighed, remembering all the beautiful trifles which had once been hers, that she had taken so much for granted; then she resolutely put them from her mind. She had left her old world behind for ever, and if she were to make a new life for herself she must not be always looking backward. Indeed, she would not do so again.

Looking about her with interest as Susan led the way downstairs, Magdalene discovered that she liked the house her rescuer had brought her to. There was something comforting about the soft mellowness of English oak, and she was charmed by the bright colours of the tapestries that covered tables, window-seats and walls. The furniture was mostly large and cumbersome, but the carving was of a gentler style than she had been used to and was somehow soothing. In the dining-hall a great buffet ran the length of one wall, its shelves filled with the sheen of polished pewter. In the middle of the room was a long, heavy table with bulbous supports and important-looking chairs stood at either end; along both sides were plain benches. The board was set with silver-gilt candelabra, a high domed salt, also gilded and platters to match. Venetian glass goblets and wine jugs with silver handles sat side by side with huge dishes filled with freshly-baked bread, fruit, cheeses and cold meat.

Knowing that Nicholas Treggaron was a man of simple tastes, the girl wondered if this display had been made for her benefit, and was touched by his thoughtfulness. When they knew each other better, she would tell him that it was not necessary to entertain her in such style, but to do so too soon would be an insult.

'Doña Magdalene,' he said, as she shyly approached the little group of men standing by the fireplace, realising now that there were other guests beside herself. Of course this was not all for her! 'How lovely you look this evening.' Nicholas Treggaron took the hand she offered and raised it to his lips briefly. 'May I present my friend Anton Barchester – and this gentleman is Sir Francis

Drake. Sir Francis has ridden from London with a message from Queen Elizabeth, and I shall be leaving with him for the city at first light.'

'Oh...' Magdalene curtsied to the two men who were strangers to her, blushing a little as each one kissed her hand in turn. Neither of them made it a caress as Nicholas did, but she saw a friendly interest in their faces. 'I am happy to meet Captain Treggaron's friends. I hope you have not been kept waiting too long, gentlemen?'

They all denied this at once, seeming to compete with each other to pay her compliments and engage her in conversation. She was a little hesitant at first, surprised by their easy manners and complete acceptance of her. It was so different from the way she had been used to being treated. At home, she was shown respect by her uncle's friends, but her views were not sought, nor was she expected to voice her own opinions freely, but here her words were awaited eagerly.

As the evening progressed, Magdalene began to enjoy herself and her laughter rang out again and again. The stories the men told were all so amusing, though Doña Magdalene might have been slightly shocked by some of them only a short while ago! But Doña Magdalene had gone for ever, and the new woman who was emerging gradually liked the free manners of her new English friends. It seemed that the evening passed too swiftly. Before she knew it, she was saying good-night and Susan was waiting with a lighted chamberstick to show her upstairs.

'I have seldom spent a more pleasant evening,' Sir Francis said, bowing over her hand. 'Treggaron must bring you to Court, Doña Magdalene, and soon!'

She thanked him, wishing each of them a restful night and turning at last to Nicholas Treggaron. 'I – I shall not see you in the morning then, sir?' she said, hiding the disappointment she felt at losing his company so soon.

'I shall be away only a few days,' he said softly, and she sensed that his words were meant to soothe her. Giving him her hand, she felt the familiar tingle that his slightest touch aroused in her. His lips merely brushed her skin, but it brought the blood rushing through her veins, making her aware of feelings and desires she had not known a woman could feel.

'I – I shall look forward to your return,' she murmured shyly, her heart leaping as the blue eyes seemed to gaze into her very soul.

'You will have Anton for company,' he said, and now those eyes had clouded with the look she had come to dread. 'If you wish to walk or ride within the boundaries of my estate, you are free to do so – but if you go

116

beyond, you must let Anton accompany you. Promise me you will never leave the grounds without him, Magdalene!'

There was such urgency in his voice that it almost frightened her. Was he afraid that she might run away? Surely she had given him no reason to think her so discourteous!

'I shall obey you, of course,' she said, a little catch in her voice.

'It was not an order, Magdalene.' Nick frowned at his own clumsiness. Just when she was beginning to respond to him, he had brought that shuttered look to her face once more. 'I am requesting you to let Anton accompany you for your own safety, that is all.'

'Then of course I shall do as you ask.'

Magdalene smiled at him. It was not for her to question his commands. He was master in his own home, and yet so many questions filled her mind! At times he was the gentlest, most considerate of men, but when the black moods descended on him she felt that she did not know him at all. What was it that haunted him? She was certain it concerned his cousin, and she was determined to find out exactly how Cathy had died. Would Susan tell her? She would ask her this very night.

CHAPTER FOUR

'You ride well, Doña Magdalene,' said
Anton, his light grey eyes admiring the way
she sat her horse. He had asked the groom
to saddle the easiest-tempered mount in
Treggaron's stables, but she had shaken her
head and demanded to be allowed to have
her own choice, a high-spirited mare with a
wicked glint in her eyes. 'I confess I am
surprised at your skill, my lady.'

Magdalene laughed, tossing her mane of
dark hair in a manner resembling that of her
wilful mount. 'My father kept only the finest
of Andalusian horses in his stables, sir, and
he taught me to ride when I was no more
than knee-high. I think he had wished for a
son to succeed him, but as he had only a
daughter...' She shrugged her shoulders
carelessly. 'It did not seem to matter when I
was a child; it was only as I grew into a
woman that he...' She took a firmer grip of
the reins, dismissing the old memories. 'I
shall race you to that tree, Anton!'

Anton watched her go, complacently
giving her a generous start until, suddenly
realising she needed no favours, he jerked
urgently into action. He was too late; she

had reached the tree long before him, laughing delightedly as she mocked him for a sluggard. He caught his breath at her beauty, marvelling at the change in her a few days had wrought. She had seemed a little reserved the night Nick had first brought her to Treggaron Manor, and after what she had suffered it was not surprising, but this past week had been a revelation to him.

They had become good friends, sharing their leisure hours as he showed her the extent of Nick's estate and the surrounding countryside with its wide sweep of open moorland and the dominating cliffs that held back the assault of a tumultuous sea. If he had begun to feel something more than friendship for the beautiful, innocent girl, he was careful to keep his thoughts well under control. Nick's instructions had been explicit, and the bond between them was too strong to risk for any woman, however lovely she might be. Besides, he suspected that Magdalene's heart was reserved for someone else. That being so, he could enjoy her company without restraint, feeling himself privileged to witness the blossoming of her womanhood.

'I let you win,' he said, laughing as he caught up with her at last. 'It will not happen again, I promise you! Would you like to ride as far as the cove?'

Magdalene shook her head. 'Not today,

Anton. I – I want to ask you something. May we walk for a little while, please?'

He saw that her mood was serious, and dismounted, coming to help her. 'What is it? Is something troubling you?'

She saw concern in his face and bit her lip, wondering how best to begin. He had made it plain that he liked her, but Nick was his friend. Would he be angry if she asked too many questions?'

'This riding-gown I am wearing belonged to Cathy when she was about sixteen. Mrs Penrith found it in a trunk, where it had been stored since it was discarded several years ago. It– It fits me almost perfectly, though Cathy must have been a little taller even then...'

'It distresses you to wear another woman's clothes?' Anton frowned, flicking back a lock of soft fair hair from his brow. 'I'm sure it is only until Nick can make other arrangements...'

'No, you don't understand.' Magdalene stopped him. 'The clothes themselves are not important. It's just that ... I feel Cathy's presence so much, but I know so little about her. I have asked both Susan Watts and Mrs Penrith, but they won't tell me how she died... They seem almost frightened to speak of it.'

'Nick has given orders that they are not to gossip about it, I expect.' Anton looked at her oddly. 'Why does it matter so much for you?'

'Why does her death haunt Captain Treggaron?' Magdalene asked, her eyes wide and glistening with emotion. 'He told me once that I reminded him of her. I am afraid that he – that he wants me to be...'

'You think he wants Cathy to live again through you?' Anton nodded, his eyes narrowed in thought. 'Cathy meant a great deal to him, it's true. Ralph said something of the sort to me before he left for London.'

'Then I was right...' Magdalene sighed. 'He brought me here so that he could make believe she was still alive. He– He thinks of me as a substitute for her...'

'I don't know, and that's the truth,' Anton confessed. 'Why don't you ask him? Tell him how you feel about using Cathy's clothes and apartments...'

'Oh no, I couldn't,' she cried. 'It would seem so ungrateful, after all he has done to help me.'

'Nick would give you other rooms if he realised you felt uncomfortable.' Anton shrugged. 'Do you still want me to tell you about her death? It's not a pleasant story, I warn you.'

Magdalene shivered, sensing that some-thing terrible lay behind the mystery, but she had to know! 'I am aware that I have no right to ask it of you, but I need to understand,' she whispered, her face tight with pleading as she gazed up at him. 'I must know why Nick is so haunted by her memory.'

He told her then, sparing no details, and when he had finished, her cheeks were ashen. She felt the earth spinning round her, and was forced to clutch at his arm. Compared to what Cathy had suffered, her own ordeal was as nothing!

'Oh, poor, poor Cathy,' she choked, tears sliding silently down her cheeks. 'She did not deserve such a terrible fate. It was wicked ... wicked...'

'No, she did not deserve it,' Anton said grimly. 'Cathy was the sweetest, kindest girl in the world. Whenever she came into a room it was as if the sun had begun to shine. We all loved her – Ralph, myself and Nick. He blames himself because he was not here when she needed him, but Cathy had always walked safely to and from the village. Everyone was her friend. Who could have guessed that such a terrible evil would fall on her?'

'No one. It was not his fault, but now I understand why he is haunted by her death – why he can never forget her.' She gazed mistily into Anton's steady grey eyes. 'Thank you for telling me. It has explained many small mysteries that had puzzled me.'

He saw the sadness in her face, and frowned. 'I am sorry if what I have told you has caused you pain. If Nick did not want you to know the story, I'm sure it was only to spare you.'

She laid her hand gently on his arm. 'No. I – I think you may have saved me from a deeper hurt, sir. Now I know what Nick wants of me, and I shall try to please him if I can. I shall try to ease the wounds inside him.'

'Be yourself, Magdalene; no man could want more.'

She shook her head. 'It is not me he loves but Cathy's memory. Come, let us return to the house. I am sewing some fresh curtains for Nick's apartments, and I should like to have them finished in time for his return...'

'How dare you disobey my orders, Captain Treggaron?' The Queen's eyes flashed with temper. 'You were on a mission of peace and you abducted a girl of good family! By heaven! You deserve a sojourn in the Tower for this.'

Nick stared at her, keeping a tight rein on his own hot temper. Elizabeth's moods were fickle, and he knew that a wrong move could see him cooling his heels in a miserable cell for months. Besides, she had every right to be angry with him. He *had* jeopardised his mission for Magdalene's sake.

'Someone has lied to you, Your Majesty,' he said, more calmly than he felt. 'The girl was being abused by a servant of the Inquisition.

She had been wrongfully accused of being a witch, and…'

'Wrongfully?' Elizabeth was magnificent in her indignation, her eyes as bright as the diamonds that adorned her brow. 'How do you know the charge was not a just one, sir? Are you a witch-finder?'

'I know the girl, ma'am. She is young and innocent…'

'You fell in love with her, so you stole her from her home and brought her back to England with you. You are a rogue, Treggaron, and I've a mind to punish you as you deserve.' There was a faint twinkle in Elizabeth's eyes now. 'Shall I hang you? Or send you to the Tower?'

'If Your Majesty has no preference, I would rather hang.'

'God's teeth! I believe you would, rogue.' The Queen gave a harsh laugh as she stared at his proud face. His manner was bordering on insolence, and she would be well within her rights to teach him a sharp lesson. Yet there was something very appealing about that bold look in his eyes. 'Nay, Treggaron, not this time. I have need of men like you – rogue that you are! I prefer that you should return to sea and sink as many Spanish galleons as you can find.'

'Your wish is my command, ma'am.' Nick's lips twisted in a wry smile and he breathed again, but the relief was short-lived and the smile left his face as she spoke once more.

'However, the girl must be returned to her family. Don José has made a formal request through the French ambassador, and I have given my word that she will be sent home.'

'To certain death!' Nick cried, anger flaring now. 'I should have sunk that damned Spaniard when I had the chance!'

'Apparently you did. Unfortunately, he was picked up by another of his ships. A pity...' Elizabeth pursed her lips. 'I wish the girl no harm, Treggaron, but I must humour both the French and the Spaniards – for the moment. If the girl had fled the country, of course, I could do nothing... As it is, I command you to deliver her to me no later than ... shall we say six days hence? Do you understand me, sir?'

Nick stared at her uncertainly. The time allowed was impossible – utterly impossible, in fact, except by sea. Was she daring him to snatch Magdalene from beneath the noses of the Spanish again? He saw the glitter of mockery in his Sovereign's eyes and smiled inwardly. If it was a challenge, it was one he meant to accept!

'And if I were ungrateful enough to disobey you and take the girl with me, ma'am?'

'I should send one of my best captains after you. If you were caught, I should have no choice but to hang you, Treggaron.'

Laughter glowed briefly in the blue eyes. He made her a deep, elegant bow. 'If I were fool enough to be caught, I should deserve it.' As he bowed once more and reached for the door latch, he heard her soft laughter.

'I wish you fair winds, Captain,' she murmured as the door closed behind him.

Magdalene's head was bent industriously over her needlework when the door of her apartment burst open. She pricked her finger, starting up in alarm until she saw who stood on the threshold, his dark hair tossed and blown by the wind.

'Nick...' she cried gladly, her heart beginning to leap. 'You're home at last!'

He heard her use of his Christian name, but was in too much haste to wonder at it or the look of delight on her face. 'Leave what you're doing,' he commanded. 'Susan will be with you in a moment and will help you to pack whatever you need. Bring anything necessary for your comforts. It may be months before we can buy replacements now.'

'Where are we going?' she asked uncertainly, her limbs shaky as she got to her feet. 'Is– Is something wrong?'

'Your uncle has demanded your return, and the Queen has agreed.' A growl issued from his throat as he saw the fear spark in her eyes. 'Never while I live! Do you think I would give you up to those foul monsters of the Inquisition? I have seen the results of their work and I would not condemn my worst enemy to such a fate. No, you are coming with me, Magdalene. We'll put to sea and be out of reach before the time Elizabeth gave me is up.'

'You will take me with you? But you cannot disobey your Queen, Nick! You would be an outcast from your own country...'

'Perhaps – for a time.' He scowled at her. 'I'll risk it, if you will?'

'Oh yes!' Her eyes lit with excitement. She would not tell him so, but her greatest dread had been that he would be absent for months on end while she was left alone at Treggaron Manor. 'I can be ready within the hour.'

He stared at her then, suddenly aware of the new sparkle in her eyes. Taking three long strides towards her, he caught her hands in his own, holding them tightly as his gaze moved caressingly over her lovely face.

'You are as brave as you are beautiful, my Magdalene. Do not fear for the future. Whatever happens, I shall always take care of you. I swear it by all that I hold dear! Do you believe that?'

'Yes,' she whispered, her heart racing so wildly that she could scarcely breathe. 'Yes, I know it, Nick.'

And suddenly it did not matter that she

was only a poor image of the girl he had loved and lost. He was looking at her with such tenderness in his face that she felt her insides melting. No man had ever looked at her like that! No man had ever made her feel as if she were floating on a cloud into the blue of the sky. It was better to be second best than to lose all he was offering her.

'I swear I shall make you happy one day, Magdalene.'

'I am happy,' she replied, and at that moment it was true.

And then his head was close to hers. She could feel the soft warmth of his breath on her face; her lips parted invitingly and she lifted them for his kiss, wanting it, needing it. A kiss so sweet and lingering that it drew her heart from her body, making it forever his.

For a long moment he looked down into her eyes, and then he smiled. 'We have a long way to go, *querida* – and I am a patient man.'

She did not quite understand his meaning, for she knew he was not only speaking of their journey; but this was no time to ask foolish questions. Susan was at the door and all at once there was so much to do. Now she could not afford to be awkward at using Cathy's things; she knew she had no choice but to take everything she needed with her. They could not stay to buy new combs or any of the trifles she would need during the coming voyage. It might be months, or years, before she could purchase what she wanted; but now it hardly mattered. She was going away with Nick, and her heart was singing. All her caution had fled when he kissed her. She had been foolish to fear love so much: it was wonderful! She had never been so happy in her life.

Dressed for travelling in a dark green gown and cloak that Mrs Penrith had discovered in one of the many trunks stored in the house, Magdalene glanced at her own reflection and smiled. Where had that sad-eyed Spanish girl gone, she wondered. Doña Magdalene had always looked so correct with her perfectly groomed ringlets and her heavy silk gowns. This woman had wild hair that tumbled down her back and eyes like sparkling emeralds!

Giving a gurgle of laughter, Magdalene turned and ran down the stairs to where Nick was waiting for her in the hall. He came to her immediately, brushing her lips briefly with his own.

'You are beautiful,' he said. 'Come, we must catch the tide and be gone before Elizabeth sends Sir Francis to arrest us.'

'He would not do so!' Magdalene cried indignantly. 'He is your friend.'

'Yes, we are friends – but Francis owes a greater loyalty to England and the Queen.

He would do his duty, however much it pained him.'

'Then we must hurry.' She put her hand in his trustingly. 'Yet I should like to say goodbye to Anton and Sir Ralph.'

'Anton goes with us, *querida* – I could not leave my faithful right arm behind. Ralph will follow with his own ship when he can.'

'Where shall we go?' Magdalene asked as he led her outside.

For a moment his eyes seemed to avoid hers. 'Who knows?' he said lightly. 'Where the wind takes us, perhaps. Does it matter, Magdalene?'

'No.' She shook her head decisively, her eyes glowing as she gazed up at him, seeing the strength in those stern features. 'All that matters is that you take me with you.'

'Remember that always,' he said softly. 'I wanted to give you time to know me, *cara*, so that you would understand who and what I am. But now I have no choice. Remember that, if you should have cause to doubt me one day.'

What was he saying? Why should he think that she would ever doubt him?

'I shall never doubt you,' she replied, her eyes bright with emotion. 'You saved my life. What more do I need to know?'

Perhaps he was trying to tell her that there had been another woman in his life. He did not know that she understood how much he

131

had loved Cathy; she understood and she had come to terms with it. His first love would always hold his heart, she knew that, but there was so much more he had to give – and she would take all that he offered, gladly.

'I shall never lose faith in you,' she repeated as he led her out to where the horses were waiting, three for riding and three with saddlebags strapped on their backs. 'Why should I?'

The odd look he gave her was puzzling, but she could ask no more questions. Anton led her horse forward, and Nick's strong hands encircled her waist, lifting her effortlessly into the saddle.

'I've sent word on ahead,' Anton said, a note of excitement in his voice. '*Treggaron Rose* will be provisioned and ready when we reach her.'

'And Ralph – have you heard from him?'

Anton shook his head. 'No, not yet. He will be furious that he was called to his uncle's sickbed at this time. Yet he knows where he can find us.'

'Yes.' Nick frowned warningly. 'He will follow when he can, no doubt.'

Anton nodded, turning away to mount his own horse. Then they were all three riding furiously towards the sheltered cove where *Treggaron Rose* lay at anchor. And not one of them looked back.

Magdalene looked curiously around the cabin, noticing that some changes had taken place since she was last on board. The bed had new hangings, and there was a brightly coloured carpet spread over the floor luxury indeed! There were other items too; things that a lady might use for her toilette, including a small silver-gilt hand-glass, pots of powder, combs and perfume.

Raising her eyes to Nick's face, she saw he had observed her reaction to the changes. 'They are gifts for you,' he explained. 'I had no time to purchase more. When I realised we must leave so suddenly, I had them sent straight to the ship instead of the manor.'

Everything was of the finest, and the girl knew he had gone to great trouble and expense on her behalf. His thoughtfulness touched her, emotion stinging her throat as she gazed up at him.

'You bought all these for me?'

'They are but trifles,' he said gruffly. 'I had intended to take you to London so that you might choose for yourself. I am but a rough sailor, Magdalene. You are used only to the finest of everything; I did my best, but I was not sure what you would like.'

She touched the tiny silver boxes with the tips of her fingers, tracing the delicate raised patterns, her heart too full to tell him how she felt.

'You have perfect taste,' she said at last, her words stilted to hide the churning emotions inside her. 'I could not have chosen better for myself.'

What she really wanted to say was that anything he had bought specially for her would have pleased her. She longed to tell him how much his kindness had thrilled her, but she dare not show her feelings too plainly. She was not yet sure exactly what Nick wanted from her, and she knew she must not expect too much, even though he had bought these lovely things for her. He did not love her – not as he had loved Cathy. She must simply wait until he told her what role she was to play in his life. After all, he had been in the habit of buying gifts for his cousin, so his presents to herself need not mean that she was important to him.

Nick frowned as he saw the uncertainty in her face, and he cursed the misfortune which had driven him to this desperate action. He had formed so many plans on the voyage from Spain, careful plans for a future which must now be set aside until such time as it was safe to return home. Magdalene's beauty made her a queen among women, and he knew how poor his hospitality had been thus far. She had been preparing to marry a man of vast wealth, and she was the daughter of a rich nobleman, so obviously these trifles would make little impression on her. Yet there was little he could do to put matters right. For a while he had thought she was beginning to shed the chains that bound her to her former life, but now when he saw the uncertainty in her face he was afraid that the situation had forced him to move too quickly. She must learn to trust him, for only then would she be able to accept who and what he was.

Her back was turned to him, and he laid a gentle hand on her shoulder, moving it up to caress the silken skin at the nape of her neck. He felt the shiver of her response and a hot flame of desire rose up in him, tempting him to sweep her into his arms and put an end to this uncertainty. He was almost sure that she would not refuse his lovemaking – but what then? How would she feel when she learned that he lived by pitting his wits against her own countrymen – that *Treggaron Rose* had sunk the flagship of her father's fleet? If he took her now, she might hate him for it!

The caress of his hands was sending little prickles of excitement up and down Magdalene's spine. She swayed towards him, feeling the warmth of his body against her back. She waited quietly, like a sleepy kitten, knowing that she was ready to give anything he asked of her. She had always been afraid of the desire she saw in men's eyes when they looked at her, sensing they wanted only to take from her and leave her bruised and empty. Somehow she knew that this man was different: he would give as much as and more than he took.

She turned towards him, smiling, quiescent, waiting. Nick looked deep into her eyes as the desire churned in him. She was so beautiful and he wanted her badly, but he could not abuse that innocence he saw in her eyes. Others had hurt her enough; he was forever damned if he crushed that emerging spirit he had seen in her earlier. She was changing slowly into the confident woman she could be – and it was that woman he wanted! He could dominate her by the sheer force of his will, but then he might lose the prize he craved.

'I have work to do,' he said harshly, driving the wayward thoughts from his mind. 'In a few hours we shall be well out to sea and you can take the air on deck.'

'Thank you. I shall try not to get in your way.'

Magdalene's meek reply made him scowl. 'Must you always take what I say to imply criticism?' he said, hating himself for hurting her, and her for behaving in a way that brought out the worst in him. 'I was merely thinking of you. Come up whenever you please!'

He swung away from her and was gone.

Magdalene stared after him, blinking at the sudden smart of tears. What had she done to anger him? She wanted only to please him. She had been taught that it was a woman's place to please her menfolk – but nothing she did seemed right. For a moment she felt close to weeping in despair. He wanted her to be another woman, that was why he had turned from her in disgust when she was ready to give whatever he asked – but she was not Cathy. She could not be like the woman who haunted his dreams!

Suddenly a surge of anger swept through her. He was like all the other men she had ever known, after all. They all demanded obedience from her, and she was so tired of always trying to do what was expected of her! She had done her best to please Nick, but she would not try so hard in future. She would be herself – and if that did not please him, it was not her fault!

Magdalene was not in the least tired, and she did not want to rest. Her father had taken her on board his ships when she could scarcely walk, so there was little she did not know about the work involved in putting a vessel to sea though she had never actually sailed with the Don. If she kept out of the crew's way, there could be no reason for Nick to be angry with her. But if he was – well, she would have to bear it, because she had no intention of staying in her cabin for three-quarters of the voyage!

There was a decided glint in her eyes as she left the cabin and climbed the wooden ladder to the deck above. In the first flush of her gratitude, she had been willing to be anything Nick wanted her to be, but now she saw that it was foolish. The man she loved was haunted by a ghost, and the only way to help him to forget Cathy was to make him fall in love with her. She knew he wanted her in his bed, but that was not enough, mere physical pleasure would not drive the pain from his heart. He must love her so much that Cathy was no longer able to hurt him...

Nick heard their laughter from where he stood on the poop, and frowned, his hands clenching on the wheel. He could not yet see either Anton or Magdalene, but he knew they were together; they spent many hours each day walking round the deck, her hand lightly touching on his arm as she laughed up at him. It was ridiculous to feel so angry when this was what he had wanted. She had changed so much in these past weeks that he hardly knew her. Now he saw the passionate, vibrant woman he had suspected lay hidden beneath her mask of docility. It was that woman that had attracted him from the first moment they met, the secret woman that lived within her, unawakened, waiting. But it was at Anton she smiled. It was with his friend that she seemed most at ease, though she no longer had that uncertain look in her eyes when he spoke to her. Instead she appeared to mock him, almost as if she were flaunting her friendship with Anton in his face.

He was not sure where he had gone wrong. He had hoped that by giving her her freedom she would turn to him with desire in those wonderful eyes, that she would come to his bed not only willingly but eagerly – as eager as he was for her. Would it have been better if he had taken her that day when he had sensed her surrender? Yet, if she had been merely offering gratitude, he would have lost her in the end – and it was not what he wanted! There was a perverseness in him that would not settle for less than the whole. He had never been able to accept second best; there had been a time when Cathy... He must not think of his sweet, childlike cousin, that way lay only pain. Magdalene was alive and driving him wild with desire... But if Anton was the man she loved... No, that could not be. He would not allow it! She was his by right. He had not snatched her from the Inquisition to yield her to another. It was not in him to beg, and he could never use force. Was he cursed that he must always lose those who meant most to him?

'Begging your pardon, Captain, but the men would like a word with you.'

Nick turned his head, scowling at the interruption of his thoughts. 'Well, what is it?' he grunted.

His mood was self-evident and the Bos'n sucked his breath. Captain Treggaron was a good master, but he had a temper on him if pushed too far.

'It's only we were wondering when there would be some work, Captain. We've sighted three vessels this past week, but you've let them all slip by unchallenged.'

'We attack when and where I decide.' Nick's eyes glinted with anger. 'Is that clear, Bos'n?'

A frown furrowed the sailor's brow. 'Ay, it's clear enough, but the crew are restless for some action. They're blaming the wench. They say she's changed you – and brought bad luck on us.'

'Then you'd best warn every man that I'll hang the first to say it in my hearing.'

'Is that an order, Captain Treggaron?' The Bos'n's face was tight with disapproval. 'They'll not like it, I'm warning you.'

'You're warning me!' Nick cursed furiously. 'Damn the lot of you! Am I master of my own ship, or must I hang every man jack aboard?'

'There'll be no mutiny while I'm Bos'n, sir, but I thought it right that you should know the temper of the crew.'

'You've done your duty, so now do as I've ordered. We'll attack the first Spaniard that comes our way. Will that content the scurvy dogs?'

'Ay, I reckon that will quiet a few of them.' The Bos'n grinned suddenly. 'I dare say you'll feel better for some action yourself, sir.'

Nick's mouth curved in a wry smile, knowing the man was right. 'Get off my poop before I flog you, Bos'n. I have no need of your advice, sound though it may be.'

It was as near to an apology as he would get while this mood gripped Treggaron, the Bos'n knew. His eyes travelled across the deck to where the Spanish wench stood with Anton Barchester. They were saying below decks that she was a witch, but to his way of thinking, witchcraft had little to do with it. She was a Spaniard and a woman, and that made her trouble!

Following the direction of the Bos'n's gaze, Nick's eyes were bleak as he watched Magdalene teasing her companion. Damn it! the crew were right to complain, he thought bitterly. Three good chances had passed them by because he had been afraid of the moment when she must learn the true nature of their mission. It could not go on, he knew it and accepted it at last. He had given her time to know him, and if she

141

turned from him now in hatred, so be it...

They had been becalmed for three days and there was an air of tension throughout the ship. Magdalene had felt it and seen the strange looks cast her way by some of the crew. Not all, but sufficient to make her feel uncomfortable whenever she went on deck. Once she had heard a voice whisper, 'Witch...' behind her, but when she turned round, every man had his head bent over his work. She did not understand why these men resented her, unless it was because she was half Spanish. She was well aware of their hatred for her countrymen by now, though she could scarcely believe the stories Anton had told her about the cruelty her people were supposed to have inflicted on the natives of the New World.

'You say the Spanish steal the silver from the Indians, but my father was not a thief. He paid the natives who worked the mines for him; he told me so...' She had faltered as she saw the strange expression in his eyes. 'He would not murder and – and do all those terrible things you accused him of, Anton. Not my father!'

'Then he was the exception, Magdalene. Believe me, I've seen too many villages left desecrated by Spaniards.'

He had seen the hurt in her eyes then and deliberately dropped the subject. After that, he had refused to answer her questions about such matters.

'I'll not be the one to disillusion you,' he had said. 'Ask Nick if you want to know why we all hate the Spaniards; his father was tortured by the Inquisition and the family sold almost everything they possessed to arrange for his release. Heaven knows why they didn't burn him! He'd have been better off dead, and so would Nick, poor devil. He was a boy when he watched his father die in agony, and he can't forget it.'

'But my father was not one of them...' Magdalene protested.

Anton only shook his head, refusing to be drawn.

Magdalene had not forgotten that conversation. She wondered if Nick had begun to hate her, too. He was almost always angry these days, and she thought it must be that he was regretting his hasty decision to bring her on board his ship. These last few days the tension had been so bad that he could not have failed to notice it. Was he blaming her for upsetting his crew? She had tried to stay in her cabin as much as possible, but it was so hot and stuffy. There was not a breath of air anywhere.

She had been lying on the bed wearing only her shift for most of the day, feeling too weary even to eat, but the sun was dipping below the horizon now and it would be cooler on deck. Surely it could do no harm if she went up for a little while? She would go mad if she stayed here a minute longer!

Splashing her body with water that had turned tepid in the pewter jug, Magdalene dried her skin and dressed herself in one of the gowns she had altered to suit her own tastes. With the waist taken in and some of the ribbons stripped away, it was no longer Cathy's gown. Not that she allowed her thoughts to dwell on Nick's cousin any more. She had tried to please him, and then she had tried flirting with Anton, but nothing seemed to banish that bleak look from his eyes. Indeed, of late she had seen it more often.

Sighing, she dragged a brush through her long hair, pushing it back from her face and fastening it with ornamental combs. She felt too weary to bother much about her appearance. What did it matter what she looked like when everyone hated her? No, Anton at least was her friend. She was not sure of Nick's feelings towards her these days; he seemed to avoid her company, and even when they were together, she felt that he was holding back from her. Why did he never smile at her in that special way now? Was it because he had realised she could never take the place of the woman he had loved?

Emerging on to the deck, Magdalene went

to stand at the rails. The blue sky had not even the trace of a cloud, she noticed, wishing that a storm would blow up suddenly to clear the air. She could understand the tension among the sailors; this endless heat and glaring sunlight were somehow unnerving...

'Why don't you cast a spell and bring us some wind?'

The harsh voice at her back made her jump. Spinning round, Magdalene found herself staring into the surly face of a sailor she knew well by sight. She had often enough seen his angry eyes following her as she walked with Anton.

'What do you mean?' she asked. 'How can I bring the wind?'

'You're a witch, ain't you? You've cursed this ship, that's for sure.'

'No!' she cried. 'I'm not a witch – and I wouldn't put a curse on this ship if I were.'

'So you say,' the sailor muttered. 'But there's a curse on us this voyage, and you're the one who brought the bad luck.'

Several of the crew had been lounging on the deck near by, but now they were on their feet. She heard a murmur of agreement, and saw the menace in their eyes.

'She's bad luck, mate, you're right there.'

'It would be better for us if she went over the side...'

Magdalene gasped, her face draining of colour. It was happening again! Why? What had she done to turn these men against her?

'The first man who makes a move towards her dies!' Nick's icy tones sent all eyes flying to his face. 'She's my woman, and I'll kill any man who lays a finger on her – is that understood?'

He stood no more than a few feet away, a loaded wheel-lock pistol in each hand, his eyes blazing with such fury that most of the crew fell back.

'It was only a joke, Captain,' cried the man who had suggested that Magdalene should be thrown into the sea. 'I didn't realise as she was your woman.'

'Now you know!' Nick's words cut through the space between them like a lash of a whip. 'Come here to me, Magdalene. Burns, get out of her way, or I'll put a ball through you.'

The surly crewman who had started it all stood his ground, glaring at Nick. 'She's bad luck, and you're a fool if you can't see it. Besides, you're only one man. Why should we listen to you?'

'Because if you don't, I shall stick my blade through your guts, my friend! Or maybe I'll let the Bos'n give you a taste of the rope before I hang you?'

Anton's sudden arrival with the Bos'n and others of the crew who were obviously loyal took the bluster out of the seaman. He shrugged and stood aside as Magdalene ran to Nick.

He looked down at her and smiled. 'Did he harm you?'

The girl's heart leaped as she saw the caressing look she had missed so much. 'No, I am not harmed. Don't punish him, Nick. He's hot and bored ... and I, too, wish the wind would blow!'

Nick grinned as he heard the note of impatience in her voice. 'Did you hear her, Burns?' he asked wryly. 'Thank God that I don't clap you in irons. Damn it, man, we're all sick of this weather, but it will change... It always does.'

A shamefaced expression had crept over the man's features. 'I lost my head, Captain. It– It won't happen again.' Magdalene shot him a smile and his eyes slid away. 'I'm sorry I called you a witch, miss.'

'It doesn't matter...' Magdalene began, then she heard something and raised her eyes. A small pennant on the mizzen-mast had begun to move. It was only a slight breeze as yet, but it was coming. She knew it instinctively. 'Look...' she whispered. 'The wind is rising.'

Everyone glanced up; the pennant had gone limp again and the men shook their heads, scowling with disappointment, but then it began to move once more and a strangled cheer issued from their throats. The wind was coming. Now you could see it beginning to stir the sails. Soon the ship would be gliding through the water once more...

'Damn me if you ain't a witch, lass!' Burns shouted with laughter. 'You wished for the wind, and it came. Maybe I was wrong about you you'll bring us good fortune yet.'

Suddenly all the men were laughing and slapping each other on the back. The air of tension that had hung so heavily over the ship was gone.

Nick looked down at the girl by his side, making up his mind. It was time to end the uncertainty. He had told the men she was his, and that was how it must be. This unrest was his own fault for not making her position clear from the start. Once it was accepted that she belonged to him, the crew would forget that she was a Spaniard – she would simply be Treggaron's woman.

'Go below, Magdalene,' he said softly. 'I shall come to you in a little while. We have wasted too much time, and now we must talk. Do you understand me?'

She nodded, aware of a subtle change in his mood. This was the man who had held her in his arms after rescuing her from the priest. This was the man who had defied his own queen to save her from being sent back to a cruel death. She had thought him gone for ever, but now he was smiling at her in the way that set her heart racing – and oh, how she loved him! She must make no mistakes this time.

Raising her eyes, she smiled at him confidently. 'Don't be too long, Nick. I shall be waiting for you.'

The invitation in her look made the blood pound in his veins. She was not afraid of him now, nor was that gratitude in her eyes! The woman his soul had recognised had awakened at last – and she was his!

Nick's laughter followed Magdalene as she ran lightly across the deck and climbed down the short ladder to the little passage that led to her cabin. Her heart was singing with the happiness which seemed to flood through her entire body. She could not have been mistaken in that look on his face. He wanted her – Magdalene – not a pale image from the past! And he had told the crew she was his woman! She knew he had done it to shock them and make them see he would not allow her to be harmed, but he had said it, and she believed he meant it.

Soon he would come to her, and when he did … when he did, she would make him so happy that he would never wear that haunted expression again. This time she would not stand meekly waiting for his kisses; she would go to his arms eagerly and let him know that she wanted to be his woman.

How she had changed from the reserved,

withdrawn girl who was afraid to love! Those dreary days when she had spent so much time sitting in her chambers alone now seemed so far away, almost as if they had happened in another life.

Singing softly to herself, she began to undress; then a sudden thought set her searching frantically through her sea chest until she found what she wanted. Ah, there it was! A bed-robe of the finest, sheerest silk. She had found it among the things Nick had sent from London, but had never worn it.

She washed her body again from head to toe, smoothing perfume into her skin so that a haze of fragrance hung around her. Then she slipped the thin robe over her head, shivering deliciously as she felt its softness against her flesh. Sitting down on a stool, she began to brush her hair, over and over again until the shine returned and it flowed luxuriantly down over her shoulders almost to the small of her back.

Satisfied at last, she took two silver wine-cups from a corner cupboard and set them on the table with a jug of wine. They could eat later, after they had ... talked. A dreadful uncertainty gripped her for one moment. Supposing Nick had really meant them to talk, only to talk...?

At the sound of booted footsteps outside the cabin, a pale rose colour warmed her cheeks. It was too late to change her clothes again now… Then the door opened and Nick stood there, his eyes moving over her with such a hungry yearning that all her doubts fled. She saw that he too had changed his clothes, and was wearing a white frilled shirt, black velvet trunks slashed with silver ribbon and a short jerkin that tailed into the waist above a crimson sash. His hair looked damp as though he had doused himself, and his bronzed skin had a shiny, scrubbed look. A gurgle of laughter bubbled through her parted lips as she realised that he was almost as nervous as she.

She rose slowly to her feet and poured wine into two cups. It was rich and red and fragrant, similar to the wine produced on the d'Ortega estates. Smiling, she handed him one of the cups, taking the other and holding it between both hands as she waited, silently, her eyes on his face.

'What shall we drink to?' he asked at last.

'To the future,' she whispered. 'To the end of bad dreams and painful memories.' She raised her cup and sipped the wine, feeling it warm her.

'Are you ready to forget the past, Magdalene?' Nick asked, an odd, wistful note in his voice. 'Can you live for the future – a future that will be ours?'

'I – I know that there is much that lies between us. Anton has told me how you feel about – about the Spanish people…'

151

'Anton talks too much,' Nick muttered. 'What else did he tell you?'

'That– That there were good reasons for the way you feel.'

'So you know, and still you can accept all that it means?'

Was he asking if she could accept that there had been another woman in his life? It hardly mattered now. Cathy's shadow no longer hung over them; she could see it was her – Magdalene – that he wanted now.

'I want ... only to be with you,' she whispered, putting down her cup and moving softly towards him. 'I want to be your woman, Nick.'

'Do you, *querida?*' His cup joined hers on the table and he took her hands in his own, his brow rising quizzically. 'I thought perhaps it was Anton you wanted. Was I wrong?'

'Anton is my friend, as he is yours. There is nothing between us, nor could there ever be.'

'Then nothing can keep us apart, my darling.' His eyes seemed to caress her as he bent his head to touch her fingers to his lips. Gently he drew her to him, placing her arms about his neck as he enfolded her, holding her so close that she could feel the throbbing of his heart. 'You are mine,' he murmured against her ear. 'From the first moment I saw you, I wanted you for my own, but you were so innocent ... so vulnerable ... that I feared to reach out and take what I desired.'

She could feel the gentle movement of his mouth against her hair. His hand was travelling firmly but softly down her arched back, stroking her with a sensuous rhythm that made her limbs weak with longing. She sighed and swayed against him as her body melted into his, her senses swimming. He touched his lips to her throat, lifting her hair to kiss the lobe of her ear. Again his lips touched her neck, softly, tantalisingly. The tip of his tongue found the hollow of her throat, its delicate flicking sending little shivers right down to her toes. His kisses moved to her forehead, just below the hairline, feathered over her eyelids, until at last his lips found hers, parted and eager for the soul-searching possession she so ardently desired.

A thousand tiny darts of fire pricked her skin, sending a slow, surging tide of white-hot flame through her veins. She was dissolving in the heat of his passion, no longer a separate person but an extension of his being. When he bent down to catch her unresistingly up into his arms, she was almost faint with longing and the strange weakness that assailed her. She lay quietly in his arms, her own curled clingingly about his neck; her heart was beating wildly as he gently laid her on the bed, and her eyes darkened with emotion, becoming smoky with awakening desire.

'Nick...' she whispered. 'I – I know nothing of what a man asks of his woman...'

'I shall teach you, my darling. Trust me: I would never willingly hurt you.'

Magdalene shook her head; that was not what she had meant. She was not afraid that he might her, only that he would be disappointed by her ignorance. Her mother had told her that men expected more than any decent woman could give, and she wanted to give all that he desired, and more.

His kiss stilled her fears as he bent over her, one hand tenderly stroking the hair back from her forehead. Slowly, carefully, he untied the ribbons at her throat, pushing the filmy material down over her shoulders, his fingers stroking the satiny flesh and moving to cup her firm breasts. She arched involuntarily as the spasm shook her, and tried to make herself lie still, turning her face to hide her blushes in the silken pillows.

'Don't be ashamed of what you feel, *cara*,' he whispered. 'You are so lovely that it gives me great pleasure just to look at you and touch you – but I want you to feel pleasure, too.'

'I – I do...' she murmured shyly. 'I I know only wicked women feel this way...'

'Who told you that?' He arched his brow,

a flicker of amusement in the blue eyes.

'My mother.'

'She was wrong.' Nick's wry look made her giggle. 'If you are wicked, Magdalene, then I must be the Devil himself, because you fill me with delight. Don't hold back from me, *querida*. I want all of you.'

And it seemed that he meant to have all of her. There was not one piece of her quivering body that was not caressed or kissed – or both! A part of her mind was still slightly shocked at the dizzy sensation his touch aroused in her. Surely it was a sin to feel such ecstasy! Yet she would not have had him cease the amazing things he was doing to her if it meant she must burn in hell for all eternity. Indeed, if he had left her now, she would have died!

'Will you let me have all of you now?' he whispered close to her ear.

She nodded dumbly, watching as he turned from her to divest himself of his own clothes. Her breath caught as she saw the sleek muscles beneath the taut, satin-smooth flesh of his back. Then, as he turned towards her, her eyes moved wonderingly down the firm chest and flat stomach to the throbbing maleness between his thighs, and she gasped, feeling a stab of fear for the first time, and half rising on her elbow in silent protest. Then all fear was forgotten as he came back to her and she felt the burn of his flesh against hers. His hand was gently but firmly parting her legs, and she felt the fire of him close to her, seeking – no, demanding! – entry.

There was a shaft of pain as he pierced her maidenhead, but his kiss smothered her cry, soothing her as he began to move gently on her, holding his passion in check until he felt her begin to open to him, letting him push deep inside her. She moaned softly as the rhythm of his thrusting became more urgent, sending her senses on a dizzy spiral that made her ach and thrash wildly beneath him, crying out at last as an intense spasm shook her whole body.

As she surfaced from the depths of the waves of sensation which had almost destroyed her, she became aware of Nick's body lying heavily on hers as if he too was totally drained. Then he lifted his head and smiled at her, kissing the tip of her nose before he rolled away on to his back, pulling her with him so that she was on top of him, his hands stroking her back as if even now he must keep touching her.

'Oh, you are terribly wicked, my beautiful Magdalene,' he murmured. 'But don't ever change. I...' His words trailed away as he heard shouting on deck and then the sound of someone pounding at the door. He slid Magdalene's body to one side and sat up, frowning. 'What the Devil! I gave orders that we were not to be disturbed.'

'There's a ship to the windward, Captain. We need you on deck.'

'Damn!' Only the Bos'n would dare to come near at such a time. Nick's brow furrowed and then he grinned. 'Thank God the summons did not come sooner! I must leave you for a while, *querida,* but stay just where you are. I dare say it's a false alarm and we have lost too much time already.'

Magdalene caught her breath. He could not mean ... but the laughter in his eyes told her that he did. It seemed that she had pleased him well enough despite her ignorance. So well that he was reluctant to leave her.

'Why must you go?' she asked. 'What does it matter if they've sighted a ship?'

Nick had pulled on his trunks and was buttoning his shirt. 'They would not have called me if it were not important. It must be a Spanish galleon on her way home from the New World...' His eyes narrowed as he saw the shock in her face. 'But you knew – Anton told you!'

She shook her head. 'Only that your father was tortured by the Inquisition...' Her head turned in the tumbled sheets where she had so recently known such ecstasy, gripping in desperation as she tried to hide from the truth. 'You're not... You cannot be! Tell me it isn't true... Please!'

His face tightened with pain or anger; she could not be sure what the emotions she was witnessing meant. Then he turned from her, sitting on the edge of the bed to tug on his long boots.

'I thought you knew, that you had accepted it. *Treggaron Rose* is a pirate ship – at least, that's what the Spaniards call us. We call ourselves privateers, but our business is the same – to attack as many enemy ships as we can, and sink them. After we've taken whatever is in the holds, of course.'

'You cannot do it!' Magdalene's face was stricken. 'Not after what has happened between us?'

'What is between us has nothing to do with this.' He sighed deeply. 'I am sorry, Magdalene. I have to take that ship and any others that come our way. I have to do it, and I will do it, even if you hate me for it.'

She sat up, forgetful of her nakedness, her hair falling over her breasts in a fiery swathe. 'If you do this I shall hate you, Nick. My father was killed by an English privateer...' Her breath caught in her throat as she saw his stricken look. 'No... No, it wasn't... It couldn't have been...'

'*Treggaron Rose* sank Don Manuel's flagship, and if I had the chance, I would do it again.' His face hardened into granite as he saw the mounting horror in her eyes and hated her for what she was thinking, believing. 'He was a murderer of women and children, Magdalene. He destroyed everything that stood in his way.'

'No! I don't believe you,' she cried, covering her face with her hands. 'I won't believe it. You've lied to me, deceived me…'

A tiny nerve flickered in his cheek. 'I thought you knew. You said you wanted to forget the past.'

If there was a note of appeal in his voice, she blocked it out, refusing to look at him. 'No – I thought you meant your father… Cathy…' she choked miserably.

'Cathy? What has she to do with this?' His voice was harsh, and she flinched as if he had struck her. 'Don't confuse the issue, Magdalene, I haven't time to argue with you now.'

She jerked her head up, her eyes wild. 'If you go, I shall hate you, Nick.'

'Then you must hate me,' he said quietly. Then he turned on his heel, and left her alone and shivering.

CHAPTER FIVE

The door had closed behind Nick as Magdalene turned her face to the pillow and wept. Deep, painful shudders ripped through her body, almost tearing her apart. It could not be true! she protested, her sprawled fingers plucking at the sheets beneath her with jerking, agonised intensity. Nick was a pirate! This ship had sunk her father's flagship and sent him to a cruel death. Nicholas Treggaron had killed her father! He was a murderer and a deceiver, and he had callously dishonoured her. But that was not true! She had gone to him as willingly as any harlot.

Shame stung her like the lash of a whip. How could she have given herself so freely to a man like that? She had been blinded by his smiles, the looks that could turn her flesh to molten fire; but she had also seen the black moods that could change him into a stranger. For weeks – no, it was months now – they had been sailing apparently aimlessly, and she had been too wrapped up in her obsession with the man to wonder what his intentions were. Perhaps she had thought Nick meant to trade with the

Indians of the New World for silver as her father had, but he had told her that Manuel d'Ortega was a plunderer, and a heartless slayer of women and children. It was a lie! She would never believe it. She could not, for that would mean all her memories of the father she had loved were false...

A thunderous roar shook the ship and sent her mind reeling. *Treggaron Rose* was attacking the Spanish galleon. Nick had given the order to fire. No, it could not be happening! It was a nightmare, it must be, she thought desperately, but another deafening roar told her that it was no dream.

She crawled across the bed to peer out of the cabin window. It was still light enough to see the Spanish ship, which was so close to them that it seemed there must be a collision. Suddenly she realised that this was exactly what Nick intended; the shots were merely a warning of his determination to board the galleon. She wondered why the Spanish ship had not tried to escape, realising almost at once that it would have been impossible for her captain to outsail the lighter, faster English vessel. She had heard her father say, time and again, that the only chance of escaping a pirate attack was to sail in sufficient numbers to warn off any raider that might cast a greedy eye over a treasure-ship. A single vessel was an easy target for the English guns.

A jarring shudder went through *Treggaron Rose* as the two ships touched. She heard shouts and the sound of running feet, and then the crack of a harquebus. Suddenly there were terrifying yells and screams, the clash of steel against steel as the hand-to-hand fighting began.

Magdalene turned away from the window as she saw men swarming across the side of the ship, cruel-looking knives clenched in their teeth as they used ropes slung from the rigging to swing themselves across the rails. It was horrible, worse than she could ever have imagined – and it was her own people who were being killed! People who had deserted her, a little voice whispered somewhere in her subconsciousness. She would have been dead by now if it were not for the Englishman...

Covering her face with her hands, she rocked back and forth in silent agony. Who was right? Nick and Anton who said these galleons carried cargoes bought with the blood of innocents, or her father who had always had a pretty gift for her when he came home after a voyage?

It was too difficult a question for her to answer. She only knew that she hated this violence and destruction. Even if the galleon were carrying stolen treasure, could it be right to shed more blood? Could it ever be right for one man to kill another? She was only a woman; a woman whose emotions were torn and mangled by what she had just learned. She prayed desperately for the fighting to cease. Let it be over soon!

The battle sounded very fierce on board *Treggaron Rose,* and for the first time it occurred to Magdalene that the Englishmen might be losing the struggle. Was that why the Spaniards had not tried to run – because they were confident of their superior strength? Supposing it was so... Supposing Nick were killed? The thought shocked her. No, it could not – must not! – happen. Anything was better than that. She did not care if he sank a dozen galleons if only he survived!

Suddenly she could not bear to be shut up in the cabin, not knowing what was going on. No matter what Nick was or what he had done, she did not want him to die. Dressing hastily, she ran towards the little ladder leading to the hatch and scrambled up it, her heart racing as she looked out. The scene that met her eyes was one of utter confusion, making her gasp in horror. The fierce hand-to-hand fighting was still going on; the Spaniards were refusing to give in tamely, though many of them already lay dead or dying, their blood staining the decks. Some of the awful, still bodies belonged to members of Nick's crew, she noticed. But where was he?

Her eyes moved frantically around the deck. Oh, where was he? There was Anton, fighting strongly, though he was being attacked by two Spaniards at the same time and was hard pressed. Fear for him made her bite her lips. He was her friend, and she did not want him to die. She felt relief surge through her as his blade ripped through one of his opponent's wrists, making the man lose his weapon and sink to his knees. Now that the odds were fairer, Anton was pushing forward, forcing his enemy back. Now his blade hand found its mark... But where was Nick? A sick terror rose in her. Surely he was not one of those bloodied corpses lying on the deck!

Then she saw him. Like Anton, he was facing two opponents, but he was being forced backwards, up the short flight of steps to the poop. Fear gripped her heart. Their quarrel was forgotten. She loved him, and she could not bear it if he died! His foot had slipped, and a Spanish blade ripped through his sleeve, leaving a thin trail of crimson. But what was that behind him? Another Spaniard! No, the odds were too great; he must be killed.

Screaming Anton's name, she pointed wildly, crying to him to go to her lover's assistance. Miraculously he heard her cry and understood, thundering across the deck to attack one of Nick's oppressors. Now

Treggaron was aware of the dangers from behind; his sword came up swiftly, entering a Spanish throat, and in a split second he had turned to face the new attack – but not before the Spaniard's blade had pierced his shoulder.

Magdalene saw him stagger. She screamed as the Spaniard thrust forward again. 'Oh no! Please God, don't let him die,' she sobbed, fear making her head spin crazily. She buried her face in her hands, unable to watch, shivering violently as she heard a man's scream of agony. 'No... No...' she whispered. 'Don't let it be Nick. Please don't let it be Nick.'

Suddenly a hush fell over the battleground. The yells were stilled and the fearful clash of steel had ceased. Magdalene knew instinctively that it was finished – but who had won? She uncovered her eyes, hardly daring to look towards the spot where she had last seen Nick, but he was there. Oh God, he was alive! She saw that he was clutching his shoulder as the crimson tide trickled between his fingers. He was wounded – but he was alive. Relief washed through her, making her faint and weak.

All around her she was aware of men, wounded or simply exhausted by the fight. A handful of Spaniards had survived; they had thrown down their swords and were looking uncertainly at one another, as if wondering whether their conquerors would be merciful in victory. Magdalene wondered, too.

'Take the prisoners below.' Nick's voice rang out, directing his weary crew. 'We'll deal with them later.'

What did he mean? Magdalene asked herself. Would the survivors be murdered in cold blood or tortured by their enemies? She shuddered at the thought, and then pushed it from her mind. It was not her concern. She could do nothing to influence the fate of these men. Accepting it, she felt better.

Emerging on to the deck, she started towards Nick. He was wounded, and for the moment nothing else mattered to her. Around her she could hear the moans and cries of the wounded, and the stench of blood sickened her. In a little while she would do what she could to help some of these unfortunates, but for now only one man was important to her.

To reach the poop, she had to pass the pitiful few Spaniards still alive. They were being herded together and searched for weapons before their captors allowed them to go below to the small hold where they would be imprisoned. As she passed, a man turned his head sharply to look at her, astonishment in his face. 'Magdalene,' he cried. 'Magdalene, is it you?' He started towards her, but was roughly pushed back into line.

Magdalene swung round to look at the prisoners, and her heart jerked as she saw the man who had called her name. He had received a slight flesh wound above the knee, but was otherwise unhurt.

'Don Rodrigo!' she said, feeling a wave of sympathy for his plight. 'Are you in pain?'

'Only a little, my lady.' He smiled at her. 'But how came you to be on board this accursed ship?'

They had spoken in Spanish, and several dark looks were directed at them both by the English crew. Magdalene sensed that this was not the moment to show pity for one of the prisoners: too many had died on both sides!

'I cannot help you for the moment,' she said, giving him a warning glance. 'Perhaps later...'

She saw that he had understood her message, and she moved on towards the poop. Anton was looking at Nick's shoulder, and pressing a pad of linen torn from his shirt against it. He smiled welcomingly at her as she approached, but she hardly noticed. Nick was staring at her so coldly, with a look almost of hatred in his eyes.

'I saw you were wounded,' she said hesitantly. 'Will you come below, and let me bind your shoulder for you?'

'Anton will see to it,' Nick's voice grated harshly. 'I would not want you to stain your hands with my blood.'

She flinched at his bitter words and the look of anger in his eyes. 'I – I want to help,' she faltered awkwardly. 'There are so many wounded.'

'Go below and keep out of the way.' His words seared her. 'The crew are used to caring for themselves; they don't need you.'

'Let her help the men,' Anton said, giving her a sympathetic glance. 'It might be for the best.'

'Damn you!' Nick growled, jerking with pain as the pad was pressed tight against his shoulder. 'I care not what she does – so long as she stays out of my sight!'

Magdalene flinched beneath the murderous contempt of his gaze. He hated her – he could not bear the sight of her! What had she done to make him look at her like that? They had quarrelled before he left her, but there was something more, something so powerful that it had driven all the softness from his heart. Was it because she was a Spaniard and so many of his men were dead?

She turned away quickly before the tears pricking her eyes could start to flow. He had no right to speak to her that way. It was she who had been wronged. She had said she hated him for what he was and what he had done, but fear for him had shown her that her love was too strong to be denied. If she had been able, she would have wielded a sword herself to save him when he had been in danger. Although it would not be easy to forget that he had caused her father's death, she had been prepared to try, but he no longer cared what she felt. Perhaps she had never been more to him than a pleasant way to pass an idle hour.

The pain inside her was tearing at her heart, but she would not let him see how much he had hurt her. Raising her head proudly, she walked across the deck to where the Bos'n had begun to inspect the men's injuries.

'Will you let me help you?' she asked. 'I promise to do whatever you tell me.'

He glanced up at her, recognising the sincerity of her request. 'If you've the stomach for it, lass, I should be grateful for your help.'

'Thank you.' Magdalene smiled at him. 'Tell me what I should do.'

'You can wash the blood from this man's wound, for a start. He was lucky, and a simple bandage will be all that's needed. Can you manage that?'

'Of course. Please leave him to me. You have so many to tend.'

Another member of the crew brought her water and rolls of soft linen. *Treggaron Rose* seemed to be well prepared for an eventuality such as this – but, of course, this was not the first time it had happened.

Pushing the tormenting thoughts from her mind, Magdalene knelt down by the injured sailor. His right arm was sticky with blood, but as she washed it away, she saw that the Bos'n was right. He had received only a scratch, and needed very little attention. Yet he was grateful for the small service she did him, grinning in a friendly way as she passed to another man more seriously wounded.

Working side by side with the Bos'n and one or two others, Magdalene noticed that the rest of the crew were busy transferring the cargo from the Spanish galleon. One rope used to haul a particularly heavy chest across the rails snapped, and the resounding crash it made when it hit the deck caused her to glance round in alarm. The wooden coffer had split open, spilling its contents far and wide so that they rolled some distance. Something came to rest a few feet away from her, and she saw that it was a large idol fashioned out of solid gold. The work was very strange, unlike anything she had ever seen. Stolen from the Indians who had probably worshipped at its shrine, she realised, feeling a wave of sickness sweep over her. Proof, if she needed it, of what both Anton and Nick had told her.

Biting her bottom lip, she returned to the task of binding a shattered kneecap. If Don Rodrigo had stolen the cargo he was carrying home to Spain, perhaps her father had done the same. He had lied about how he came to be in possession of so much treasure because he did not want his family to know the truth. It was a bitter truth, and one she did not want to accept. Yet, were Nick and his crew any better? The Spaniards stole their silver from the Indians, and the English took it from them. If there was a difference, she could not see it at this moment. It was as she had always believed until she met Nick: men were all cruel, and one was no better than another. She had been a fool to believe otherwise, even for a moment.

Disillusion flooded through her. Despite all Doña Maria's warnings, she had given her love to a man who was not worthy of it – to a man who did not even love her. He had wanted her and he had taken her, perhaps more considerately than many would have done, but still he had used her for his own pleasure... A tiny voice in her head told her that it was not so, but she ignored it. Fear for Nick's safety had made her weak for a time, but he had rejected her offer of help. She had tried to reach him, but he had shut her out. Now she hardened her heart against him. So that when at last he came to stand beside her, just as the rosy dawn was breaking over a dark sea, she would not turn her head to look at him.

'You have done enough,' he said, his voice

still cold. 'Go below now, Magdalene.'

She glanced up then, defiance in her eyes. 'Some of the injured still need attention...'

'That was an order,' he growled. 'Do as I say, or, by heaven, I'll take you below myself!'

Her eyes flashed with scorn as she got to her feet. 'I would rather die than let you touch me again,' she said clearly. 'If you ever try to...'

'...seduce you?' He laughed bitterly. 'Forget it, Magdalene. Ralph warned me from the start that I was a fool to take you with me. Maybe I should have left you to the tender care of your uncle.'

'Perhaps it would have been better if you had,' she said quietly. Her eyes flicked proudly over his handsome face. 'It would have saved me from the distasteful attentions of a murderer.'

She saw the colour leave his face and knew that her cruel words had reached him. Turning away, she walked wearily across the deck, feeling the tiredness flood over her. All she wanted to do was to sleep and sleep – but would she be able to rest in the bed that had held both her and Nick such a short time ago?

Sleep claimed her eventually, though she tossed restlessly for a while, breathing the scent of his body where his head had lain on the pillow and remembering with pain the joy she had known so briefly. Then, at last, she succumbed to the demands of her weary body. It was late in the afternoon when she finally opened her eyes to find Nick standing by the bed, watching her with a strange expression on his face. Why had he come? Surely he did not imagine she would welcome him to her bed after the way he had spoken to her last night?

She shrank from him, holding the covers to her naked breasts. In her weariness she had tumbled into bed without bothering to don her nightclothes, and from the way Nick was staring at her, he seemed to imagine her nakedness was an invitation to join her. Well, she would soon disabuse his mind of that idea!

'What do you want?' she asked coldly. 'If you try to touch me, I shall scream.'

A faint smile briefly lit his face. 'Scant good it would do you if you did! Remember, the crew believe you are my woman – they would merely grin and get on with their work!' The amusement deserted him abruptly, leaving his features like carved stone. 'I have no intentions of forcing my unwelcome attentions on you, Magdalene. I came to see if you had recovered enough to eat some food.'

She saw the tray of hot soup and thick, coarse bread on the table, and frowned. 'That was thoughtful of you, but unnecessary. I can prepare my own meals.'

'I wanted to talk to you, Magdalene. Bos'n told me you asked about tending the wounds of the prisoners. You will not endear yourself to my crew by showing too much sympathy towards Spaniards.'

'Have you forgotten that I am of Spanish blood?' Her eyes flashed angrily at him. 'Should I ignore my own people and let them die of their wounds simply to please your crew?'

'They have been attended to; I saw to it myself after my own men were settled. Bos'n will make sure they have whatever they need. We are not as heartless as you seem to think us.'

She held her tongue, knowing she had accused him unfairly. What– What will you do with the prisoners?'

'Don Rodrigo's men fought bravely – too bravely!' Nick glared at her, anger grinding at him as he saw the doubts in her eyes. What was going on in that stubborn head of hers now? 'If we meant them harm, they would be dead already. The galleon I shall sink before we reach the islands, but the prisoners will be put ashore, and eventually one of their own ships will pick them up.'

'The islands?' she asked curiously.

'There is one on the horizon,' he replied. 'We must stop there to replenish our stocks of food and water. If it seems a suitable place, we shall leave your countrymen there, but only if they can survive until a ship calls to reprovision.'

'And Don Rodrigo?' She wrinkled her brow. 'Could you not leave him his ship? If he gave his word that he would never return to the New World?'

Nick's harsh laughter made her flinch. 'The word of a Spaniard? I would as soon trust a serpent. Your ... friend may think himself fortunate to be alive. My men would hang him, given half a chance.'

'You would not allow that? You said he fought bravely...' Magdalene stared at him in disbelief, hardly recognising the man she loved in this cold-eyed stranger.

'Are you asking me if I would hang him, or telling me you know I would not commit murder?' He gave her a look of disgust. 'Don't bother to answer! I know you believe me capable of accepting a man's surrender and then running my blade through his back.'

'I do not...' She broke off in fright as his eyes glinted.

'Do you not? But you think me a murderer, Magdalene. You said as much.'

'You– You told me that your ship sank my father's galleon. What did you expect? You should have told me the truth long ago.'

'Yes, that much is true.' A tiny nerve ticked in his throat. 'Don Manuel would not

176

surrender. He returned our fire, preferring to go down with his ship rather than let us board her. It was his own choice, Magdalene. If he had surrendered, he would have been given the same choice as Rodrigo and his men. We sink as many ships as we can and take their cargo, but we do not kill unnecessarily. We are not like the Spaniards. If they had defeated us last night, they would have killed every man on board. Your people, as you call them, take no prisoners.'

'I don't believe you,' she whispered, horrified.

'No?' His brows went up. 'Then I see no point in continuing this conversation. We should reach land before nightfall. I shall be going ashore, but you will stay on board until I send for you. If I send for you. Is that understood?'

'Yes.' She gazed up at him miserably. Now she was to be treated as a prisoner! Did he hate her so much? 'Yes, I understand you, Captain Treggaron.'

Nick stared at her and his fists clenched at his sides. By God! If she looked at him in that way again he would... The blood pounded at his temples; he had never struck a woman in his life, but he was closer to it at this moment than he had ever been before. The taste of ashes was in his mouth as he turned away and went out. In that moment he almost felt himself bewitched. No other woman had ever roused these feelings in him. Another second in that room, and he would have... Self-mockery glinted in his eyes and he laughed, the tension easing out of him as he realised exactly what he wanted to do to her.

'Treggaron, you're a fool,' he said softly. 'But, given the right timing, it might be worth the risk... After all, she can't hate me more than she does already.'

Magdalene knelt on the bed, watching as the island loomed closer and closer. It was still light enough to see the fringe of white sand and the dense mass of trees covering the hill that seemed to run its entire length. It was only a very tiny stretch of land, she realised, looking at it wistfully, but it would be pleasant to go ashore for a little while. It was unfair of Nick to go on land and leave her stuck on the ship after so many months at sea! There might be a stream where she could take a bath; she had only been able to wash herself all over, using the water sparingly of late because supplies were running low. She had tried washing her hair in seawater, but that made it sticky and uncomfortable.

Seeing a small boat leave the ship, Magdalene pressed her face against the window, experiencing a sharp longing as she saw Nick sitting in the prow. She should have been going with him! If there had been any way she could have got ashore herself, she would have disobeyed him; but short of swimming the quite considerable distance to the beach, she was unable to find any method of flouting his orders. Unfortunately, it had never been considered necessary for her to learn to swim, and she was not brave enough to jump overboard in the hope that Nick would turn back to pick her up. From the expression on his face when he left her earlier, he might well decide to let her drown.

She watched as the rowing-boat touched the sand and the men jumped out to haul it further up the beach, her face tight with annoyance. How could Nick leave her on board while he went off to enjoy himself? Frustration made her pound at the pillows. Oh, she would make him pay for this somehow! But what could she do to cause him to feel the way she did at this second?

When the idea first popped into her head, she dismissed it. She wanted to annoy Nick, but he would be furious if she dared to do what was in her mind! No, she couldn't, she dared not... But it would serve him right if she managed it!

He had said he would sink the Spanish galleon before they reached land, but he had not yet done so. She was anchored in the bay only a short distance from *Treggaron*

Rose, and a man could swim that distance easily. She knew Rodrigo could swim, because she had heard him telling Isabella so. It was probable that the other surviving Spaniards could also swim… But dare she try to set them free?

'Oh, he would be so angry,' she whispered, a wicked glint in her eyes. It would punish him for all the terrible things he had done to her.

She would attempt it, she decided, but could it be done? There were still several men on board, so how best to distract their attention while the Spaniards slipped over the side?

Going up on deck, she saw to her surprise that only two men were actually on guard. If any more remained on board, they had already sought their hammocks. Neither of the two unfortunates looked very pleased about being left to watch the ship while most of their companions had either gone to the island or were sleeping comfortably below deck. Magdalene smiled. The poor things looked thirsty, she thought, so why shouldn't she give them some wine? No, rum would be better; from the tales her father had told her, it was much more potent than wine. She knew that Nick had a supply in the small cabin he had taken for his own use after giving up his own to her. She would fetch a jugful – or two! – for these thirsty sailors.

Her eyes were sparkling as she made her way to Nick's cabin. The unlocked door opened as she pushed it. Inside, she let her eyes travel around it slowly, her heart jerking as she saw a torn, blood-stained shirt tossed on the floor. It made her pause for a moment as she remembered her fear for him when he was in danger. What she was doing might make him so angry that he would abandon her on the island, too... No, no, he would never do that, she reassured herself.

She noticed that his clothes were strewn about the room, as if he had just taken them off and dropped them where he stood. 'Untidy man,' she muttered, bending to pick up a jerkin, and then, recalling how angry she was with him, she threw it down again. She was not going to start looking after him!

Seeing a small barrel of rum, she took two pewter jugs from his cupboard and filled them to the very brim, carefully pegging the cask when she had finished. Oh, how cross Nick was going to be when he found out that she had given his own special rum to the crew! She tried not to imagine what he might do if she succeeded in helping the prisoners to escape. It would be time enough to face his wrath when she must.

There was surprise in the eyes of the two sailors when she handed them the jugs, but it soon turned to pleasure as they tasted what was inside.

'You looked so thirsty,' she said, smiling innocently at them. 'It's a shame you couldn't have gone to the island, too.'

'Our turn tomorrow – yours, too, miss.'

'Yes, I expect so,' she said lightly. 'Don't work too hard. After all, the ship is quite safe here, isn't it? The island looks uninhabited.'

'Ay, there's been no sign of life on shore,' the sailor agreed.

'Well, I think I shall go to my cabin and get some sleep. Good-night.'

'Good-night, miss. And thank you for thinking of us.'

Magdalene was thoughtful as she went below. How long would it take the men to drink the rum – an hour? Two at least before it began to take effect. She might as well lie down for a little while. She wouldn't undress, but simply lie there and rest. If her plan was to have a chance of success, she must give the crewmen time to become drowsy.

She had not meant to fall asleep, but somehow she did, waking with a jerk to find the cabin in darkness. Drawing the window curtains aside to peep outside, she saw there was a crescent moon shedding sufficient light for her to find her way about the deck, but not so bright that the prisoners would be immediately seen when they went over the side.

Her heart was thudding as she went up on deck, walking softly across to where the dark shapes of the two sailors were slumped against a coil of rope. They were fast asleep and snoring gently. So far, so good! she thought, smiling to herself in the darkness. Now all she had to do was to go down to the hold and lift the bar that held the hatch in place. It was heavy, but she thought she could just about manage it.

A small sound made her glance swiftly over her shoulder, but there was nothing to see. The crew were all still on the island or sleeping soundly in their hammocks. The night was warm and silent, with only the whisper of the waves against the side of the ship. She paused for a moment to gaze towards the land; in the moonlight, the beach was pure silver and the mountain had a dark mystery that tantalised her. It was spiteful of Nick to keep her on the ship, and she was justified in what she was doing! Besides, there could be no harm in setting the prisoners free. They would simply take their ship and go home, doing nothing that could hurt anyone.

All was still as she went back below. If there were more than two guards on board, they certainly had no intention of leaving their quarters tonight. She held her breath as she reached the lower level and saw the hatch with the heavy iron bar securely across it. It was going to be a little more difficult than she had imagined, but she would do it somehow. She had not come this far to turn back now. She took two steps towards it, then opened her mouth to scream as a shadowy figure lunged at her from out of nowhere. What was happening? A hand covered her mouth before the scream could escape, and a strong arm encircled her waist, lifting her off the floor as she began to struggle.

'Scream, and it will be the last thing you ever do!' Nick's voice hissed in her ear. 'You little fool! I thought you were up to something when I found the look-outs asleep and two of my jugs lying by their sides. None of them would dare to touch my rum, so I knew you must have given it to them. It didn't take me long to work out why.'

She had stopped struggling. He took his hand from her mouth and swung her round to face him. She could hardly see his grim features in the dim light, but she did not need to see: she could feel the fury oozing out of him.

'Do you know what would have happened to you if you had succeeded in setting the prisoners free?' he demanded. She shook her head, suddenly aware of the seriousness of her actions. It had all seemed like a grand jest until now. 'The crew would have marooned you on the island – that's if they didn't just put you over the side! You would have been a traitor, and not even I could protect you from them then.'

'I – I didn't think about the crew,' she choked, her throat closing. 'I just wanted to annoy you, because you left me here and went ashore without me.'

Nick gave a sigh of exasperation. 'Should I have taken you, and exposed you to any number of unknown dangers, you foolish child? I don't know this island. The inhabitants could have been unfriendly. The way some of these people have been treated, they might have attacked us on sight.'

'What do you mean – the way they have been treated?' Magdalene stared at him, trying to read his expression in the gloom.

'There are islands not far from here where whole villages have been wiped out.'

'By– By Spaniards?' Her voice wavered. 'That's what you're saying, isn't it?'

'Yes, it's usually by the Conquistadors – but not always. Ships call in to trade with the natives and end by plundering and...' His voice was a harsh croak. 'You called me a murderer and perhaps by your standards I am, but neither I nor my men have ever killed women and children. All my crew know that I'd hang any man who violated a woman. I don't stop them enjoying themselves, but if they want a woman, they pay her father for her. In that way there's no trouble and our ship is always welcome.'

Magdalene's lips were dry. 'I – I'm sorry. I've behaved badly. I promise it won't happen again.'

'You can be damned sure of that,' Nick's voice grated. 'The next time you try something like this, I'll make a present of you to the crew!'

He didn't mean it. She knew that he was only threatening her to punish her for what she had done, or was he?

Nick's fingers closed over her wrist, pulling her towards him, holding her pressed against his iron-hard chest so that she felt the heat of his breath on her face.

'I've had enough of your tantrums, Magdalene! Just be warned that I won't allow even you to flout my orders on board ship.'

He pushed her in front of him, towards the ladder leading to the level above. She stumbled and he grabbed her arm, thrusting her before him, an angry grunt issuing from his throat.

'Be quiet, you troublesome wench, and watch what you're doing! I don't want anyone to hear us. There'll be hell to pay if any of the crew realise what you planned to do!'

'Where are you taking me?' she quavered,

her knees shaking. He sounded so angry.

'To your cabin; where else?' He made a little sound of disgust in his throat. 'You deserve to be punished, but I'm damned if I'll give you the satisfaction of reproaching me again. Your punishment will be in knowing that your beloved Rodrigo will not now be allowed on the island until we've blown his ship out of the water.'

'So you're going to leave him here?'

'Yes. Why?'

They had reached her cabin now, and he pushed her inside, pausing to strike a tinder and light the candle in the lantern that hung from a hook in the ceiling. Its thick, oiled glass shed a yellow light on her face.

'You were willing to risk your life to save that damned hidalgo. Or were you planning to go with him?' Suspicion hardened his features and he gripped her shoulders, his fingers digging into her flesh as he studied her expression. 'Is that it? Were you planning to run away with him?'

'No.' She stared up at him defiantly, hoping he would not guess what was in her mind. 'You know I can't go back to Spain – ever.'

He nodded, his brow furrowing in thought. 'And if it were safe for you to return, would you have gone?'

Magdalene did not understand why he was so concerned about her intentions. He had refused to let her bind his shoulder, ordering her out of his sight, and he had looked at her as if he hated her. So why should he care what she did? She felt a surge of rebellion. Her situation was impossible! Whatever she did, she was wrong.

'Naturally I should go home if I could,' she said, lifting her head to stare at him with haughty pride. 'But I cannot – and you know it.'

'So you will stay with me because there is nowhere else to go?' Nick's face tightened with what might have been pain or anger, she could not tell which. 'Well, at least I have the truth from you now. Good-night, Magdalene. Tomorrow you shall see the island…'

There was such a look on his face that it frightened her. 'You– You won't leave me there?'

He laughed mirthlessly. 'It might be better for all of us if I did! But don't worry, my lovely one, I'm not as heartless as you seem to think. I gave you my word that I would always look after you, and I shall, whether it pleases you or not!'

With that last threat, he turned on his heel and left her to stare after him in distress.

She sank on to the edge of the bed, trembling all over. What a strange mixture this man was, she thought, feeling bewildered by his sudden change of mood. One moment he was threatening her with all manner of terrible punishments, the next he was promising that he would always take care of her. What was she to make of it all? It was impossible to understand him!

The island was every bit as enchanting as Magdalene had imagined as she stared at it from the ship. The sand was fine and soft beneath her feet, and the green mass behind it turned into a riot of colour as she entered it shadowed coolness. Rich crimson, palest pinks and mauves; the shades and variety of the flowers were seemingly endless. Huge trumpet-like blooms thrust out boldly in the lush greenery, while a delicate yellow blossom shyly hid beneath its sheltering spread. Here and there a jewel-bright bird fluttered through the trees, making her cry out in delight as she saw its beauty.

'Why, it's – it's paradise,' she cried. 'And yet you say no one lives here?'

'No. It's completely uninhabited,' Nick answered, smiling inwardly as he saw her incredulous joy. 'There are many such islands scattered hereabouts. This one is much too small to support a large community, but there is an abundance of food, and a small group of men could live here for years if need be.'

'So you are determined to leave the prisoners here?' Magdalene stared at him uncertainly. 'You will not let them take their ship and go home? Surely they could do no harm to anyone now!'

'My orders are to sink as many Spanish ships as I can.' Nick frowned, wondering why he felt the need to justify himself to her yet again. 'Even if I wanted to let them go, I could not, Magdalene. Besides, it's not such a terrible fate, is it? To be marooned in paradise...'

She heard the softer note in his voice and bit her lip, knowing in her heart that he was being more than generous to his enemies. 'No, perhaps not. Forgive me – I am being very foolish.'

Nick smiled, and she felt her heart catch. There was such a wide chasm between them, but it might not be impossible to bridge that gap even now – if only he still cared for her!

'I shall leave you to explore,' he said. 'You can come to no harm, but be sure to stay on this side of the island so that I can find you when it's time to leave.'

'What will you do until then?' She looked at him wistfully, wishing that he would spend the time with her in this beautiful place. Perhaps the magic of the island would bring them together again, she thought.

'I shall be helping my men to gather food and water. We may be at sea for many months, and we must take what we can at every opportunity. I shall not be far away, and there is nothing to frighten you here.'

She nodded, smiling slightly to hide her disappointment. He was not in one of his worst moods this morning, but he was certainly holding back from her. She could not reach him through the barrier he had erected between them.

A restless night had left her no nearer to understanding the man she loved; for she did love him, she knew it in her heart. She might fight him still, she might blame him for her father's death, but she could not stop loving him. He had only to smile at her and she felt her whole body beginning to melt.

Sighing, Magdalene walked slowly through the trees, stopping every now and then to examine a flower or an unusual plant. The sound of birds calling to one another was all around her, making her even more aware of her aloneness – even the birds had their mates. She tried to count how many different types of birds there were, but it was impossible to be sure because they fluttered from tree to tree, leading her further and further into the interior. She had been walking for some time when she heard a curious sound. She paused to listen, turning her head from side to side as she tried to decide from just what direction it was coming. Turning in towards the sound, she walked swiftly, in eager anticipation. Could it be...?

'Oh...' she breathed as she saw the waterfall. 'It's so beautiful.'

The sparkling water tumbled from high on the hill, down over several little ledges into a pool below, casting up a fine spray that hung like diamonds in the sunlight until they vanished in the swirling pool. Magdalene watched it for some time, entranced by its glory. She had loved the fountains in the gardens at home, but this was beyond anything she had ever seen. Kneeling beside the pool, she trailed her fingers in its delicious coolness. How she would love to immerse her whole body in it! Alas, it was far too deep for her to venture in.

Her eyes were drawn to the waterfall itself. About halfway up there was a wide ledge – wide enough for her to stand beneath the water and catch it as it fell. Did she dare? Why not? There was no one to see her, no one to scold her for her boldness.

She got to her feet, studying the ascent to the ledge. It was steep, but she could see footholds. If she removed her gown and petticoats now, she could easily manage the climb in her shift. Her fingers were trembling with impatience as she pulled off her clothes, letting them fall in a careless heap on the ground. Then she began the slow journey up the side of the hill.

Several times she stumbled, catching at overhanging branches to steady herself, and once she grazed her hand and knee; but at last she had reached her objective, and the elation that filled her as she gazed out from her vantage-point was worth all the effort. She could see the strip of silver sand, and beyond it the clear, endless blue of the bay where both ships still lay at anchor, basking sleepily in the sun. For a moment she wondered why Nick had not yet sunk the galleon, then she pushed the troublesome thought from her mind. Just for a short time she would forget everything and enjoy her stay in paradise.

Throwing off her shift, she edged her way behind the waterfall, which seemed very noisy now that she was actually beneath it. Holding out her hands to catch the fine spray, she splashed her face and arms, giving a little scream as the cold water sent shivers through her. Oh, how glorious it is! she thought, creeping a little further forward so that the icy droplets fell on her feet and legs. She gurgled with delight at the joy of it, becoming bold enough to stand almost at the very edge of the rock, so that she was completely beneath the fall of water, twisting and turning freely as she lifted her face in a moment of ecstasy.

It was at that moment that Nick saw her. He had heard her laughter before he realised where she was, and his breath stuck in his throat as he looked up. For a second he was spellbound by the sheer beauty of the woman. Even in his wildest dreams, he had never imagined her like this ... her innocent enjoyment ... the light, joyous sound of her laughter ... the perfection of her slender body. It stirred him deeply, sending a tide of desire surging through him. She was his woman, no matter what, and he wanted her. God, how he wanted her at this very moment! Always, he had been able to control his passion, indulging in the game of love for pleasure or amusement, but the feeling inside him now was something more. A burning need to possess that divine creature who was driving him wild with her childlike sporting beneath the waterfall.

Suddenly, he knew he was going to take what he wanted. She had yielded to him once, and she would do so again. He would smother her protests with kisses until she could no longer hold out against him. He would make her forget that she hated him, even if only for a little while. She was his, and he would let nothing stand between them!

A surge of excitement went through him as he pulled off his boots and stripped the clothes from his body. Laughter lit the blue eyes as he began the climb to Magdalene's ledge, his bare feet finding the way surely and easily. It took him half the time it had taken the girl, and he was grinning as he edged his way behind the water, imagining her surprise as he joined her at her sport.

He moved beneath the fine spray, his hand reaching out to take hold of her arm – and then she turned and saw him. A little start of surprise made her step backwards, her foot slipping on the edge of the rock. She gave a scream as she felt herself tipping backwards. Nick moved desperately towards her, his hands almost grasping her wrist as she screamed again and fell.

'Magdalene, no!' Nick yelled, his face twisting with agony as he saw her falling ... falling ... into the foaming spray as it emptied into the pool below. For one brief moment that might have been all eternity, he watched as she was swept beneath the water – and then he dived from the ledge.

The impact as he entered the water was such that it drove the breath from his lungs, and he felt a crushing force squeezing his chest. The pain in his injured shoulder was like a shaft of ice, but he ignored it, surging upwards, using the power of his muscular legs to bring him swiftly to the surface, his eyes searching desperately for the girl. He caught sight of something being tossed by the foaming water, catching her as she was dragged under once more. Surfacing, he held her head above the water, swimming on his back as he dragged her to the edge, and up on to the grassy verge.

Kneeling over her limp body, he turned her head to one side, pressing both hands against her abdomen and pumping with a rhythmic motion. She gave a little choke, opened her eyes, and then rolled over to vomit, before slumping on her back.

Thank God he had been in time, before she had had time to swallow too much water! He saw the graze on her forehead, touching it to reassure himself that the skin had not been broken. It could only have been a glancing blow.

'Are you hurt anywhere else?' he asked, his eyes exploring her body anxiously, as his hands moved surely over her limbs, seeking to be certain that she had no real injuries. 'You were lucky. No bones seem to be broken. You must have hit your head and lost consciousness...'

Magdalene's eyes were closed, but she moved her head negatively. 'I can't swim,' she whispered. 'I was drowning...'

'You can't swim – and you were under that waterfall?' Nick ejaculated, his voice harsh with fear. 'You little fool! Didn't you realise you might fall?'

She opened her eyes again, her breath coming in tiny, sobbing gasps. 'I was never allowed to bathe. It felt so good ... so good...'

Tears were flowing silently down her

cheeks as he gave a groan, gathering her to him, holding her close as she wept, his lips moving tenderly against her hair.

'It doesn't matter, my lovely one,' he murmured softly, caressingly. 'You're safe now. I told you, no one and nothing will harm you again. It was my fault you fell. I frightened you.'

'No, I wasn't frightened, only startled.'

She had stopped shivering now, and Nick laughed. 'Well you scared the life out of me, my girl! When I saw you fall, I thought I'd lost you.' She gave him a faint smile and he grinned. 'I shall have to teach you how to swim before I let you loose again, shan't I? Now lie still, I'm going to fetch your clothes.'

'I can...' she began, but was silenced by his look. She turned on her side to watch as he quickly gathered up their things and came back to her. 'I left my shift up there.'

'I'll get it later,' he promised.

She wondered what he was doing as he picked up his shirt and bent over her, beginning to dry her body; she noticed that the wound on his shoulder had begun to bleed sluggishly and tried to protest that she could look after herself, but she still felt weak and shaky, and it was so pleasant to lie in the sun and let him tend her. When he had wiped the last of the water from her body, he squeezed what he could from her long hair, taking care not to pull the roots, and lifted it clear of her neck to fasten it with a ribbon he tore from his shirt. Then he began to dress her, raising her hips to slide on two layers of petticoats and tie them at her waist. She sat up so that he could lower her gown over her head, smiling shyly. His fingers fumbled with the tiny buttons at the opening of her bodice, and she laughed.

'Let me do it, Nick,' she whispered, feeling a tingle at the base of her spine and knowing that she wanted him to go on touching her. 'You will catch cold if you don't dry yourself…'

His grin told her that he was well aware of what was happening to her – to them both! 'I had it in mind to do more than bathe with you, *querida*,' he admitted, a wicked glint in his eyes. 'But I have been well served for my evil thoughts. I'll not deny I want you – you know it without my telling you – but I should be a brute indeed to take advantage of you now.'

He moved away to dress himself, ignoring the thin trickle of blood down his arm, and slinging his wet shirt over his shoulder. He smiled as he gave her his hand, pulled her gradually to her feet. 'Can you walk?'

'Yes, of course,' she said stoutly, took one step forward and swayed dizzily. 'In a moment…'

He chuckled, bending down to sweep her

198

up in his arms despite her protests. 'Be quiet, *cara*. What am I to do with you, my wilful Magdalene? Ralph said you would be trouble, and surely he never spoke a truer word!'

She sighed and laid her head against his chest, feeling content to let the future take its own course. This man of many moods was so much stronger willed than she, and she had no reserves left with which to fight him, even if she would.

'Perhaps you should beat me if I am so much trouble,' she murmured, her hand moving lazily at the nape of his neck, exploring the smooth skin beneath his wet hair and sliding down over the top of his back.

A groan issued from his lips and she felt the tiny shudder run through him. 'Maybe I will, if you torment me enough, woman,' he growled, but she knew there was no anger in him, and she smiled.

Instinctively she knew that the island had worked its little miracle, after all...

CHAPTER SIX

Magdalene yawned and stretched, sitting up in bed as she realised that the hour was late. A lantern had been left burning on the table, and she knew Nick must have been in to look at her while she slept.

She had slept for hours! She had protested when he had insisted she must rest, but she felt much better for it. The little graze on her forehead stung a bit, and her body had tender spots all over as if it had been bruised by the impact of her fall, but otherwise she felt wonderful.

At the time she had not fully understood all that was happening, but now she realised that Nick must have dived from the ledge to rescue her so swiftly. How brave and strong he was – and how much she loved him! Her cheeks grew warm as she remembered the way he had dried her body so gently, dressing her as if she were a child. He had wanted to make love to her then; she had known it, just as had known that she would have responded to his kisses. Yet he had controlled himself, caring for her so tenderly that she felt he must love her. Surely no man would do the things he had done for her unless he cared deeply?

Outside a thinning moon shed a path of silver light across the sea. Magdalene could see the rowing-boat pulled up on the shore from her window, and she frowned. What were the men doing on the island at this hour? Was Nick with them? She pulled on her clothes hastily, suddenly wanting to be with him, to feel his arms round her and listen to the thunder of his heart as she had earlier. This time she would show him that she wanted his loving. There must be no more doubts between them, for the love that bound them was too strong to be denied. In her heart she had accepted that what both Anton and Nick had told her concerning her father was true, though a part of her mind still rejected it. Yet she knew she must learn to keep her memories locked away in a secret corner of her heart where they could hurt neither her nor the man with whom she wanted to spend the rest of her life...

The roar of cannon-fire ripped through the stillness of the night, shocking her with its unexpectedness. It set her body trembling with fright, and it was several minutes before she could gather her wits. Where had the shot come from, she wondered dazedly. Not from *Treggaron Rose*, of that she was certain. Were they being attacked? It must be so! Yet they were an easy target, anchored as they were in the bay, and if they had been hit, she would have felt the impact.

She ran from the cabin, her heart thumping painfully against her ribs, liked a caged bird beating its wings on the bars. What was happening? As she burst on to the deck, to her amazement she saw that there was a third ship in the bay, and it was firing on the Spanish galleon. Watching in bewilderment, she saw the galleon shudder beneath the barrage of fire; and suddenly it was ablaze, flames shooting high in the air to turn the night sky orange. The stench of burning assailed her nostrils, and the smoke was carried towards her on the breeze, making her cough and hold a kerchief to her mouth. She could hear the awful crackle of burning wood, catching her breath as sparks flew in a flurry of red-hot flecks; then there was a sharp explosion and the galleon split in two. Water rushed over it, dragging it down in a swirling whirlpool until at last it was gone.

Magdalene crossed herself and shivered. Who was on board the third ship, and why had she fired on the galleon? More important; perhaps, would it fire on *Treggaron Rose* next?

She glanced over her shoulder, and saw that she was not the only one who had been watching the sinking of the Spanish ship. Most of the crew were staring at the spot where she had been, a strange hush seeming to hang over them. Why were they not cheering? She knew that there was not a man among them who was not glad to see their enemies' vessels destroyed – and yet they hung together in small groups, almost as if they were waiting for something...

A man had just come on board. As she stood fixed to the spot where she had witnessed the dreadful spectacle, he came slowly but purposefully towards her, his face tight and cold – as if she were somehow responsible for this mood of tension that hung over the ship. She felt a stab of fear in her stomach. What was happening?

'What is wrong?' she whispered, her throat dry.

'I gave the order to sink the galleon,' the man said, and she gasped as she realised who it was, seeing his face clearly now for the first time.

'Sir Ralph! So it's your ship in the bay,' she said, feeling a cold trickle down her spine as she met his hard look. 'I knew the galleon was to be sunk – but why now, this evening? Something has happened. I know it has...'

Sir Ralph was staring at her strangely, almost as if he were hiding something from her – something so terrible that he was afraid to speak. Fear clutched at her heart. Was it Nick? Had he been hurt? Even as the chill went through her, she saw the man she loved come on board, with Anton close behind him. They stood just a little bit behind Ralph, all three looking at her silently. The tension was so brittle that she felt ill and her senses swam. What was making them act in this way?

'Go to your cabin, Magdalene,' Nick said, his voice curiously flat. His eyes were wearing that bleak look she hated, and his nostrils were flared as if he were experiencing some dark emotion. 'I have to talk to you ... to tell you...'

'No,' Anton said quickly, laying his hand on Nick's arm warningly. 'Let me explain to her. You are not...'

'No!' Nick's eyes glittered angrily as he shrugged off the restraining hand. 'This is something I have to do myself. She has to face the truth.'

'Tell me what?' Magdalene cried, her eyes wide and full of dawning fear. 'What is so terrible that you hesitate to tell me?' And then suddenly she understood why the ship had been sunk so dramatically, and why the crew were staring at her. The colour drained from her face and she swayed on her feet. 'Rodrigo ... his men ... you've...'

'Don Rodrigo is dead,' Nick said coldly, his words searing her like the lash of a whip, making her recoil in horror. 'I killed them myself; I do not regret it and, if I had to, I would do it again.'

'No...' she whispered, her face stricken as

she looked at him in disbelief and saw a bitter stranger. This was not the man who had cared for her so tenderly this morning... But that man was a false image, donned at will like a mask. The real Nicholas Treggaron was a cruel, ruthless murderer. 'You lied to me,' she said, her voice rising shrilly. 'You told me you would set the prisoners free on the island when we left...'

'The others have been freed,' Sir Ralph interrupted. 'Let Nick tell you why he...'

'No!' she screamed, her face blazing with hatred. 'I'll listen to no more lies from any of you! You are all liars and murderers and I hate you all. All of you! I mean it, Nick!'

He looked at her and his face was suddenly weary, but she did not see his tiredness or the pain. He had deceived her too many times, making her believe terrible things about her own father, pretending that he and his men were prepared to be merciful – and he was worse than any Spaniard. He had killed Rodrigo out of spite or jealousy, she knew not which. The hurt of his betrayal was so dreadful that she wanted to strike back at him, to wound him as he had wounded her. She had believed in him, but he was as false as all the others!

'Liar! Murderer!' she cried, suddenly running at him to beat at his chest in her agony of spirit. How could he have acted in such a cowardly way?

'Stop her,' Sir Ralph yelled urgently, and Anton moved swiftly to catch her round the waist, dragging her clear as she struggled to renew her assault on Nick.

'Be quiet, Magdalene,' he hissed furiously. 'You don't know what you're saying.'

'Let me go,' she sobbed, kicking and biting at his hands as he tried to restrain her. 'I hate him … I hate him! I want to kill him as he killed my father and now Rod–' Her words trailed away in astonishment as she saw Nick sway on his feet. Before her startled eyes he crumpled to his knees, looking at her with such soul-searing agony that she was silenced.

'Get her out of my sight,' he muttered chokingly. 'For God's sake…'

His bitter words were lost as he slumped forward to the deck, lying so still that Magdalene thought he was dead. She screamed wildly over and over again until Anton slapped her face hard; then she began to weep, sinking into a little heap on the deck as he abandoned her to go to Nick. She bent her head, burying her face in her hands and rocking back and forth as the tears flowed. Why had no one told her he was injured? Why had they let her attack him in a senseless temper? She hadn't meant to hurt him. She hadn't realised … when she felt a hand on her shoulder, she looked up fearfully.

'Is– Is he dead?' she whispered in dread.

'As near to it as a man can be and still live,' Ralph replied harshly. 'Don Rodrigo's blade almost found its mark. An inch higher, and he would have pierced Nick through the heart. He didn't quite manage it, but you succeeded where he failed.'

'No ... I didn't know ... I didn't mean it,' she whispered. 'I thought he had deliberately deceived me.'

'You should have given him a chance to explain.'

Magdalene took the hand he offered to pull her to her feet, sensing his disapproval. She was trembling, sick with misery as she watched several members of the crew gently lift their Captain and carry him below.

'I must go to him,' she said, trying to pass him, and failing. 'Please let me go.'

'I can't. His crew would never stand for it. They respect him to a man. Some of them damn near worship him. Surely you must know that by now? They heard you say you wanted to kill him, and most of them already distrust you. They would have put you over the side long ago, were it not for him. If you nursed him and he died, they would kill you.'

'But I love him so much,' she whispered, her face contorting with pain. 'I was upset when I said those terrible things. I was angry with him for lying to me. He promised that

Rodrigo and his men should go free...'

'And he intended to keep his word,' Sir Ralph said, his strange look making her stare at him intently. 'If I had come but a few hours later, this might never have happened.'

'What do you mean?' She did not understand him. Why should his arrival make any difference?

'I brought grave news from England,' Sir Ralph went on, almost as if she had not spoken. 'It was what I had to tell him that made Nick break his word to you, Magdalene. You should blame me, not him.'

'Please,' she begged. 'Please you must tell me what you mean.'

'There was a girl,' Sir Ralph said. 'She was not as beautiful as you, but she was dear to all of us...'

'You– You're talking about Cathy,' Magdalene whispered, her mouth suddenly dry. 'Anton told me how she died...'

'Then you know her death has haunted Nick for months. He knew who one of her assailants was, and he forced a duel on the man, but the Queen prevented it from taking place. She imprisoned Chevron in the Tower and he was ... persuaded to give the name of one of his accomplices, though he died before he could give the final name. The name he did yield was that of a young man – a man who was a visitor to England. He had come to find a market for his wines...'

Magdalene felt the deck move beneath her feet. Everything was whirling around her as she clutched at his arm for support. 'You are telling me that Rodrigo was one of the brutes who attacked Cathy... No! Oh no, it can't be true... Not Rodrigo!' But even as she denied it she was recalling the way he had tried to force his kisses on her in the gardens of Don Sebastian's home. Nick had arrived before it had gone too far, and neither of them had thought it more than a young man's foolishness. But what would have happened if Nick had not come when he did? Would she have suffered the same fate as Cathy, or would Rodrigo have remembered who and what she was in time? Then, if what Ralph was saying was true, she had misjudged Nick. She could understand why he had challenged Rodrigo to a duel. She raised her eyes to Ralph's. 'That's why Nick...'

'Yes, of course. Once he knew the truth, there could be only one outcome. Both Anton and I begged him to let one of us do it, knowing that you had a fondness for the Don and would blame Nick for his death.'

'No,' she whispered miserably. 'I have never cared for Rodrigo – except as a fellow-countryman and the betrothed of my cousin. It was only that I thought Nick had deceived me deliberately. That he was not the honourable man I believed...'

Ralph frowned, his eyes intent on her face. 'If that is true, it only makes things worse.'

'Why?' she stared at him desperately. His face seemed to be somehow very far away so that she could scarcely see it.

'Nick had him at his mercy. One thrust, and the Don would have died, but he hesitated at the last moment – and in that moment received the wound that may yet kill him.'

'He– He hesitated?'

'Momentarily – because he thought of you and the pain it would give you.'

'And yet Rodrigo is dead?'

'Nick's blade found its mark more surely than the Don's. If it had not, Anton or I would have finished the business.'

The blackness was closing in on her, but she knew she must see Nick. She must tell him that she was sorry, that she loved him. She must tell him now, before it was too late!

'I must see him...' she whispered, clutching at her companion's arm in desperation, but the rest of her words were lost in a sigh. She swayed, and Sir Ralph caught her as she fainted.

Afterwards, Magdalene never knew how many days she had lain in a fever. Someone came to her and bathed her forehead, touching water to her cracked lips until she could swallow a few drops. She thought it was Sir Ralph, but did not know him until the day she opened her eyes to find herself in a strange cabin with the large man bending over her. She gave a little cry and tried to sit up, but he pressed her back against the pillows.

'You have been very ill,' he said gently. 'It was some kind of a fever, but I think it has left you at last.'

'Where– Where am I?' Magdalene asked, her voice a harsh croak. 'Water... Can I have some water, please?'

'Of course.' He slid his arm beneath her shoulders, lifting so that she could swallow. 'Just a little, child. Not too much at first.' He smiled at her kindly. 'You are on board *Catherine,* my ship. I brought you here the night you were taken ill.'

'Nick...' Her eyes grew suddenly dark with fear as she remembered. 'Is he...?'

'He was holding out when I last spoke to Anton. Anton has command of *Treggaron Rose,* and will let us know if the worst should happen.'

'How?' Her fingers moved restlessly on the covers. 'How will you know?'

'While Nick's pennant flies from the mizzen-mast, he lives.'

'And it still flies?' She tried to lean across the bed to make certain for herself, but fell back weakly. 'Tell me, is it there?'

Her distress touched him and he looked out of the window to ease her. 'It flies bravely, child, as bravely as Nick will fight for his life. He is no coward; he will live if he can, no matter how terrible the pain he has to bear.'

'And I have given him so much pain,' Magdalene sobbed, tears of weakness flowing down her cheeks. 'I shall not be able to bear it if he dies believing I hate him.'

'You will bear it if you must, as we all shall. His friends love him too, you know.'

His tone was a little harsh, and she looked at him miserably. 'You blame me for what happened, don't you? Nick said you had warned him against me, and you were right! I have brought him nothing but trouble.'

'No, I do not blame you, though I have always believed that you two were so far apart that it could bring only unhappiness for both of you. You are a Spaniard and a Catholic – how could Nick marry you, even if he wanted to?'

She bit her lip. 'He– He does not have to marry me. I love him. I have made no demands on him. I would be his – his woman...'

'At sea for a few months that might be acceptable, but what about when we return to England, as we shall very soon? Will you live as his mistress then? Could you bear the shame of it? Could you let him bear the dishonour he would feel he had brought on you? You are a woman of gentle birth, Magdalene, not a whore he has taken from the streets.'

She blinked hard, trying to stem her tears. 'If he lives... If he forgives me, I shall do whatever he asks of me.'

'Nick has sworn to protect and care for you. He will forgive you if he lives, but if you become his mistress, you will be doing him a terrible hurt. While he loves you, he would never think of marrying another woman. He will have no legitimate heirs, Magdalene. Will you rob him of that?'

'You are cruel,' she whispered. 'Why do you say these things to me? Do you hate me because I am a Spaniard?'

Ralph sighed, shaking his head. 'Forgive me, child, I meant not to hurt you. Nick is my friend. I love him as a brother, and I was thinking only of his good, but perhaps I was wrong. Do not listen to me. Nick will decide for himself when he is well again.'

'Only let him be well, and I shall ask for nothing more.'

'I am a fool,' Ralph said, smiling at her now. 'You love him truly, and perhaps the rest does not matter. Now, I shall leave you to rest and in a little while you shall have some nourishing broth. You must try to eat it, child, for it will help you to regain your strength.'

'Thank you. I shall try to swallow a little.'

She closed her eyes as he went out, fighting the waves of despair that washed over her. Sir Ralph believed that she was to blame for what had happened to Nick; she knew it, even though he had denied it. He thought she would ruin his friend, and perhaps he was right. She had been named as a witch, and it seemed that she was an evil spirit, a curse on the man she loved. She had brought him nothing but bad luck, and now he was close to death, believing she hated him. They would not even let her see him because they feared she might harm him!

She thought then that it might have been better for everyone if she had died. Why had Sir Ralph bothered to nurse her through the fever when everyone hated her? Yet she knew he could not let her die even though she was his enemy; if Nick lived, he would still keep his promise to protect her, because he was a man of honour. At last she knew it with a deep certainty, and with that knowledge she slept peacefully at last.

The pain was closing in on him; it was all around him, filling his mind, racking his body unbearably so that he could not stop himself crying out. He was aware of Anton sponging the sweat from his brow, aware of it despite the mist that clouded his sight.

'Tell her...' he muttered through clenched teeth, the beads of perspiration breaking out once more as he made the effort to speak. 'I have to tell her ... Anton...'

'She isn't here,' Anton said gruffly. 'Lie still, my foolish friend, or your wound will break open again. She knows all that she should know: Ralph told her himself.'

'Ralph told her...' Nick's fingers curled around the other man's wrist with a strength born of desperation. 'She knows ... but she is not here... Then she still...'

'We thought it best,' Anton began, but he saw that the sick man was no longer listening. Nick had brief moments of lucidity, but for the most part he lay in a semi-conscious state, halfway between life and death. And perhaps it was for the best: no man could bear the pain he was suffering for too long. Only the strength of his will had kept him alive this long, but he was getting weaker...

The days seemed endless, each one so like the one before that they passed in a meaningless blur. Every morning on waking Magdalene looked at the pennant on *Treggaron Rose,* and it was the last thing she saw before she closed her eyes at night. While it still fluttered in the breeze, it meant that Nick lived, and that she could somehow struggle through another weary day.

She went on deck as little as possible, not wanting to be in the way. Sir Ralph's crew treated her with cool politeness, but she knew that they had all heard about the way she had flown at Nick in a rage when he was wounded; they all knew that she had said she wanted to kill him – and they all blamed her for his being so close to death.

Twice the monotony of the long voyage was broken when they sighted Spanish ships on their outward journey to the New World.

Catherine engaged both after a warning shot across their bows. Neither captain offered to surrender, and both galleons were sunk with the help of *Treggaron Rose*. Since the ships had not been carrying valuable cargoes, the only motive for the attacks was to sink the vessels, and Sir Ralph had been quite blunt about it.

'It is my duty to sink as many enemy ships as possible,' he said. 'Spain and England are at war, and have been for years. It pleases your king and my queen to pretend it is not so, but Philip prepares an armada against my country, and I would be a traitor if I did not do what little I can to put off that evil day.'

Magdalene accepted what he said without argument. She stayed in her cabin while the fighting was going on, shutting the roar of the cannon out of her mind as best she could. She knew that Sir Ralph was right about the armada, and for the rest it was naught but confusion. She did not know where her loyalties lay any more. She was half English, half Spanish – torn between conflicting emotions. All she really knew was that the man she loved was desperately ill, and she wanted to live to see him again. So she could only feel relief when the fierce battles were over and the two English ships sailed on victoriously. She did not doubt the skill of the Englishmen; they seemed to outsail and out manoeuvre the heavier galleons time after time. So perhaps the victory was theirs by right. Men would always fight; it was their way, and she had been a fool to protest so much. She was merely a woman with no fortune to recommend her, and in the eyes of many that made her of less worth than a horse or a hunting dog. Despite the black moods that sometimes possessed him, Nicholas Treggaron was someone special, and if he died she would never find his like again.

She could only pray that he would live, and she did pray on her knees night and morning. She asked pardon for her sins without the benefit of a priest, and felt that God listened to her prayers. If the comfort she received from following the ways of the heretics was wrong, then she did not care. Let it be so. She had been born and raised a Catholic, but the doubts had always been there in her mind. She would not be the first to turn to a less rigid creed, and though a priest would condemn her as eternally damned, she felt renewed and strengthened by her faith. For it was never God she had doubted, simply a doctrine.

And so the days and weeks passed, and the two ships sailed on towards England. The captain of *Treggaron Rose* lay on his sickbed and she could only watch for the pennant fluttering in the breeze. She had wronged the man she loved, but how dearly she was paying for it now! She ate little, and grew so slender that her clothes hung on her loosely, and her hair was dull from lack of brushing.

Would this voyage never end? How long must she suffer the torment of uncertainty? How long before they would let her see Nick again?

'She has asked to see you, Nick. Will you not speak with her now?'

Nick glared at his friend from the bed that had held him captive for so many weeks. 'Damn you, Anton! I have given you my answer several times. I shall see her when I am able to greet her on my own two feet, and not before. I'll not give her the satisfaction of seeing me like this – a weak fool who can scarce stand!'

'As you wish.' Anton's brows rose half mockingly. 'Yet she could do you little harm if I were here. Besides, I doubt she ever meant to. Magdalene has a temper, my friend ... rather like you.'

The blue eyes glinted with ice. 'I need no explanations from you. I don't fear what she might do. I know exactly what she is – and what was in her mind. She thinks me a murderer and every foul thing that breathes.'

'Are you sure of that?'

'Get out of here!' Nick cursed as the pain began again. 'I can see she's bewitched you, damn you!'

Anton gave him an odd look, but shrugged his shoulders and left the cabin, knowing that nothing would move Treggaron when he was in this mood.

Once the door had closed behind him, Nick lay back, shutting his eyes as he fought the weakness that swept over him. His wound had begun to heal at last, but the pain scarcely left him – and he felt so damned weak. He had been wounded before many times, but he had never come so close to dying, nor had he ever felt so helpless... Like a child, he thought bitterly. It made him angry, very angry – and the grinding inside him helped to fight the physical pain he was enduring, but nothing stopped his mental agony.

Magdalene had asked to see him – now, after all this time! He could guess why, he thought, his mouth twisting coldly. She had decided he would live, and she was concerned for the future – her future! Well, he had had plenty of time to think about that, lying here during those hazy, fever-racked nights when only his desire for revenge had kept him hanging on to the slender thread of life. Oh yes, he had thought about the future, and he knew just what it held for that Spanish witch...

The weather was growing colder as they neared the shores of England. Magdalene wore the travelling cloak Mrs Penrith had found for her whenever she came on deck now. Her clothes were very shabby after so many months at sea, but it did not matter. Nothing seemed to matter much these days.

Storms had threatened their progress for more than a week, but they were through the worst of it. Ralph had told her that another week would see them safely home, but what then? What did the future hold for her?

It was towards the end of the week that Magdalene saw something that almost made her faint. A man was standing on *Treggaron Rose's* deck, staring intently towards *Catherine,* and the sight of him sent her heart on a dizzy spiral. It was Nick! He was alive... He was alive! Oh, God be praised! he was well again. She could not see his face clearly enough to tell how much the long weeks and months of his illness had changed him, though she knew there must be some. No man could come so close to death and escape unscathed.

He stood very still for a long time, then he turned and walked away. She thought that he moved terribly slowly, and her heart caught with pain. He was well enough to come up on deck, but he was so weak even now. She felt tears prick her eyes. How she longed to hold him in her arms and try to ease his pain!

Why would they not let her speak to him now? Surely they could not still believe she would harm him! Her longing to be near him was so great that she decided to ask Ralph if it would be possible for her to go on board *Treggaron Rose,* but when she did, he shook his head and frowned.

'You will see Nick when we reach England; you can speak to him then.'

'I want to see him now,' she said desperately. 'It has been so long. Please let me talk to him just for a little while?'

'Nick has refused to see you yet,' Ralph replied, frowning as he witnessed the shock in her face. 'I should not have told you if you had not pressed me. I sent him word some weeks ago that I thought he ought to speak with you, but he was adamant in his refusal. I'm sorry, Magdalene. Truly. I have been touched by your suffering – I like not to see you thus.'

The kindness in his voice brought the tears to her eyes. She could not look at him, and hurried away to the privacy of her cabin. Then she wept until she could weep no more.

At last the storm of grief left her. It was clear that Nick no longer wanted her. Somehow she must find a new life for herself, away from him. She knew instinctively that he would stand by his promise to look after her, but she did not want his charity. Since there was no one she could turn to for help, she would have to find some kind of work – perhaps as a ladies' maid. Or as a child's nurse? She could teach children to read from a hornbook and form their letters with a quill, but would any English family employ a Spaniard to look after their children?

Lifting her head proudly, Magdalene decided that she would work as a tavern maid if need be, but she would not be a burden to a man who did not want her.

They had reached England at last, and were anchored beneath cold grey skies. Magdalene shivered as Ralph helped her into the rowing-boat that would take them ashore. She sat straight and stiff as the men pulled towards the beach, keeping her eyes averted from the tall figure waiting on the sand. At last she would see Nick, but it was too late for apologies now. Too much time had elapsed, and he had grown to hate her. If she had any pride at all left, she would use it to prevent him guessing her misery.

Ralph helped her out of the boat, giving her a little nod of reassurance. She smiled slightly, her limbs feeling so weak that she could hardly put one foot in front of another. How could she face Nick, knowing that he hated her? But she must – she had no choice. She walked slowly until she was almost level with him, then she lifted her eyes to gaze into his face.

He was much thinner than she remembered, and he had streaks of grey in his hair at the temples. She almost swayed, imagining the pain-filled nights and days which had put them there. The longing to reach out and touch him was so strong it nearly overpowered her, but she fought against it, controlling it at last and giving him a cool smile.

'I am glad to see you well again, Nick.'

'Are you?' He sounded bitter, and she chewed her lip, knowing that she had brought this on herself. 'Anton will take you to the manor. I must ride at once to London, and Ralph goes with me. We shall beg an audience of Her Majesty.'

'But– But she said she would hang you!' Magdalene drew her breath sharply as she saw the mockery in his face.

'She is welcome to hang what's left of me, if she's a mind to it,' he rasped. 'Anton has instructions to see that you are provided for in that eventuality.'

'I was not concerned for myself.' Magdalene drew herself up proudly, refusing to let him see how his sarcasm had hurt her. 'I shall not be a burden to you for long. As soon as I can find work, I shall do so.'

Anger flickered in the blue eyes. 'Would you shame me now? I brought you to England, and I shall provide for you. If you try to run from me, I'll have you found and brought back, no matter where you go. Damn you, Magdalene, I'll hear no more of this! Do you understand me?'

'I understand you, but you have no rights over me.' Her eyes flashed angrily at him.

'I have the right of possession,' he said coldly. 'Anton will guard you well, my proud beauty. You will stay at Treggaron Manor until I send for you. If I choose to send for you.'

'But why?' she whispered, staring at him miserably. 'You do not want me.'

'Do I not?' he asked softly, and the look in his eyes made her draw back in fear. 'As yet, I am too weak to show you what I want of you, but I grow stronger every day. I told you once that I was a patient man, and I can wait for what I want.' His eyes were very bright as he looked at her, reminding her of a bird of prey. 'And what do you imagine that might be, Magdalene?'

'I – I don't know,' she croaked, terrified by the cold fury she witnessed in him. This was a stranger – a man she did not know. 'Unless– Unless you want revenge?'

His laughter was harsh and bitter. 'I knew you would understand, my lovely one. Yes, I want revenge. I crave it as a man dying of thirst craves for water – and when the time is right, I shall take what I want, whether you yield to me or not!'

Gasping, Magdalene shrank back from him. She had never seen him like this – there was such coldness in his eyes. This was not the man she had given her heart to but a cruel stranger, forged in the fires of hell he had endured. His message was plain enough, and she knew that he had fed on his anger over the past months, drawing strength from it and the will to live. He had wanted to live so that he could take his revenge and make her suffer as he had suffered, but she had already paid so much. Could he not see it in her eyes?

Sorrowfully, she realised that his anger would not let him see the truth; he had not noticed how thin and pale she was. He saw her as he wanted to see her – and that was as some kind of evil spirit who had blighted his life. For a moment she gazed into his eyes, then turned away from the blazing hatred she found there. She cast down her lashes, refusing to let him guess her pain, and then he had swung away from her and was walking briskly towards the waiting horses – horses he must have sent for as soon as he landed.

'He does not mean all those terrible things he said to you,' Ralph muttered, unable to look at her. 'Before God, I've never seen him look that way. The man I knew could never have spoken thus to any woman. I know not what has come over him.'

'He– He hates me,' she whispered, lifting her stricken gaze to his. 'He hates me – and he wants to hurt me.'

'God help him, I think he does,' Ralph said. 'I'm sorry, I must go now, but here comes Anton. He will take care of you now, and Nick will relent, never fear.'

'Anton will make me his prisoner,' Magdalene whispered as her companion strode away. 'But what does it matter what I do or where I go? Nothing matters now... Nothing.'

She looked at Anton, seeing the grim expression on his face as he came towards her. Merciful heavens, did he, too, hate her? Was there no one she could turn to for comfort? Then he smiled at her and held out his hand.

'It has been too long, Magdalene,' he said.

'I have missed you...'

Magdalene shivered, despite the huge fire burning in her apartment. It was cold, colder than she had ever experienced; but she was warmly dressed and the weather did not worry her. It was the lack of news from London that had brought a frown to her brow.

It was ten days since Anton had escorted her to the house which was to be her prison, though she had not been treated as a prisoner. Mrs Penrith had exclaimed at her thinness and immediately embarked on a campaign to put the colour back in her cheeks. She seemed to claim the girl as a long-lost daughter. Possets, warming broths and hot spiced ale were brought to Magdalene so often that she could hardly manage to consume them all, but the housekeeper would not go away until she did, and already the difference was noticeable. She had begun to regain the weight she had lost, and it suited her.

Susan's sister Hanna had been summoned from the village to act as her personal maid, and as a result the dark locks had started to shine once more. Hanna had taken charge of Magdalene's meagre wardrobe, clucking with dismay at the salt-stains on the gowns she had worn throughout the long months at sea.

'It is not fitting that you should wear these rags,' she said, shaking her head. 'I don't know what the master can be thinking of. Miss Cathy was always provided with everything she needed.'

'But I am not Miss Cathy,' Magdalene said. 'Besides, it does not matter what I wear.'

Neither Mrs Penrith or Hanna agreed with her. The housekeeper had searched through the trunks stored in some dark corner of the manor, finding two warm winter gowns that had belonged to Cathy, and Magdalene was grateful to have them. They were made of a serviceable woollen cloth and did not become her particularly, but she hardly noticed. If it were not for the insistence of others, she would have neglected her appearance entirely. What good was it to have her hair prettily dressed if Nick was not there to see it? And even if he had been, it would not make him love her. Her stupid behaviour on the night he had fought Don Rodrigo had turned his heart against her, and she did not think anything she could do would alter that. The future seemed bleak and hopeless, but she did not know what to do about it.

She was gazing aimlessly into the fire when someone knocked at her door. Calling out that whoever it was might enter, Magdalene did not turn her head until she heard the scrape of a man's riding-boots. Hope and a kind of fear flared in her; but when she twisted round, she saw that it was Anton.

'Would you care for a ride, Magdalene?' he asked. 'Despite the cold, it is a fine morning and the air would do you good. You spend too much time indoors.'

'Why not?' Magdalene stood up obediently. It did not matter to her whether she rode or not, but Anton had been kind to her and she did not want to worry him. All these people were so concerned for her, and she was grateful for their charity – but there had been no word from the man who constantly filled her thoughts. She feared for his return, and yet she feared it too – feared the hatred she would see when she looked into his eyes.

'You will need a cloak,' Anton said. He saw one lying on a chest and picked it up, putting it carefully around her shoulders. His hand brushed her cheek as if by accident, and she glanced up, surprised at the expression she caught on his face. Before she could be sure she had seen it, he had himself under control once more and was smiling. 'Come, you will enjoy yourself once we are mounted. I have given instructions that you shall ride the mare you favour.'

'Thank you,' she whispered, her pulses flicking with an odd excitement. She was not quite sure what that look had meant. Physical desire could mean many things, and he was not necessarily in love with her. But if he were...? If he were, he might help her to escape from a situation she disliked.

Perhaps if she were to flirt with him a little? Magdalene glanced at his face as he walked beside her, along the gallery and down the stairs. In his own way he was as attractive as Nick, though he did not set her limbs on fire whenever he looked at her. Yet his smile was pleasant, and she liked him well enough. He was her friend. She would not object too much if he kissed her – but supposing he demanded more as the price of his help? She knew instinctively that she could never yield to him as she had to Nick, with her heart and soul as well as her body. No, that would be too high a price to pay for the freedom she desired. But perhaps Anton would be satisfied with less: a smile, a touch of her hand, a kiss...

When he lifted her on to her horse's back, she noticed that his hands lingered a little longer than was necessary about her waist, and she smiled down at him, a hint of mischief in her eyes.

'This was a good idea, Anton,' she said, feeling a surge of pleasure as she looked about her at the bare fields, and trees that were covered in a frothing of white frost. She had sat moping indoors for too long. It was good to be out in the fresh air again, and to feel the bite of the wind on her face. 'Shall we ride as far as the cove?'

'Whatever you wish, Magdalene. You must know that I would do everything in my power to make you happy.'

'Everything?' Her brow went up mockingly, and she gave a little toss of her head as she urged her mount to a gentle canter, leaving Anton to mount hurriedly and follow behind. She must not ask him for help too soon, she thought. His loyalty to Nick was still strong and would not be easily overcome.

Glancing sideways as she heard the sound of pounding hooves closing on her, she laughed invitingly and urged the obliging mare to a faster pace. Soon they were galloping side by side, both enjoying the exercise and the sting of the wind on their faces. The air was cool, but deliciously crisp, making the blood sing in their veins as if it were wine they breathed instead of merely air. Now truly Magdalene was enjoying herself, and her laughter was light and joyous; the smiles she gave her companion were genuine, with no thought of the future.

Yet when he suggested they should tether the horses and walk on the beach for a while, she could not resist flirting with him a little. The smell of the ocean was in her nostrils, reminding her of so many happy days when she had strolled round the deck, knowing that Nick's eyes were following her... The memory brought such a surge of pain that she turned to Anton with a brilliant but wavering smile.

'Are you not bored having to stay here with me when you could be at Court?' she asked, sighing deeply as she brushed her hand against his arm.

'I have no desire to go to Court,' Anton replied, staring at her oddly. 'Why should I be bored?'

'Oh, I don't know. Surely men like to enjoy themselves...' She opened her eyes wide at him, her lips pouting provocatively. 'Have you no lover waiting eagerly for your return? You have been many months at sea...'

Anton grinned. 'I dare say a few ladies of my acquaintance would be pleased to see me, but I have no need of them as yet. Don't play games with me, Magdalene. I know you too well.'

She stopped walking and looked up at him, a hint of laughter in her eyes. 'Oh, it was foolish of me to think that I could fool you – or that you would ever betray Nick's trust! I know that I can never mean as much to you...'

'Once, I would have agreed with you.' Anton's face was suddenly serious as he looked down at her. 'I have tried to hide my feelings for you since the first time we met. You were Nick's woman and I knew you loved him. I decided then that I could not hope for more than to be your friend – and I was content, because you wanted it so. Now I am not sure how either of you feels...'

'He hates me, Anton. He keeps me only because he wants to punish me for what happened on the island. Perhaps I deserve it, but...'

'No, you have not deserved what he has made you suffer. Do you think I am blind? I have seen how thin and pale you were – how much he has hurt you.' Anton tipped her chin up towards him. 'And you think you want to escape from him, is that it? Are you sure you know what you want, Magdalene? If I thought you really meant it, I would take you with me now and risk Nick's anger.'

'If you would help me, I could find work somewhere...'

'You would never need to work,' Anton said. 'I should take care of you, and if one day we parted, there would always be another man. You would never manage alone, Magdalene. Wherever you went, men would look at you and want you; better a protector who cares for you than some brute who would force you to his bed.'

She stared at him, a cold knot forming in her stomach. 'That is plain speaking, sir, and

I will be as plain. I had not thought to exchange one form of bondage for another...'

'You misjudge me,' Anton said with a careless laugh. 'You would not find me a jealous tyrant. We should both be free to live as we please, and you would discover I can be generous. All I should ask would be your company for perhaps a year, longer if we were both happy with the arrangement. After that, I swear you could take your pick of a dozen wealthy protectors.'

It was a bitter disappointment. She had believed Anton her friend, but he demanded so much in return for his help. Perhaps it was true that she could never hope for freedom; as he had said, there would always be a man to look at her with lust. It was the curse of beauty and she was so vulnerable; alone and friendless, she would be at the mercy of any man who offered her employment. Better to take the protection of a gentleman than be forced to act the whore for a tavern-keeper! And yet there was a part of her that knew she would rather die than bed with any man but Nick.

'You must allow me time to consider your offer,' she said at last. 'I – I know it was meant kindly, but...'

'Kindness has nothing to do with it.' Anton gripped her shoulders, pulling her against him fiercely. 'If it had been anyone but Nick, I would have taken you from him long ago.'

His hungry mouth fastened over hers and she felt the passion in him, letting him kiss her, but making no response. His embrace was not unpleasant but her blood did not race wildly in her veins. He let her go after a moment, a wry smile twisting his lips.

'You're still in love with him,' he said. 'Why don't you tell him so and put an end to this nonsense?'

'I cannot,' she whispered. 'It is too late. If he knew how vulnerable I am he would use my love to destroy me. Oh, don't you see? That's why I have to leave him!'

'In his present mood he might,' Anton agreed. 'I have known Nick to be angry before, but never for this long or to this extent. So what will you do?'

'I don't know. Perhaps his anger will have cooled when next we meet. Perhaps he will let me go.'

'And if he won't?' Anton flicked her cheek with his finger. 'You would forget him in time, Magdalene. I should not make too many demands on you at first. Remember I am there if you decide to leave him.'

'I shall not forget.'

It might be better to live as Anton's mistress than bear the coldness of Nick's anger, and yet... Would she ever be able to forget the way she had felt when he held her in his arms? She did not think so.

Anton nodded, smiling oddly. 'In the meantime, I am still your friend. We should return to the manor now, but the ride has done you good; you have more colour in your cheeks. Mrs Penrith will be pleased with me at least.'

Magdalene laughed. She gave him her hand and he helped her to mount. Glancing up at the cliffs, she pointed to something that had been puzzling her.

'What is that for, Anton?'

He followed the direction of her gaze, and frowned. 'It is a beacon. The Queen ordered that they be built the length and breadth of England. It is a warning system in case of attack.'

'Attack by the Spaniards?' Magdalene guessed the reason for his frown. 'Will it come soon?'

Anton shrugged. 'Last spring Sir Francis paid a little visit to Cadiz and burnt many of Philip's ships. But the war must come; it has been threatening for too long.'

A shiver ran down her spine and she had a strange sensation as if she were falling. Suddenly she could hear the roar of cannon-fire and the screams of dying men all around her. The stench of blood was so strong that she almost fainted.

'What is the matter?' Anton's concerned voice reached her through the mists. 'Are you ill, Magdalene?'

'No…' The vision had faded as swiftly as it came. She shook her head, not wanting to tell him of what she had seen. 'No – it was nothing. I felt faint for a moment, that's all.'

He stood looking up at her anxiously. 'Perhaps you should rest for a little while before we ride back to the house. Was it something I said that upset you?'

'No, just a foolish moment.' She smiled at him. 'I promise you I am perfectly well. Come, I will race you home.'

She jerked on the reins, startling the mare to a spanking pace. Her premonitions had always frightened her, and this one was too terrible to speak of. She had seen such a horrible scene of carnage, as if a tremendous battle had taken place; and among the dead and dying men she had seen a face she recognised – but she would not let herself believe that it was a warning. She would put it out of her mind and forget what she had glimpsed.

She glanced over her shoulder, seeing that Anton was following close behind, and waving so that he urged his horse to catch up with her.

As they cantered into the courtyard, Magdalene was immediately aware of the flurry of activity. Servants were busy unloading a wagon full of packages, and a groom was leading a horse towards the stables. It was obvious that someone had recently arrived,

238

and her betraying heart gave a leap of joy. Was it Nick?

Then a man came down the steps of the house to greet them, and the faint hope died. She hid her disappointment and smiled in welcome as Sir Ralph came to help her to dismount.

'I had not expected to see you here,' Anton said. 'Is Nick with you?'

'Come inside,' Ralph replied with a frown. 'I have bad news, I'm afraid.'

'Bad news?' Magdalene's heart lurched. 'Nick is not ill again?'

'No, he was well enough when I last saw him, but that was five days ago.' Ralph looked at his companions, unable to hide his anxiety. 'Nick has been arrested on a charge of treason and taken to the Tower.'

'Arrested?' Magdalene cried, the world seeming to whirl around her. 'For treason? Then he will hang!'

'Surely Elizabeth will not hang him,' Anton said, his eyes narrowing sharply. 'She intended him to spirit Magdalene away... It was a challenge understood on both sides, though not spoken.'

'It seems she is angry with him for some reason, though I know not what. When we reached London, Nick asked for an audience at once, but was told to present himself in ten days. Then, the day before he was due, they came to arrest him. I have tried to gain a hearing of Her Majesty, but she will not see me.'

'But we must do something,' Magdalene cried. 'We cannot stand by and do nothing while he hangs!'

'The Queen has sent me word that I am to bring you to London, Magdalene. It seems that your uncle has made a further request, through the French ambassador, for your return.' Ralph frowned. 'I believe that must be why Nick was imprisoned – to make certain that he could not snatch you away this time.'

A wave of nausea swept over her but she fought it down, knowing that Nick's life might depend on her obedience to Queen Elizabeth's commands. 'If Her Majesty has sent for me, I must obey. Perhaps, if I return to Spain, she will relent and set Nick free.'

'I fear it is some kind of bargain she has in mind,' Ralph agreed grimly. 'If she would be see me, a generous gift from the prize Nick took might help to soften her heart towards him. It was his intention to present her with a chest of silver, but before it had even arrived he was on his way to the Tower.'

'We must leave for London at once,' Magdalene cried, starting towards the staircase. Then she stopped and looked down at her gown in dismay. 'But what shall I wear? I cannot plead Nick's case before the Queen like this!'

'I have thought of that. You will find suitable clothes waiting for you upstairs.' Sir Ralph smiled at her benevolently. 'From what I have seen, you will be dressed as finely as any lady of the Court.'

'You have brought clothes for me?' She showed her surprise as she glanced at his face. 'That was indeed thoughtful of you. I do not know why you should do this for me.'

He laughed, dismissing her thanks with a wave of his hand. 'I am only the courier, child. It is Nick you should thank. He has spent a small fortune to provide a wardrobe worthy of a queen, most of which awaits you in London, though I dare say he can afford it easily enough.'

Magdalene gaped at him, feeling bewildered. Why should Nick buy her beautiful clothes, now, when he hated her? He had given her small gifts before, but nothing on the scale that Sir Ralph was indicating. Or was it really Sir Ralph who had provided her with the necessary clothes himself? She knew he had felt sorry for her when they parted because of the way Nick had treated her, and this might be his way of helping her. Perhaps he hoped to please her by saying the gifts came from Nick. Whatever the truth, she must not embarrass him by doubting his word.

She smiled shyly at him. 'Then I thank you for your part in the business, sir. Now, if you

241

will excuse me, I must prepare for our journey. Mrs Penrith will bring you whatever refreshments you care for.'

Her rooms were full of packages: so many that she could scarcely find a passage through the mounting piles. Hanna and Susan were watching the resulting confusion with obvious anticipation, and Magdalene laughed at their hopeful faces.

'You had best begin to open some of them,' she said. 'I have no time to examine all these things now. Will you help me to find a travelling-gown? There should be one among all these...' She indicated the variously-shaped parcels. 'I must leave for London shortly.'

Neither girl needed a second bidding, and they began to untie the strings, exclaiming in delight as they uncovered one treasure after another. Brocaded bed-hangings in rose and silver; rolls of velvets, silks and satins followed one another from the wrappings in swift succession; fine linen, laces, gloves of embroidered leather, and others of silk – and still the servants brought more boxes.

Hanna finally found the trunk they were seeking and lifted the elegant gown from its hiding-place with reverent fingers. It was fashioned of velvet in emerald green and trimmed with black ribbon; there was a short cloak to match, banded and embroidered in black, and a tiny hat with a swirl of fluffy black plumes pinned by a large silver brooch set with a huge black pearl. There were shoes, too, with shiny buckles and high, shaped heels.

'Oh yes, this will suite you to perfection, miss,' Hanna said with evident satisfaction. 'It you won't take Susan long to shake out these creases. By the time I've dressed your hair, it will be ready for you. We shan't keep the gentlemen waiting long.'

'Are you coming with me, Hanna?' Magdalene looked at her doubtfully.

'You're never thinking of going to London without me?' The girl looked shocked. 'Someone must look after your clothes! Besides, you can't travel with two gentlemen without a maid. It wouldn't be right. What would all those fine ladies at the Court think?'

Magdalene smiled, remembering the months at sea when she had been the only woman among a crew of more than a hundred men. She had managed then, but Hanna was right, circumstances had changed. If she were to hold her head high at Court, she could not afford to give anyone a reason to gossip about her. Especially if she hoped to gain the Queen's goodwill – and she must, if Nick were not to die!

She looked at the confusion all round her.

Many of these things were meant to transform her apartments, and seemed the kind of gift a man might give to his intended bride. Perhaps they really were from Nick, but why had he gone to so much trouble for a women he hated?

It was a mystery, but it gave her some hope. If Nick had bought these beautiful things for her, he could not be as angry as she had feared. It did not matter that she would never use them; it would be enough to know that he did not hate her. At least then she might be strong enough to face the cruel death that awaited her when she was handed over to the Inquisition!

CHAPTER SEVEN

The velvet travelling-gown suited Magdalene to perfection, fashioned as it was to accentuate her tiny waist and full, firm bosom. She blushed as she saw how low the bodice dipped across her breasts, so that they were hidden only by a ruffle of exquisite lace; but Hanna assured her that sometimes even the Queen of England wore gowns every bit as daring as this one. If Magdalene were not to be dismissed as a country nobody, she must do the same.

When the outfit was completed with a pair of the softest leather gloves and a silver-handled riding-crop, she had to admit that she had never owned anything quite so becoming. Whoever had chosen it had done so with skill and care, but was it Nick or Ralph?

There was a flutter of apprehension in Magdalene's face as she walked downstairs. Would the men waiting for her think she looked too bold? There was no mistaking the hot glow in Anton's eyes, and she did not have to wonder at his opinion of her new clothes. Ralph smiled and said that she looked very pretty. She thanked Mrs

Penrith, who embraced her warmly and warned her to take care in the wicked city, and followed the men outside.

Hanna was already seated pillion behind the groom. Three riding horses and two with saddlepacks were ready waiting. Anton helped Magdalene to mount, but this time his hands did not linger about her waist, though she sensed the underlying passion he held in check, a passion he dare not show too plainly lest Ralph should notice and think him disloyal. He would never have spoken so plainly of his feelings if Magdalene had not pushed him to it, and she knew that he was as concerned for his friend as any of them. He would prefer to fight Nick for her rather than steal her while the other man was a prisoner in the Tower. What a tangled web fate had woven about them all!

They rode in silence, wanting to cover as much distance as possible before nightfall. Magdalene's thoughts were sombre as she kept pace with the men; she knew her own future was unavoidable, and she had accepted it. At least she would no longer have Nick's wrath to face, but what of him? He had suffered enough pain because of her, and only if she knew he was safe could she go to her own death with fortitude. It would not matter what happened to her if Nick was alive.

'Only a few more miles, and then we shall rest for the night,' Ralph smiled at her. 'You are not too tired?'

She shook her head. 'No. I am anxious that we reach London as soon as possible. I am afraid that the Queen will be angry if we delay.'

It was an hour or more before the inn was finally reached. It was a respectable house of red brick and timber, its yard bustling with ostlers and travellers in search of a bed for the night, and Magdalene noticed several well-dressed gentlemen as Ralph led the way into the parlour. This was a large, open room with a huge fireplace where a spit was roasting meat; above the hearth in a niche in the wall, a little dog was treading a wheel that churned on endlessly, his efforts ensuring that the travellers' meal would be thoroughly cooked.

The host came hurrying towards them, almost bending his stout body in two as he showed them to a table set in a corner near the fire.

'If your honours had come but half an hour sooner, you could have had your supper in my private room. Alas, a party of gentlemen have already taken it for the evening.'

'We shall sup here well enough,' Sir Ralph said. 'But I trust you have rooms for this lady, my friend and myself?'

'Yes, if your honours would not mind sharing. I have a small chamber for the young lady, but I am afraid your servants must make do with the stables.'

'Hanna can sleep with me,' Magdalene said. 'She will be company in a strange room.'

The arrangements for their accommodation made, the weary travellers sat down to enjoy the delicious meal their host put before them; pigeon pie, York ham, and pork roasted to its succulent best and served with apples boiled in their skins. A quince tart, cheeses and a jug of the landlord's best ale, spiced and sizzling from a red-hot poker, completed the feast.

'If I eat any more, I shall burst,' Magdalene declared, stifling a yawn. 'Forgive me, gentlemen, I must seek my bed if we are to have an early start in the morning.'

Anton stood up. 'I shall see you to your bedchamber.'

She smiled and shook her head. 'No, stay and finish your ale. It is not necessary to come with me.'

He watched her go, frowning. Ralph looked at him, arching his brow. Anton was obviously infatuated with the girl, though he was trying hard to hide it.

'You had best go after her,' he said. 'She is so innocent that she has no idea of the danger she risks in this house, decent though it is. A dozen men have eaten here tonight, and not one of them could keep his eyes from her. She is too beautiful for her own comfort, and men were ever fools where such a one is concerned!'

Anton nodded, his face thoughtful as he threaded his way between the benches and tables. He had recognised a few of the faces here tonight, and it was for that reason he had been anxious that Magdalene should reach her bedchamber safely. As he emerged from the parlour to the hall, he saw that Ralph had been right to send him after her. A dishevelled buck was deliberately blocking her path; from the glazed look in his eyes and his slightly unsteady gait, it was clear that he had already drunk more wine than was good for him.

'Ah, Magdalene,' Anton said, 'there you are. Shall we go up now?'

'Yes. I have been waiting for you,' Magdalene said, following his lead and feeling a surge of relief at his arrival.

'She is with you, Barchester?' The drunken buck gave a foolish laugh. 'If I'd known that, I wouldn't have approached her. You shouldn't leave such a delicious morsel to wander about on her own – some hungry man is bound to gobble her up!'

'You are drunk, Lord Allingham! If you care to repeat those words in the morning, I am sure I can accommodate you. My sword is at your disposal, sir.'

There was no mistaking the glint in Anton's eyes, and the young aristocrat turned pale. 'You misunderstood me, Barchester. I meant no offence to you or your lady.'

'Then kindly stand aside and let us pass.'

His command was hurriedly obeyed, though resentful eyes followed them up the stairs and along the landing until they disappeared from the drunk's view.

'I should have let you come with me in the first place,' Magdalene said ruefully. 'I'm sorry, Anton. You won't really challenge him to a duel, will you?'

He laughed scornfully. 'That rabbit will be gone from here long before morning. I couldn't make him fight if I wanted to! If I called him a coward to his face he'd probably bow and thank me – though I have wondered...' He frowned. His suspicions were not for her ears, but if he could prove them, he would kill Allingham whether he would fight a duel or not. 'Take care if you meet that man again, Magdalene. He has a spiteful nature and may well try to take his revenge on you.'

'I don't expect we shall meet him again,' she said, unaware of the dark suspicions in his mind. 'Look, Hanna is waiting for me. Thank you for helping me, Anton.'

'Reluctantly, I shall let you go to your

maid's watchful care,' he replied with a grin. 'But remember that my offer still stands. When Nick is free, I shall try to take you from him, I warn you.'

She laughed and shook her head. By the time Nick was released – if he was! – she would be on her way to Spain. She knew better than to say it, however, for Anton was just enough in love with her to risk spiriting her away as Nick had done, and she dared not let him do it. Instinctively she felt that such a flagrant disobedience of the Queen's orders would seal Nick's fate.

'When Nick is free, many things may happen,' she said lightly.

She walked away from him, and he watched until she was safely inside her chamber before he turned aside.

Magdalene stared at the row of elegant gowns hanging in the huge Flemish armoire which ran the entire length of one wall of her bedchamber. Ralph had promised her that clothes fit for a queen were awaiting her in London, and now she saw that he had not exaggerated. She had never possessed such beautiful dresses in her life. It was not that the material was finer – she had always been used to the best – it was the sheer elegance of the styling. They had been selected by an experienced eye, and the colours were all calculated to show off her hair and colouring to its best advantage. Vibrant shades that she would never have dared to choose for herself, but which she saw were perfect for her when she held them against her in front of a small Venetian mirror.

Her apartments were smaller than those at Treggaron Manor, but they were furnished with the care and excellent taste that had been expended on her gowns. Bed-hangings of pale primrose and gold blended with the softness of silver-gilt toiletries and the deeper yellow of the window curtains. The whole effect gave her the illusion of sunshine, and she wondered if that had been the reason behind its design. If so, someone had been very thoughtful on her behalf.

Selecting a pale lilac gown ornamented with tiny bows down the length of the deep stomacher, Magdalene sat patiently while her maid dressed her hair in a soft swirl round her head, covering it with a net of silver caught with seed-pearls. It was the most demure of her dresses, worn with a pale blue ruff of delicate French lace, and the girl hoped it would not offend the Queen, as she feared some of her other dresses might. She could not appear before the English Queen half naked! Whoever had chosen her gowns seemed determined that she was to be a leader of fashion ... and a bold one, at that!

She was to be carried to the palace in a

covered litter, with Sir Ralph and Anton to walk by her side, and a stout porter to clear the way ahead. If it had not been for the inevitable end to her interview with the Queen, Magdalene might have enjoyed her first sight of London. Certainly, it was far noisier than she had expected, with the rattle of cart-wheels on cobbled streets and the raucous voices of the costers crying their wares. They seemed to be selling everything from fresh milk to a linnet in a wooden cage, and they came eagerly to her litter, pressing her to buy until her escorts ordered them away.

The streets themselves were narrow; the half-timbered houses on either side had upper storeys with overhanging windows that seemed almost to touch at times, and there were colourful signs hanging outside the merchants' shops. Every now and then a woman would throw open the shutters of a bedchamber and cry a warning to those below as she emptied slops into the already filthy gutters. The stench from the gutters was sickening, especially when they passed the rotting corpse of a cat that no one had cleared away, and Magdalene was glad of the silver pomander filled with sweet-smelling herbs which she had found amongst her things. She saw that her escorts also carried pomanders, and she knew that they were considered invaluable to help to protect their owners against the plague.

Many curious eyes were turned in Magdalene's direction when she entered the palace, and she glanced nervously at her companions for reassurance. The knowledge that she was dressed as well as any lady present helped her to keep her head high as the whispers followed her through the echoing corridors.

At last they reached the antechamber to the royal apartments, and the two men halted outside. 'You must go in alone, Magdalene,' Sir Ralph said, giving her a sympathetic smile. 'Her Majesty will send for you when she wishes to see you.'

'Can you not come with me?' She was suddenly very afraid, looking at him appealingly.

'Her Majesty has not granted me the favour of an audience, Magdalene; but if you should have the chance, tell her that I have a special gift I would like to present to her.'

She nodded, fighting her nervousness as she entered the antechamber alone and found to her surprise that she was not the only one waiting there. She was, however, the only woman; of the three men, one was young and handsome, the other two were older and rather serious-looking. Probably ministers of the Queen's council, Magdalene thought. They glanced at her once and then went on with their conversation in low voices; the young man smiled at her, but she did not respond. Her nerves were strained tautly, and she almost jumped out of her skin when a tall, thin lady came into the room and called her name.

'Doña Magdalene, you are to come with me.'

The councillors exchanged annoyed glances. They had already been waiting some time, and it was likely that they would be left to cool their heels a deal longer, until it pleased the Queen to see them.

'I am Lady Barbara Manners,' the woman said as she led Magdalene into the next chamber. 'Her Majesty is intrigued by your story and is impatient to meet you. She may ask you several questions, and do not be afraid to answer her truthfully. Her tongue is often sharper than her temper.'

Magdalene thanked her, grateful for the advice and friendly smile that went with it. Lady Barbara indicated that she was to wait in the well-furnished withdrawing-room while she went through into a third chamber, the door of which was concealed by thick curtains. It was several minutes before these were held aside to allow another woman to enter. Instinctively Magdalene sank into a deep, reverent curtsy, remaining with her head bent until Elizabeth spoke.

'You may rise, young woman.'

Magdalene obeyed, finding that the Queen's bright eyes were looking at her inquisitively but with no actual malice. She herself was struck by Elizabeth's air of vitality. She was an impressive woman with short, fiery hair worn in tight curls, and strong features; not beautiful, but, the girl thought, a woman who would always command attention whenever she entered a room. Her gown was of heavy white silk thickly encrusted with gold embroidery and sewn with pearls and precious stones. A stiff collar stood up at the back of her neck and curved in flattering wings on either side of her face; it was fashioned of some gauze-like material and kept in place by a hidden frame. A frosting of tiny diamonds made it glitter every time she moved. Around her throat were several ropes of thick pearls, one of which was so long that it reached the deep V of her stomacher.

If Magdalene was impressed by the Queen's magnificence, it seemed that Elizabeth was equally pleased by the girl's modesty. She let her eyes travel over the lilac gown, noting the way Magdalene's hair had been hidden in a net, and smiled with secret amusement as she guessed the Spanish girl's motives. At last she nodded, an odd smile playing about her mouth, as if she were about to enjoy herself.

'They tell me you are a witch, Doña

Magdalene. Is it the truth?'

'No, Your Majesty. I have no magical powers, nor have I ever wished for them.'

'Is it not true that you can sometimes see into the future?'

Magdalene bit her lip. How had the Queen learned so much about her? 'It is unfortunately true that I do – sometimes – seem to have a vision, but I am not a witch.'

'These visions – do they come to you often?' Elizabeth looked at her curiously. 'Could you read the future for me?'

'I have no power to tell fortunes,' Magdalene said. 'When the vision comes, I – I am frightened by it.'

Elizabeth nodded. 'I have heard others say the same. So you swear to me that you are not a witch. Why, then, are these accusations made against you? Tell me the truth, girl, for I shall know if you lie to me.'

'I have no reason to lie, ma'am. I was accused of murdering the man I was to marry, but I am innocent. They said I brought about his death by witchcraft, but I do not know how to work spells, nor would I have killed him if I had. Don Sebastian was a good man, and I – I liked him.'

'You liked him. You were happy to marry him?'

'My marriage had been arranged for me, and I was prepared to accept my duty then, Your Majesty.'

'Your duty – hmm…' Elizabeth pursed her mouth. 'Unfortunately, others neglect their duty to me, but we shall speak of that later. Now, tell me more of your arrest. It has been said that you were also accused of being a heretic. Are you not a Catholic?'

'I was born and raised as such, ma'am, but – but there were doubts in my mind. Foolishly, I spoke to a priest more plainly than I should. It was he who brought the charges against me.'

'Yes, I have heard of this.' Elizabeth's eyes were piercing. 'And what is the truth, girl? What faith would you follow if you were free to choose?'

Magdalene hesitated momentarily, then she met the Queen's gaze boldly. 'If I were free to choose, I would ask that I might be instructed in the English faith, ma'am. I know so little of it, but I believe that it would bring me much happiness.'

'A wise choice,' Elizabeth said. 'Since you are now in my country and your mother was an English woman, I am minded to see that your wish is granted. I shall send my own chaplain to you.'

'You are gracious, ma'am. I thank you for your kindness.' Magdalene swallowed hard. 'I shall have need of my faith when I am sent back to my uncle. Yet I shall go willingly, if – if Your Majesty could grant clemency to Nicholas Treggaron.' She lifted her eyes to the Queen's. 'If he disobeyed you, ma'am, it was to save me from a cruel death. His loyalty to you was never in question.'

'Ha!' Elizabeth gave a harsh laugh. 'So you would plead the rogue's cause, now – are there not enough wagging tongues to speak for him? Am I to be plagued by the wretch's friends?'

'Sir Ralph Goodchild craves an audience, ma'am. He– He has a special gift from Nicholas Treggaron.'

'Would you attempt bribery?' The Queen's eyes flashed with anger. 'Be quiet, you foolish girl, before I lose all patience with you and your troublesome lover! When I am ready, I shall decide Mr Treggaron's fate, you may be quite certain of that!'

'I meant not to offend you, ma'am.' Magdalene clenched her hands into tight fists.

'You have been guided by fools! If I wished to punish Treggaron, he would be beyond your help ere this, girl. Your impudence deserves some punishment, but I shall be merciful...' Elizabeth regarded her thoughtfully. 'You shall receive instructions from my personal chaplain, and I shall hear his reports of you. Then I shall decide what to do with you, Doña Magdalene. Go now, and tell Treggaron's friend that I may see him. He must present himself every day until I am minded to grant him an interview.' A glint of amusement showed in the Queen's face. 'We shall test Sir Ralph's patience a little, I think.'

Remembering the long-suffering councillors waiting in the antechamber, Magdalene's eyes lit with sudden laughter. The Queen had an odd sense of humour, but she rather liked her. Lady Barbara might be right, she thought. Elizabeth was not really as angry as she pretended to be. It was as if she enjoyed teasing her victims, testing their loyalty to her while she threatened and bullied.

'Your Majesty is generous,' Magdalene said. 'I thank you for listening to me.'

'I have promised nothing,' Elizabeth said, her brows arching. 'But I am sworn to protect all those who follow my faith, and I have no love of those fanatical priests who would burn me if they could. Ay, I know it. I know how they hate me. They would set another in my place, if they could, but they'll not succeed while I hold the hearts of my people.'

She waved her hand, dismissing the girl. Magdalene curtsied, backing from the room, her head whirling. She did not understand what was happening. Apparently she was free to leave. Why had the Queen not arrested her? From Her Majesty's last statement, it would seem that she was not to be handed over to the Inquisition, but could that really be true? Or was Elizabeth merely playing with her, giving her the illusion of freedom while she worked out her secret masquerade? No, somehow Magdalene did not believe she was so cruel... Then that must mean that she at least was to be spared, but what of Nick? What fate awaited him?

Nick opened his eyes, staring at the stone walls of his cell as he began painstakingly to count the cracks once more. He must do something, or he would lose his mind! How long have I been here now? he wondered, impatience churning inside him. I could only have been a few days, but already the tedium was driving him mad. He had been treated more as a guest than a prisoner – he had blankets in plenty, a fire, food and wine – but the inactivity was a nightmare. At first he had paced the floor of his cell like a caged animal, but now he had taken to lying on the bed, staring blankly at the wall while his thoughts tormented him. He had been so certain that the Queen would see him, would listen to his arguments, and now he was justly served for his impudence. He had angered Elizabeth once too often, and this was her reply.

The sound of a key grating in the lock made him turn his head. Was it supper-time already? Instinct made him get to his feet as a heavily cloaked figure entered the cell. He stared in disbelief for a moment, then dropped to one knee, his head bent.

'Your Majesty...'

For once in his life Nick found himself lost for words. Even when he rose to his feet and met the mocking gaze of his sovereign, he could not force himself to speak. That she could come to this place... Was it to taunt him? He looked into her face, wondering.

'What am I to do with you, sir?' she asked at last, and he glimpsed the glint of humour in her eyes.

A wry smile curved his mouth. It was her wit and her courage that had first drawn his loyalty to her. 'You should hang me, ma'am. I doubt not I deserve it.'

'Indeed you do,' she answered sharply. 'You disobeyed my orders to bring Doña Magdalene to London, and I have received many tiresome letters from her uncle, also the demands of various Catholic churchmen from several countries. They tell me she is a witch, and they say I must return her to Spain for the just punishment of her crimes.'

Nick looked at her uncertainly. Why was Elizabeth telling him all this? She had challenged him to snatch the girl, and he was powerless to alter her decision. Did she want him to beg? He would not crawl, even for Magdalene's sake, though the thought of her condemned to a cruel death had haunted him constantly these past days, making him fret at his impotence. Yet, as a

262

prisoner, there was nothing he could do to help her.

'I can only ask you to believe that she is innocent of any crime, ma'am.'

'Ha!' Elizabeth bridled. 'Have you no more to say, sir? She pleaded for your life. Indeed, she offered to return to Spain if I would grant you clemency – your life for hers.'

'No! No, I would sooner hang.' Nick's eyes glowed with blue fire. 'She is innocent of any crime, I assure you!'

'As it happens, I am inclined to agree with you, so for the moment, the girl is safe enough, Treggaron. You need have no fear for her, but what have you to say for yourself?'

He frowned, staring at her in some confusion. 'Forgive me, ma'am, I do not understand you. I have angered you, I know, but...'

'You have been ill,' Elizabeth interrupted impatiently. 'How dare you risk your life in a foolish duel, sir? You should have hung the Spaniard and had done with it! How many times must I tell you I have need of your services? England has need of you!'

'You– You are angry because of the duel with Don Rodrigo?' Nick was amazed: he had never even considered that as a likely explanation for his imprisonment.

'God's teeth, man! Am I always to be

served by fools? Understand that I have heard of a threat against your life, and you are here for your own protection, you will remain here until I am satisfied that your health is sufficiently recovered...'

'The Tower is scarcely an ideal place to recover one's health, ma'am,' Nick remarked wryly.

Elizabeth laughed, her face alight with mockery. 'It seems I was misinformed. I was told you were a broken man, almost on your deathbed.'

'At the moment, I am near bored to death!'

'Hmm... Well, I shall send my physician to you, and then we shall see.' The smile left her lips. 'Take care, Treggaron! I have received reliable information that there are those who would be very happy to see you in your grave.'

'I dare say I have my share of enemies, ma'am. I have sent too many Spaniards to the bottom of the ocean.'

'I am not sure that your enemies are all from that direction, sir. I believe you should look much closer to home.'

A thoughtful frown creased his brow. 'Has this anything to do with Lord Chevron?'

'If I knew who was behind the plot, your enemy would be here instead of you, sir. Believe me, had I not acted when I did, you might even now be dead.'

'I am grateful for your concern, ma'am...' Nick's face was stiff with pride. 'But I am well able to protect myself.'

'Indeed? This is fine gratitude, sir!' Humour glinted in her brilliant eyes. 'I offer you my hospitality, and you will have none of it! Well, maybe you have learned your lesson now, Captain Treggaron. In future, remember I value your life too highly to have it risked for a chivalrous notion.'

He made her an elegant leg. 'Forgive me for my churlishness, ma'am, but I could wish you held me in a little less esteem...' His eyes sparkled with wicked mockery as they travelled round the cell and returned to challenge her. 'Delightful as my stay here has been, I should be happy to leave now ... with your permission?'

'When my physician tells me you are strong enough to defend yourself, sir.' She laughed harshly. 'Come, Treggaron, you have a fire, food and wine; what more could you want?'

She was teasing him, and yet there was iron beneath the velvet softness of her words. His sojourn in the Tower might have been in part for his own protection, but he knew that it was also a warning. Elizabeth was telling him that she would not stand for more disobedience. Chevron had been punished for his crimes, and the affair was over. Nick accepted it at last, knowing that the fierce desire for vengeance was no longer in him. Cathy was dead, and he must look to the future. Don Rodrigo's death and his own illness had left him feeling bitter and drained, but it was time to put the nightmare behind him; from now on, the only revenge he would seek would be that he intended to exact from Magdalene. As he imagined the form that revenge would take, an icy flame lit his eyes.

He met the Queen's gaze with a grin. 'What more could I want? Why, nothing, ma'am ... I am entirely at your disposal.'

'God's teeth, you rogue!' Elizabeth cackled her delight at his obvious return to health. 'Methinks I should hang you after all!'

Magdalene threw down her embroidery in disgust, boredom making her feel as if she could scream. She had already been in London for a whole week, and still there was no word of Nick's well-being. The Queen had kept her word in the matter of her personal chaplain, and the girl had begun a course of instruction. A little to her surprise, she had found the man to be well-spoken and intelligent, with a sense of humour, and he listened to her opinions; although they differed in some respects, she found there was a great deal of common ground between them and she had begun to look forward to their discussions. Already she knew that she would not find it difficult to accept the English doctrine ... were she to be allowed to remain in the country. As yet, there was no confirmation of that from the Queen.

Apart from the hour she spent with the chaplain each morning, Magdalene had only Anton's occasional visits to relieve the tedium of her days. Ralph was spending all his time at Whitehall in the hope that he would be permitted an audience with the Queen, but for the moment he had been left to cool his heels in the antechamber with several other impatient courtiers. Elizabeth was said to be in a difficult mood. Ever since she had signed the death-warrant for Mary Queen of Scots, she had been prone to periods of regret and guilt. She had never wanted to put that unfortunate woman to death, and had protected her for nineteen years against the vengeance of her own ministers, but the foolish Mary's plotting with Philip of Spain had forced Elizabeth's hand. Mary had willed her right to the English throne to Philip, and for many years he had been slowly gathering his forces for an invasion. The whole of the Catholic world would unite in their delight if he could manage to snatch the throne of the heretic queen who had held it so securely in the palm of her hand.

Elizabeth had been strengthening her defences for some time. She, who hated the thought of war with Spain, knew that it was inevitable. She had used every device she could to contrive to stave it off for as long as possible, allowing her loyal sea-captains to harass and plunder the Spanish ships, while pretending anger against them to the Spanish King and declaring herself his true friend. Until Walsingham's spies had discovered Mendoza's plotting with Mary Queen of Scots, she had allowed Philip's ambassador to attend her Court, but he had been dismissed, never to be replaced. For years she had cleverly dangled the prospect of marriage and a share of her throne in front of the noses of a host of suitors, but no one now believed that she would marry. Indeed, her most trusted advisors now counselled her against it. Mary's son James was her heir, and he had been brought up as a Protestant. Until such time as the throne fell vacant, England was more than satisfied to have their Gloriana unwed.

So Elizabeth had put off the evil hour, but now the year of 1588 was upon her. It had been forecast as a year of terrible disasters, and the English Queen's spies had told her that the Spanish armada was in the final stages of its long preparation, in spite of the efforts of Sir Francis and others of his kind. It was little wonder, then, that the Queen's temper was uncertain in these difficult times.

Magdalene was vaguely aware of all these things. Anton had explained so much to her, telling her of his conviction that Elizabeth would not hang Nick, despite her apparent anger with him.

'Her Majesty knows she needs the loyalty of all her sea-captains, Magdalene. Depend upon it, she is merely giving him a sharp lesson. If she really wanted to punish him, do you think she would send her own chaplain to you?'

Anton's reassurances were all she had, and she had come to rely on his daily visits, for without them she would have had only the company of her maid. Apart from her audience with the Queen, she had not ventured outside the house for a whole week. She was afraid that if she did, she might be out when Nick returned.

Hearing the scrape of heavy footsteps on the stairs, the girl got to her feet expectantly, but as she heard Anton's voice at her door, the hope died in her. Yet she was smiling as she bade him enter.

'I came as swiftly as I could.' Anton's manner had a new vitality about it. 'There's news at last, Magdalene!'

'News? About Nick?' Her eyes lit up and she moved excitedly towards him. 'Tell me... Tell me at once.'

He took both her hands in his, laughing with genuine pleasure. 'Ralph has seen Her Majesty. He was allowed to present Nick's gift, and was told that he is soon to be released.'

'Oh, Anton, that's wonderful news!'

Magdalene looked up at him, her face glowing with happiness. In that moment she looked so beautiful that Anton lost his head. With a slight groan, he took her into his arms, kissing her and releasing her only when she struggled against him. As he saw her distress, he was at once contrite.

'Forgive me, I should not have done that.'

'No, you should not,' Magdalene agreed with a rueful smile. 'But I forgive you, Anton. You are my friend, and I know you were excited because Nick is being set free.'

'I am happy for him,' Anton agreed, 'but can you not see what this means, Magdalene? While Nick was in the Tower I could not betray his trust, but now I, too, am free – free to press my cause with you. If you wish it, I shall tell Nick that you have chosen to place yourself in my protection, and you need never see him again.' He looked at her expectantly. 'Well, will you leave him for me?'

Magdalene was hardly listening. Even as he had begun to speak, her attention was drawn beyond him, to the tall, silent figure who stood in the open doorway. The colour drained from her face, and she could neither speak nor move as her limbs turned to water and her head spun dizzily.

'Answer him, Magdalene!' Nick's icy tones made her flinch. 'I am as interested as Anton to hear your reply. Which of us is to be the fortunate man?'

Anton swung round with a muffled oath, his face shocked and disbelieving. 'Nick! We heard you were to be released soon... How are you?' He saw the other man's expression, and frowned. 'For God's sake, man, don't look like that! Neither of us intended to deceive you.'

'I have no doubt that you intended to act honourably,' Nick drawled, his mouth twisting in an ugly sneer. 'When would I have received a visit from you? After you had set Magdalene up in some secret hiding-place? Or were you planning to fight me for her?'

'Don't be a fool,' Anton growled. 'I'm no coward, and you know it! I have no wish to fight you, but I'll not run from a duel, if you force one on me.'

'You'll not take her from me while I live!'

'Damn you!' Anton yelled, angry now. 'You behaved as if you hated her, refusing to see her and treating her worse than you would a common whore!'

'Perhaps because she is a uncommon whore...'

The insult was deliberate. Magdalene's

271

face was deathly pale, and she felt sick. This had to stop. She would not allow them to quarrel over her like two dogs over a bone.

'Anton, please go now,' she whispered, managing to speak at last. 'I – I am grateful for your kindness to me, but my answer has not changed.' Seeing the hesitation in his face, she looked at him pleadingly. 'Please leave now. I want to be alone with Nick.'

'If you wish it.' Anton frowned, shooting a strange glance at Nick. 'She has not betrayed you, Treggaron. You have my word on it. If you harm her, you'll answer to me!'

'I am at your disposal, sir.' Nick laughed harshly. 'I was warned of an enemy, but I had not thought to find treachery so close at hand. I trusted you above all others.'

Anton winced as he heard the bitterness in his friend's voice, knowing that no explanations would heal the breach between them now. 'I'm not your enemy, but I love her. And I'll take her from you yet.'

Nick merely inclined his head, the contempt he revealed making it clear he had no fear of Anton's threats. 'You may try!' he said.

Rage flared in Barchester's eyes, but a look of desperate appeal from Magdalene stayed his hand even as it moved towards his sword. 'Don't forget that I shall be near by if you need me,' he said, then with another angry glance at Nicholas, he went out.

They heard the clatter of his boots down the wooden stairs, and the silence stretched between them as they stared into each other's faces.

Magdalene swallowed hard, her throat dry with fear. 'It was not what it seemed, Nick. You must believe me.'

'Must I?' Nick's gaze seared her with its icy contempt. 'I suppose, like Anton, you will swear that you have not betrayed me?' His brows rose in a polite enquiry that mocked her.

'Since you would not believe me, it is useless to try,' she replied bitterly. 'I know you hate me, but you should not blame Anton. He is still your friend, whether you know it or not. He would not have spoken if I had not asked him for help.' She raised her eyes to his, the tears burning but unshed. 'Will you not let me go, Nick? Not to Anton, but away from you; a quiet retreat where you need never see me again.'

'Do you want to leave me so much, Magdalene?' There was a sudden bleakness in his face, making her stare at him in confusion. 'I must have treated you more harshly than I had thought.'

'I do not understand you,' she faltered. 'I realise you hate me now, and that you can never forgive me for the terrible things I said to you that night. Ralph... He told me why you fought Rodrigo. I would never have flown at you in a temper had I been told you were wounded. You must know I never meant all those cruel words I flung at you! You *must* know it, Nick?'

He saw the mist of tears in her eyes and hesitated, torn between his desire to punish her for all the agony she had made him suffer, and the other, confusing, emotions he felt were a weakness in him. She looked so innocent as she pleaded for understanding, but his doubts made him wary of speaking too plainly. He had seen the intimate smile she gave Anton, and a nagging jealousy churned in him. Was she what she seemed outwardly, or a scheming wanton? Had he been deceived in her from the start?

Memory stirred in him, and he recalled the night he had found her struggling in Don Rodrigo's embrace. Had he saved her from an unwanted assault on her virtue, or interrupted a lovers' quarrel? He was no longer sure of anything. How bitterly she had denounced him when she learned of the Spaniard's death – so bitterly that he had been convinced of her passion for the Don. Now his closest friend was so infatuated with her that they had become enemies, yet she could still look at him with those accusing eyes and ask for understanding! If she were in truth a cheat and a liar, he was a fool and would be well rid of her, but if she was the woman he had once believed...

A surge of panic went through him as he looked down at her, and he knew that he could not let her go, no matter what she was. Nor could he reach out to her as he once had. His soul was in torment once again, and he reacted in the only way that was left to him.

'I believe that you would not have struck me if you had known I was wounded,' he said coldly. 'Even I must grant you some compassion. Yet I think you meant the words as you spoke them. Too much has passed between us for things to be as easy as they were.'

'Then let me go, Nick.'

'No!' Anger surged in him suddenly, his eyes blazing with an unreasoned anger as he seized her wrist. 'Why should I let you go? I saved your life, and you belong to me. You are mine my property, and I intend to keep you! At least, until you no longer please me.'

A gasp was torn from her as she saw his expression. 'You can't mean... You don't want...'

'Oh yes, I do want you, Magdalene. That hasn't changed, though sometimes I wish that I could be free of you!' he muttered, his fevered tones striking terror into her heart. 'Once I thought I loved you, but that was before I knew you for what you are. Now, I despise you... Still, you are desirable, and you please me in bed.' He laughed harshly. 'I shall keep you for a while.' He flicked the stiff yellow lace that formed a ruff around her neck. 'After all, I have paid for the privilege and you owe me something, I think?'

She recoiled from him, her eyes dilating with pain. 'So it was you who bought these things for me?'

'Of course.' He frowned. 'Who else would it be?'

She shook her head, knowing that she had deceived herself. Ralph had always denied any involvement other than delivery.

'I – I did not know,' she whispered miserably. 'Ralph brought them to me...'

'Did you imagine that he, too, had fallen for your charms?' His voice was sharp with scorn.

'No...' She choked on the bile that rose in her throat. 'I thought he was sorry for me.'

'You thought Ralph pitied you?' Nick's eyes were intent on her face. 'Why, because you had only cast-off clothing to wear? It was never my intention that it should be so. Had we not been forced to leave England so hastily, it would have been rectified long ago.'

'I would rather wear old clothes than be bought and paid for like a whore,' Magdalene flashed, becoming angry now. 'Do you imagine that buying me expensive gowns will make me accept your embraces with anything but loathing?'

He moved a little closer to her, his breathing laboured. 'You were as eager for my bed as any woman of the night, and I shall make you so again, my beautiful wanton Magdalene. Even if you fight me to the end, I shall have you!'

She looked into the cold eyes and shivered; he was a cruel stranger, not the man she had loved. That man could never have made these threats. As the fear showed in her face, he moved towards her with sudden urgency, taking her by the shoulders to pull her hard against him. Her heart was hammering in her breast as he bent his head towards her, and she steeled herself to resist the onslaught of his kisses, knowing that already her treacherous body was responding to the call of his desire. Her lips were softening in helpless longing; the wanting rose up in her despite her determination to give him nothing, and she almost swayed to meet his demanding body. Then she took hold of her emotions, blocking out the yearning he aroused in her by his nearness. If he wanted her body, he must take it without her consent. She would not yield to him now!

Making a supreme effort, she wrenched away from him, pride stamping her fine features. 'Force me to your bed if you will.' She spat the words at him. 'You have made me your prisoner, but you cannot make me your slave! I do not love you, and I shall not surrender to you willingly again.'

She saw anger and pain in his eyes. For a moment she thought that he would indeed take his revenge on her – and instantly! Then the hot glow faded and his mouth curved in bitter lines. She thought briefly that there was disappointment in his face, as though he had expected a different reaction from her, then his expression became icy.

'So ... you do not love me.' His voice cracked with harsh emotion. 'Now we have the truth at last. Yet you will stay with me, Magdalene, because I shall keep you, and because I shall kill any man who tries to take you from me! If you value Anton's life, remember that!'

She recoiled in horror from his fury, half thinking that he would strike her. For a second he stared into her face with such a terrible expression that she felt almost faint. Then he turned abruptly on his heel, leaving her pale and trembling. For several minutes she was motionless, unable to move as the pain intensified inside her. Then she sank to her knees, covering her face with her hands as the tears slipped silently down her cheeks and the agony of her heart raged mercilessly.

Why had she denied her love for him, when she had wanted so much to be with him again? What madness was in both of them that they must seek to hurt each other? She had lashed out at him in self-defence, needing to protect herself against the cruel barb of his taunts, but she had lied. He thought she was a wanton, to be bought with elegant gowns and fancy trifles; but she loved him. She should hate him for his callous treatment of her, but he had put his mark on her too deeply for her to break free. She belonged to him, and she knew she would stay with him no matter what he did not because he made threats against Anton's life, but because she loved him. But he would never know it!

Pride came to her rescue at last. She lifted her head, the tear-stains dry on her cheek. Let him do his worst! No matter what he did, no matter how many times he tried to break her spirit, she would never confess her love...

'This has just arrived for you, miss!' Hanna held out a roll of parchment, fastened with wax and stamped with a royal seal. 'The messenger said it came from Her Majesty.' She looked at the girl in awe.

Magdalene took the parchment with shaking fingers. It was three days since Nick's release, and during that time she had scarcely seen him. They had met twice on the stairs, when she had gone down to take a turn about the garden at the back of the

279

house, but he had given her no more than a brusque nod in passing. It seemed almost as though he wanted to avoid her, as if he could not bear to look at her. She was bewildered and confused, keeping to her own rooms as much as she could, to avoid another quarrel.

A frown creased her brow as she looked at the parchment in her hand, and she was reluctant to open it. Without Anton to turn to for comfort, she felt very insecure. Was this message from the Queen the summons she had been dreading? Was she at last to be delivered to her uncle?

Her fingers trembled as she broke the seal, and her eyes scanned the brief letter hurriedly. At first she could scarcely credit what the large, bold script stated, and then she gave a little gasp of surprise. Elizabeth had written personally, saying that she was well pleased with the reports from her chaplain, and that she had decided to accept Magdalene as one of her ladies-in-waiting. The girl was to present herself at Court without delay. Tonight the Queen's Men were presenting a new performance of Master John Lyly's play *Campaspe,* a story of the rivalry for a captive girl's love between Alexander the Great and the painter Appelles, that was a great favourite with the Court. And Magdalene was commanded to attend!

'Her Majesty has summoned me to Court,' she said, looking at Hanna in dismay. 'What shall I do?' How could she attend the Court when Nick was determined to keep her close.

'Why, you must obey, of course.' Hanna shook her head. 'You are never thinking of refusing…' Her comment went unanswered as the door was flung open and Nick appeared on the threshold, a scowl on his face.

'You may go, girl,' he grunted.

Hanna bobbed a curtsy and departed hastily. Like every other servant in the house, she was aware of the black mood that had gripped her master since his return from the Tower. By the expression on his face just now, there was no sign of its abating!

'You have Her Majesty's letter, I see.' Nick glared at Magdalene, as she remained silent. 'I, too, have received a message from Elizabeth. It seems I am to escort you to Whitehall this evening.'

'I – I can find another escort,' the girl faltered as she saw his nostrils flare with temper, 'if you do not wish to trouble yourself…'

'I have no doubt that Anton would come running if you snapped your fingers,' he drawled. 'However, it is Her Majesty's wish that I accompany you.'

'Thank you.' Magdalene's voice was polite

but cold. 'The Queen has graciously appointed me to be one of her ladies. Does that mean I shall have to live at the palace?'

His mouth curled in a mocking sneer. 'If you imagine this is your chance to escape from me, Magdalene, you are sadly mistaken! I may be forced to let you go for a little while, but once I explain the situation to Her Majesty, she will understand.'

'What situation?' She stared at him, puzzled. He would scarcely tell the Queen of England that he meant to keep her as his prisoner!

'You will be informed of my plans when I have spoken to Her Majesty,' he said, his eyes hard. 'For the moment, you need only concern yourself with your gown for this evening. You should wear the burgundy velvet...'

'Why?' she interrupted, annoyed at his peremptory manner. 'Will you tell me what I must wear, now?'

'This evening is your first appearance at a Court function,' he said with forced patience. 'Please allow me to guide you in this, Magdalene. I have my reasons.'

'I think you enjoy issuing orders to me!' she retorted. 'I shall wear a gown of my own choice.'

'As you please,' he shrugged carelessly. 'I had intended to ask if you would care to be rowed down the river to Southwark to visit the Bear Gardens, and perhaps take luncheon at an inn – but since my company is obviously distasteful to you, I shall leave you to your own pleasures.' He bowed stiffly. 'Until this evening.'

Magdalene tapped her foot with frustration as he left her. Why could he not simply have asked her if she would like to eat with him? She was bored by her enforced idleness and would have loved to spend the day as he had suggested. She was tempted to run and accept his invitation, but pride held her back. He would take it as a sign of weakness, and he would use anything he could to break her will! She must be constantly on her guard against any pretence of kindness in him, because he had clearly shown that he expected to be paid for what he gave.

Tonight, at least, she would be in carefree company. And, after that, her future would be in the Queen's hands...

CHAPTER EIGHT

Magdalene studied her reflection thought-fully. She had chosen a gown of thick gold silk, the overskirts heavily encrusted with embroidery and tiny seed-pearls. The neckline was square, and skimmed her breasts so that they were hidden from view only by an edging of exquisite lace. Her ruff was of the finest gauze and shaped like wings over a support of thin wire; little tear-shaped pearls dangled from it, matching those on the full, padded sleeves of her dress. She looked elegant, and the clothes were entirely suitable for the occasion, but something was missing. Wrinkling her brow, she tried to decide what it was, finally realising that she needed something round her throat – a string of pearls, perhaps? Since she possessed none, there was nothing to be done, and it was merely a whim of vanity. Her appearance would not be a disgrace to anyone.

Ready at last, she left her bedchamber and walked slowly downstairs, her emotions mixed on this her first evening at the English Court. As she descended to the hall, she heard the sound of male voices, and recognising both, she was not surprised to find Sir Ralph with Nick. He gave her a friendly smile as he entered, and her response was warm.

'Sir Ralph,' she exclaimed. 'How pleasant it is to see you again!'

He looked a little surprised at her welcome, but took her hand and kissed it. 'You look charming, Magdalene. That gown becomes you well. An excellent choice for this evening, if I may say so.'

'Thank you.' Magdalene could not resist a glance at Nick, expecting to see anger in his eyes. Instead, there was wry amusement.

'Unfortunately I neglected to ask what colour you would be wearing this evening,' he said, a hint of mockery in his voice. 'I have a gift for you; a trifle I thought might please you, but I fear it will not go with your gown.'

Magdalene stared at him suspiciously. He reached inside his black velvet doublet, taking out a small object wrapped in silk, and came forward to hand it to her. She hesitated and then accepted it reluctantly, knowing that she could not make a fuss in front of his friend – and that that was the reason he had waited until now to give it to her! Managing to keep her hands steady, she unwrapped the parcel and gasped as she saw what Nick had given her. It was a large oval cabochon ruby, set with pearls and suspended on a heavy gold chain. Compared to the jewellery worn by many ladies at Court, it was a simple piece, but the sheer magnificence of the stone took her breath away. She had never seen another to rival it. Suddenly she knew why Nick had suggested she should choose the burgundy gown, and a stab of regret pierced her. She could still wear the pendant, but the effect would not be quite as dramatic.

'It– It is beautiful,' she faltered, meeting his eyes uncertainly. If he had given it to her when they were alone, she might have refused it and accused him of trying to buy her favours, but what was the use? He had already given her so much that she would achieve nothing by being churlish. 'I shall wear it, even though it does not quite match my gown,' she said, suddenly decisive.

'Let me put it on for you,' Nick offered, a faint smile on his lips. 'You may find the catch awkward at first.'

She gave it to him, turning so that he could place it about her neck and fasten the clasp. He found it difficult to do so without crumpling her standing ruff, and his fingers brushed against her flesh, sending a tiny trail of fire coursing through her veins. He felt the little shiver that occurred as he touched her, and frowned. Seeing the expression in his eyes, Magdalene knew that he would have questioned her, but Ralph's presence saved her from any interrogation.

'How does it look?' She turned away from Nick's burning gaze, soliciting an opinion from his friend.

'Perfect,' Ralph replied gallantly. 'But I think we should be leaving. It would not do to be late.'

His reminder relieved any tension there might have been between them, and with one accord they moved towards the door, which was opened by a servant. As before, Magdalene was carried in a litter, while the porter went on ahead and the two gentlemen walked at her side. In addition, this evening, two burly servants accompanied them a few paces behind, both armed with thick cudgels in case they should be set upon by the beggars who haunted the dark streets. Although these vagrants were beaten, branded and driven from the city, they often returned, even though to do so would incur a severe punishment. Only those unfortunates who could prove their inability to work by reason of deformity would be given food and shelter by the city fathers; the others were considered criminals and were treated as such. Fortunately, their numbers were not as great as they had been at the beginning of the Tudor dynasty, for England was prospering beneath Gloriana's rule.

Magdalene's entrance caused a little stir among the assembled courtiers. It was clear that everyone knew just who she was, and they stared at her with varying degrees of curiosity; some smiling politely, others inclined to be hostile to this stranger in their midst. Especially, she noticed, some of the other women.

She kept a cool smile on her lips, ignoring the whispers and glances that bordered on rudeness, looking about her with interest. For perhaps five minutes the three new-comers stood alone, then one or two gentlemen drifted over, claiming acquaintance with either Nick or Sir Ralph. They stayed to talk and laugh, their eyes moving over the girl's lovely face with obvious admiration, and in time they were followed by others. There was quite a crowd round Magdalene when Lady Barbara Manners came to fetch her.

'Her Majesty wishes you to attend her,' she said, and the girl felt her moment of triumph as she saw the surprise and jealousy in the eyes of certain women who had been ignoring her.

Lady Barbara was as friendly as she had been at their first meeting, introducing Magdalene to several more of the Queen's ladies who were waiting in the royal chambers to escort their mistress, and the girl was soon put at her ease. She learned that her duties would be merely to gather with the other ladies each day at a given time, and to accompany the Queen on her walks in the gardens or to one of the many entertainments Elizabeth enjoyed. It might be that they would hunt, or visit the tiltyard at Greenwich, or perhaps the bull and bear houses across the river at Southwark – or merely dance a galliard or two in the mornings. Since she was not a lady of the bedchamber, she would not be expected to help the Queen to dress and she need not live in the palace; all that was really required of her was that she should smile pleasantly and help to amuse her mistress.

When the Queen emerged from her bedchamber accompanied by those most privileged of her women, she nodded approvingly at Magdalene, bidding her welcome. Elizabeth was in a mood to be merry, and her ladies did their best to oblige her as the whole party walked to the great chamber, where the entertainment was to take place. The main play was preceded by a rollicking farce, which made the Queen laugh so much that it brought tears of mirth to her eyes. Seeing their sovereign was in high good humour, the courtiers relaxed, and after the players had given their performance, Elizabeth conferred her blessing on those of her ladies who wished to dance.

Magdalene was at once approached by two gentlemen she had met briefly earlier in the evening, both of whom vied with each other for the honour of leading her out on to the floor for the first dance. Eventually, one was persuaded to give preference to the other, on the strict condition that the next dance was his. Finding herself suddenly in great demand, Magdalene's cheeks flushed with pleasure. It was a long time since she had been in company, and she was enjoying herself. Turning to greet a new partner with an expectant smile, her heart jerked as she saw who had approached her.

He bowed elegantly before her. 'Will you not give me the honour of a dance, Magdalene?'

Nick's look made her breathless all at once. He was smiling at her in his old way, his eyes seeming to caress her, and she could feel her body tingling with anticipation. Wordlessly she gave him her hand, letting him lead her out to join the other merrymakers. The musicians were playing at a slow, stately pace that required lightness and skill from the participants, and Magdalene was surprised by the grace of her partner. A wry smile tugged at the corners of her mouth. It seemed that he danced as well as he did everything else! She tried to harden her heart against him, but the music, gaiety and sheer pleasure of the evening combined to defeat her. How could she be cold to him when the slightest touch of his hand was enough to send her senses on a dizzy whirl?

'Shall we walk in the gardens for a while?' Nick's whisper sent a shiver through her. She knew she ought to refuse him, but the excitement had gone to her head like wine, and she wanted to be alone with him.

'It– It is a little warm,' she said, needing an excuse to spare her blushes. She could not let him guess that she was longing to be kissed. And yet, when he smiled at her, she could almost believe that they were as close as they had once been, and that all the bitter words between them meant nothing.

Nick took Magdalene's hand, urging her towards a door as she hesitated. The entrance obviously led through to an open gallery and then to the gardens, and she glanced nervously at the Queen, wondering if her departure would be frowned on. To her surprise, she saw that Elizabeth was smiling at her approvingly. Apparently she understood and consented, but why? What had Nick been saying to her?

Outside the night air was cool, and Magdalene shivered. She heard an owl hoot from a nearby tree, jumping at the eerie cry. Nick glanced at her and smiled, keeping a firm hold on her hand as he drew her towards a secluded shrubbery. She tried to pull back now, the cooler air clearing her mind and making her aware of the solitude in the gardens. Had she been wise to let him bring her here? Now the doubts began to crowd in on her, and she remembered her determination to hold herself aloof from him. Was she so weak-willed where he was concerned that a smile could destroy her?

Gazing up at him, she tried to read the odd expression in his face. 'Why have you brought me here?' she asked.

Nick's wicked grin made her heart leap. 'To do this,' he said, and reached out for her, pulling her into his arms and holding her close so that she could feel the thudding of his heartbeat. Before she could protest, his mouth was covering hers, kissing her tenderly but with a possessiveness that brooked no argument.

Magdalene's head told her that she should resist, but her heart defied all common-sense. Such a surge of longing swept over her that she found her body moulding itself to his without her conscious volition. Her arms wound themselves round his neck, and her mouth softened beneath his, parting to invite the teasing entry of the tip of his tongue. She felt desire rising in her, making her tremble as his lips touched her throat and moved downwards to skim the soft mounds of her breasts.

'Nick, I...' she murmured, but his lips silenced her, and she could not speak when at last he released her.

'I could not resist a few moments alone

with you,' he said, touching her cheek with the tip of his finger. 'You are even more beautiful than when I first saw you, *querida*.'

'Am I?' Magdalene gazed up at him, shy and uncertain. Was this tenderness just another mood? Did he really care for her, as his words seemed to imply, or was this all a part of his plot to coax her into his bed?

His laughter was soft and full of mockery. 'Come, Magdalene, you do not need to ask. You must have seen the answer in a score of faces this evening. There was not one man present who could take his eyes from you.'

She smiled and tipped her head to meet the challenge of his look. 'Were you jealous of them, sir?'

'Yes.' His eyes gleamed. 'I am jealous of any man who looks at you or touches you, but soon it is they who will be envious of me.' There was a note of triumph in his voice and it made her stare at him in suspicion.

'What do you mean?'

'In a little while Her Majesty will announce our marriage.'

'Our marriage?' she gasped. 'What are you saying?'

'Her Majesty has given her gracious permission for us to marry. Indeed, she is insistent that it shall take place soon, and at Court, so that everyone can see that it has her approval...' He broke off as he saw a flash of anger in her eyes. 'Now what ails you, wench? I thought it would please you to be wed here instead of in a village church.'

Anger was beating at her temples, making her head spin. So that was what this was all about! The Queen had demanded that she should come to Court, preventing him from keeping her a prisoner – but once she was his wife, he could do whatever he pleased with her. It would be a simple thing to leave her at Treggaron Manor and pretend that she was not well enough to attend the Court. It was a clever plot; and he was making it sound as if the marriage was by royal command, thereby catching her neatly in his web. By gaining Elizabeth's permission, he had cut off her only retreat! Why else would he present her with a *fait accompli?* But she would not be trapped so easily! She would not go meekly to a bitter bride-bed, there to pay the price he demanded as his revenge.

'No,' she said. 'No, I shall not marry you. You cannot force me to obey you. I know you hate me, and you will marry me because it is the only way you can keep possession of me.'

'You little fool!' His eyes were cold again as he felt the frustration grind inside him. 'God forgive me, must I beat some sense into you?'

He stared at her furiously, his hands itching at his sides. No other woman had ever roused such a terrible rage in him. Sometimes she drove him so hard that he could scarcely keep his hands from her slender throat. At this moment he wanted to shake her until the bones rattled in her body, and yet his desire for her had never been stronger. She was the proudest and the most stubborn of wenches, but she was the only woman he had ever wanted as badly as this. And he was determined to have her!

'Beat me if you will,' Magdalene said, her eyes bright with unshed tears. 'I shan't marry you simply because the Queen has given her permission. I shan't! I have the right to choose for myself.'

Her bottom lip trembled and he laughed, suddenly reminded of the night on board his ship when she had lain in his arms. 'You foolish woman,' he chided. 'Do you imagine I would go to so much trouble to have you if I did not care for you?'

She looked at him doubtfully. 'But you said you did not love me?'

'And you said you hated me?'

Nick smiled, and she felt her heart begin to race wildly. If he did indeed love her, she would be a fool to throw away her chance of happiness, but could she, dared she, believe him?

'Are you saying that you do love me?'

'Perhaps...' His brows rose maddeningly. 'What do you think, Magdalene? Am I a devil? Or merely a man who is prone to doubts and fears, just like you?'

'I ... don't know.'

He touched her cheek with his fingers. 'Will you not give me the chance to show what my feelings are for you? Agree to the marriage tonight, and if you have not learned to trust me in three months' time, I shall give you your freedom.'

'You would let me go, even though Her Majesty has approved our marriage?'

'Yes, if you tell me that it would bring you only unhappiness.'

'Why did you not simply ask me if I would marry you?' She looked at his face intently, trying to read what was in his mind. 'Were you afraid I would refuse?'

'Yes. After the terrible things I said to you, who could blame you?'

She smiled a little tremulously. 'I have said as much and more to you, sir.'

'Perhaps you had good reason.' His eyes were serious. 'I fear I have a wicked temper, Magdalene. I am a jealous man, but I shall try to curb this failing in future.'

Suddenly she knew that she would agree to the marriage. It had always been inevitable, for good or ill. If he loved her, then to be his wife was all she desired, and if he did not... But she would not let herself dwell on that possibility. He had asked her to trust him, and she wanted to accept the offer of peace between them. She would make herself forget the cruel things he had said to her, and perhaps he would forget the accusations she had flung at him. They must try to put all the bitterness behind them, for if they did not, there was only pain in store for both of them.

She looked up at him, feeling slightly faint, as though what was happening was somehow unreal. 'Then we had best go in, sir. Her Majesty will be wondering what has happened to us.'

Nick drew her towards him, his lips brushing hers briefly. 'Ralph told me that you were ill after we parted on board my ship,' he said. 'I did not know that, Magdalene. He also said that you never loved Rodrigo, so why did you plead for him so desperately if he meant nothing to you?'

'He was my countryman, and my cousin's betrothed. I was confused, torn by old and new loyalties. I would not have asked you to spare his life had I known what kind of a man he really was. I hold you blameless in the matter of his death, Nick. He deserved to hang for what he did to Cathy.'

'Thank you.' Nick's smile made her tremble. 'I have decided to put the past behind me. I shall seek no more revenge for

Cathy's death.'

'I am glad. Truly, I am glad, Nick!'

'And your father's death – can you forgive me for that?' His eyes questioned her anxiously.

'I forgave you long ago.' She laid her hand on his arm. 'Will you not forgive Anton? He is still your friend, Nick.'

'He meant to take you from me if he could.' Nick's eyes glittered. 'He betrayed me, Magdalene. Do not ask too much of me.'

'You said you would not be jealous any more?'

'I said I would try to curb my failings.' He laughed harshly. 'Perhaps in time I may forgive him, but things can never be as they were. I should never trust him near you again.'

She sighed, a deep sadness inside her. It was wrong that such a long-standing friendship should end because of her. Yet if she pleaded Anton's case too strongly, it might only make things worse. She had learned to be wary of arousing her lover's jealousy.

'We should go inside now,' she said. 'If we stay here much longer, people will start to gossip.'

'Let them,' he replied, his eyes gleaming; but he took her towards the palace.

Magdalene stood perfectly still as her maid

lowered a gown of cream silk heavily embroidered with silver thread and seed-pearls over her head and began to fasten the laces at the back of the bodice. The girl fingered the stiff material with nervous fingers. It was the most beautiful dress she had ever seen, and it had been commissioned especially for her wedding. Her wedding! The thought sent little tingles down her spine. In one hour she would be Nick's wife.

It was two months since she had allowed him to persuade her into giving her consent; and though he had promised her three months in which to change her mind, the Queen had insisted on a spring wedding. As Nick's behaviour had been exemplary since that night, Magdalene saw no reason to hold out against the royal command. So today was the occasion of her marriage, and in the morning they would set out on their journey home to Treggaron Manor, where they were to spend some time alone.

The ceremony was to take place in Her Majesty's private chapel with only a handful of witnesses, and afterwards, if the weather were fine, a cold collation would be provided for the guests in the gardens. Already the sun was shining, and Magdalene had watched from her window as the servants scurried about making preparations for the feast.

She had spent the previous night in the

palace, in a room found for her by Lady Barbara, who was to be her matron of honour. Sir Ralph had agreed to give the bride to her husband, and Nick was to be supported by another of his friends. It should have been Anton who stood by his side, but the breach between them had not been healed. Magdalene had hoped that, since he was so soon to be her husband, Nick could find it in his heart to forgive his former friend, but any attempt to plead Anton's case led to a coolness between them, and she dared not attempt it. Nick was generous, charming and attentive, paying court to her as if there had never been any bitterness to thrust them apart; but she felt that he held a part of himself aloof from her, and she knew that he was still fiercely jealous. She had only to smile too warmly at another man to bring a scowl to his face.

Perhaps his jealousy would wane once she was his wife. Magdalene could only pray that it might be so. Ever since she had agreed to marry him, he had not tried to make love to her, kissing her briefly when they met as if he were deliberately holding his passion in check. It might be that he would feel more settled once they were man and wife and he was sure of her.

A knock at her door made Magdalene turn expectantly. She smiled as Lady Barbara entered.

'Are you ready, my dear? You look lovely – but then, you always do.'

'Thank you.' Magdalene touched the string of creamy pearls at her throat – one of the many gifts Nick had given her – and took a deep breath. 'Is Sir Ralph here?'

'He is waiting outside. Shall I tell him to come in?'

'Yes, if you will.'

Lady Barbara went out again, and Magdalene took a last glance in her mirror. Her hair was partially hidden beneath a delicate silver head-dress, and her standing ruff was of the finest silk gauze. She was satisfied that Nick would be pleased with his bride's appearance.

'Magdalene, you are ready?'

She turned to Sir Ralph with a look of welcome. 'Yes, sir. I am grateful to you for supporting me today.'

'It is my privilege and my pleasure. Especially for such a beautiful bride!'

She blushed at the compliment, looking at him pensively. 'Once you told me that I could bring Nick only unhappiness. Do you still feel the same way?'

Taking her hand, he raised it briefly to his lips. 'Pray forgive me for my foolish warning, Magdalene. It is true that I once believed it was so – but then I discovered the depth of your love for him.' He frowned oddly. 'I believe in his heart he loves you, child, but he is much changed. I have pleaded for a reconciliation with Anton, but he will not listen to me. It is a pity that he should carry such bitterness in his heart.'

'Yes,' she said, her eyes misty. 'It was my hope that he would ask Anton to support him today.'

'And mine.' Ralph gave himself a mental shake. 'We must not let it spoil your wedding day, Magdalene. Come, we should go now, or we shall be late.'

'I am ready,' she replied, her heart fluttering as she laid her hand lightly on his arm.

In less than an hour Magdalene would be his wife. Nick held the precious thought as he finished dressing, knowing that he ought to be satisfied at last. She would be his, and no man could ever take her from him. Why then was there still this nagging ache inside him, this dull suspicion that would not give him peace? It was his fault, he knew it. She gave him no cause for jealousy, though he watched her every movement with the intentness of a hawk, hating himself for what he did but unable to control the hot jealousy of his eyes. Oh why could he not believe her when she swore she had not betrayed him with Anton? Anton ... his friend... Sometimes the anger burned so deeply in him that he felt sick. Sick of the man he had become. How could he ask for

Magdalene's love and trust, when he would not let himself trust her?

His eyes were full of a wry amusement as he surveyed his own appearance. 'Fine feathers, Treggaron,' he murmured, his lips twisting. For once he had abandoned the severe black he usually favoured, choosing maroon and silver to harmonise with his bride's colours. He slipped a fine ruby ring on his hand, donned a short velvet cloak and his hat, then buckled on his sword. He would remove it for the ceremony, but a man would be a fool to walk unprotected through the streets of London. Besides, only last night the Queen had once again warned him of unknown enemies. It would be foolish to take careless risks.

He was frowning as he walked alone through the quiet streets; the city was not yet fully awake, and the rumble of a water-cart was all that disturbed his thoughts. His friends had arranged to attend him at the house, but had not arrived before he left. Having left them still drinking at a tavern late the night before, he doubted not that they would still be snoring in the landlord's beds. He would likely need to resort to a bucket of water to wake them!

Anton would not have needed to be dragged from a drunken slumber on such a day. The thought brought a cloud of pain to Nick's eyes. In his heart he knew it was up to him to bridge the gap between them, but he could not bring himself to do it. That Anton should plot behind his back to steal her...

He had reached the inn: a respectable house by the river that was much frequented by the younger men, who spent their days at Court and their nights in revelry. A brief enquiry of the landlord confirmed his suspicions. His friends had not yet called for breakfast and were probably asleep. He started towards the stairs, hesitating as he heard a burst of raucous male laughter from the tap-room. Were his friends still drinking? Hovering uncertainly, he heard his own name, and his blood turned to ice water as the speaker's ribald words reached him.

'So Treggaron will wed the Spanish whore! The more fool he!'

'She's a comely baggage, all the same, Allingham. What man would not enjoy the thought of such a one in his bed on a cold winter's night?'

Nick's hand gripped the hilt of his sword. He took two steps in the direction of their voices, and stopped as Allingham's sarcastic tones began again.

'If she were not warming Barchester's bed instead.' Lord Allingham gave a sneering laugh as he lounged negligently in his chair. 'He made it clear enough she was his prop-

erty when I saw them at the Craven Cock...'
The colour drained from his face as he suddenly saw a man's shadow fall across the table. 'Devil take it! Where did you come from, Treggaron?'

There was an uneasy silence as the little group of men looked at one another and then at Treggaron's face. His expression was plainly murderous, and his reputation too well known for any man present to doubt what was in his mind.

Nick's mouth twisted with scorn as he let his eyes travel over their faces. He knew them all by sight, though they were not men with whom he chose to keep company. Idle, drunken wasters the lot of them! Not one of them was fit to wipe Anton's boots.

'Damn you, Allingham, you'll pay for that insult,' Nick snarled. 'You may name the time, place and your friends.'

Allingham's clothes were dishevelled, and it was clear that he had spent the night in drinking with his cronies. He passed a shaking hand across his unshaven chin, his eyes wild and staring as he got warily to his feet.

'No insult was intended, Treggaron. If I had known you were there, I should not have spoken.'

Nick moved towards him, his fury raging out of control. He seized Allingham by the throat, wanting to choke the life out of him.

'You filthy lies disgust me,' he growled. 'Take them back, or I'll break your neck!'

A chair went sprawling behind Allingham as he was suddenly flung backwards. Gasping for breath, he stumbled, and grabbed at the table to steady himself. His eyes were sullen as he stared at Treggaron and saw the scorn in his face. 'I saw them go upstairs together,' he choked. 'She was alone; I thought her available and stopped her, then Barchester came and she went with him to his bedchamber.'

'You lie!' The pain churned in Nick and he clenched his fists, wanting to thrust his sword-point through the cowardly dog's heart. Yet something stayed his hand. Supposing it were the truth! For a long moment he stared at Allingham, hating him, then he turned and walked blindly away, his temples throbbing as the drums beat in his head. Magdalene and Anton ... together ... lying in each other's arms ... Anton and the woman who was soon to be his wife!

All thought of waking his friends forgotten, Nick strode from the inn. His face was tight with fury, his eyes glittering coldly. Nausea swept over him as he tried to gather his wits. They had lied to him – both of them! He had blamed himself for his unworthy suspicions, but he had been right to distrust her. She was a wanton after all, and he was the butt of filthy jests for

Allingham and his like. Worthless, idle scum they might be, but he found their jeers hard to swallow. He could imagine the laughter and sarcasm now that he had revealed his pain, and the knowledge was bitter gall in his throat.

He had wanted to believe in her innocence, but she was a liar and a cheat. Only a fool would take such a woman as his wife! Now that he had proof of her guilt, he would be well within his rights to disown her, to proclaim her shame for all the world to hear!

Magdalene had spent the hour before her wedding in being fêted by the Queen's women. They had given her many pretty gifts, including a crystal posset set chosen personally by Her Majesty. She had had to endure a deal of sly teasing from some of the ladies as they decked her with a bride-lace tied with rosemary, to lead her to the altar in accordance with custom.

Nervous as she was, Magdalene had been glad of the other women's chatter, but now the hour had fled and her heart pounded as she entered the chapel. Her eyes flew to Nick's tall figure as she walked towards him with her hand on Sir Ralph's arm, and her heart began to thud. He had not turned his head to look at her, as a burst of joyful music announced her arrival, and the set of his shoulders was stiff and straight. Was it possible... Could he, too, be nervous?

She kept her eyes downcast, taking her place at his side without daring to glance at him. She was dimly aware of the ceremony, and of the smiling, watchful faces all around them, her own eyes seemingly fixed on the high altar with its cross of gold. Sunlight was filtering in through a small window, making a colourful patch on the stone floor and dazzling her. Roused by a direct question from the chaplain, she gave her responses as she had been taught, and heard Nick do the same.

As he slipped a heavy gold ring on her finger, she lifted her eyes shyly to his, wondering at the sternness of his look. For the past two months she had had only smiles from him, so what was wrong? Why was he looking at her like that? Her heart sank. Surely he was not angry with her again! This time, she had done nothing to deserve such a look.

She was numbed by his coldness, hardly aware when the ceremony was over. His fingers bruised her flesh as he took her arm, almost forcing her from the coolness of the chapel. Suddenly everyone was laughing. They were surrounded by well-wishers as they emerged into the gardens and the warm spring sunshine. The feasting had begun.

It was a nightmare. Surely it was only a

bad dream, Magdalene thought, unable to force a smile to her frozen lips. She could sense the deep, cold anger in Nick as he stood at her side, accepting the good wishes of their guests with apparent pleasure. He smiled at their jests, but she knew that his smiles were false. For her, there was only anger and something akin to hatred in his eyes.

It was almost unbearable. She was being forced to smile and dance as if she were indeed the happy bride everyone thought her. She took the cup of wine someone offered and held it to her lips, but she could not swallow. Food tasted like ashes in her mouth, choking her as she tried to force down a piece of tender chicken. How long must she endure this agony? How long before she could escape? But she could not escape from the angry man at her side – ever! He was her husband now, and she feared the moment when she must be alone with him.

The courtiers had staged a mock joust; the winner's prize to be a kiss from the bride. Everyone watched with amused anticipation, sending sly glances at the groom to see how he would take the joke. Magdalene saw him laugh at the antics of the men, pretending to be amused as a triumphant victor came to claim his kiss. She saw the blue eyes narrow momentarily, as if it were taking him all his will-power to hold his temper in check.

At last it was time for the bride to leave for her husband's home. The guests were disappointed that she was not to be put to bed by her ladies, to await the coming of her lord and his friends: a custom much enjoyed by the guests, but seldom by the bride or groom. However, since the newly-weds were to set out on a long journey on the morrow, their friends were at last persuaded to let them go.

Climbing into a flower-decked coach, Magdalene dug her nails into the palms of her hands, half expecting an angry outburst from her husband the moment they were alone. She shot a nervous glance at him, biting her lips as she saw the hard lines about his mouth. He did not look at her, nor did he speak as the coach bumped and rattled over the uneven roads. Not even when they entered the house did he break his silence, striding past the astonished servants and leaving Magdalene standing alone in the hall as he disappeared into the back parlour.

She hesitated for a moment and then followed him, watching anxiously as he poured wine into a cup and drank it down in one draught. He had drunk sparingly at the feast, and surprise made her speak.

'You are angry,' she said, twisting her silk gloves. 'What is wrong, Nick? Has something happened to annoy you?'

He did not answer, merely refilling his cup and draining it once more, his back still towards her. Magdalene stared at him, her hurt and concern swept away as he ignored her, to be replaced by annoyance. Why was he behaving like this? She had done nothing to merit such boorish treatment, and she would not stand for it a moment longer!

'I asked you a question, Nick,' she said, 'and I demand an answer!'

'You demand an answer!' Nick whirled round then, his eyes blazing with such terrible anger that she fell back, her hand flying to her throat. 'By God, madam, I am minded to give you the answer you deserve...'

She had never seen him quite like this. There was a look in his eyes that frightened her, as if he had been pushed almost to the limit of his endurance, but why? What had she done? Fear was closing her throat, but she knew she had to speak. She could not draw back now.

'Yes,' she whispered, her face white with strain. 'Tell me what I've done to deserve this coldness from you? You pressed me to marry you...' Her words trailed away as a burst of harsh laughter broke from him and he came towards her.

'Yes, I pressed you to marry me,' he said bitterly. 'Now I must pay the price for my madness... I must close my ears and pretend not to hear when scum like Allingham sully my wife's reputation with their filth! I must be content to wear the horns you have given me, and smile as you cuckold me with any man who...'

'What is this?' Magdalene interrupted, her eyes dark with anger. 'Why should you believe the lies this man has obviously told you, without even asking me for an explanation? Lord Allingham is a coward! Anton told me to beware of him because he might seek to harm me...' She gasped as his eyes sparkled with fury. 'I have never betrayed you with any man. Why will you not believe me?'

'You stand convicted by your own words, madam. Allingham approached you, and when your lover came to your rescue you went upstairs with him...'

'Is that all you would accuse me of?' Magdalene stamped her foot, temper making her forget all caution. 'What fools men are! Do you really believe that I would have stayed openly at an inn with Anton if he were my lover? I do not deny that he accompanied me to my room. It was to save me from the unwelcome attentions of such as Allingham. He left me at my door, as Hanna will confirm if you ask her.'

'What has your maid to do with this?'

'She slept in my bed all that night. Ask

her, if you will not accept my word!'

Nick's mouth curved in a sneer. 'She would say anything to protect you.'

It was too much. She had borne all she could take from him. He was no longer the gentle, tender lover who had stolen her heart. His jealousy had changed him so that he was impossible to reason with, and she had heard enough of his insults.

'You are truly a fool!' she snapped. 'If I had wanted Anton, I could have fled with him while you were in the Tower. Your jealousy has unhinged your mind, sir. When you are calmer, we shall speak of this again...' She turned away from him with a haughty look, but he caught her arm. 'Pray let me go, sir. I have no more to say to you.'

'You have no more to say to me? The Devil! Madam, I shall not be pushed aside by you. I have married you despite your treachery, but I shall tolerate no more of it. You will learn respect for your husband, if I have to beat you!'

Magdalene glared at him, trying to wrench free of his grasp. 'Let me go! I hate you! You disgust me!' She gasped as his fingers bit deeper into her flesh and he pulled her hard against him. Seeing the intention in his eyes, she struck out in a temper. As he recoiled from the stinging blow, surprise mingled with the fury in his eyes. Taking advantage of his momentary hesitation, she broke away from him. He tried to catch hold of her sleeve, but she was quicker. Rushing from the room, she ran through the hall and up the stairs to her own chambers, glancing over her shoulder once to see if he were following. Relief flowed through her as she saw no sign of him.

Bursting into her rooms, she found Hanna waiting for her. 'Lock the door quickly,' she commented. 'And do not open it for anyone.'

Hanna stared at her open-mouthed, too bewildered to obey. 'But– But it is your wedding night...'

'I shall not admit him!' She looked angrily at her maid. 'Do as I tell you! He has insulted me once too often. Until he apologises, I shall be no wife to him.'

It was too late. After a moment's hesitation, Nick had followed her, arriving in time to hear her last sentence. He stood glowering on the threshold, then lifted his arm to point a finger at Hanna. 'Out!' he barked, and with a squeal of fright she obeyed. The door was slammed to behind her, and the key turned. Then Nick swung round to face his defiant wife.

'So now you would deny to me those favours you give so willingly to others?'

There was a quiet menace in his voice that shocked her. She stared at him, her heart beating wildly. As he moved purposefully towards her, she backed away from him, fear leaping to her eyes.

'No, Nick,' she whispered. 'You cannot mean to... You cannot! Not you.'

The reproach in her eyes stung him, but the bitter canker of his jealousy had been eating at him for hours. He had managed to hold it back during the feasting, pride making him act the part of a happy bridegroom. Now, the fermenting anger was boiling over, heating his brain to fever pitch. He had forgotten all the things that had first drawn him to her – the pride and passion he had sensed in her that set his blood aflame remembering only the pain he had suffered because of her. She was a thorn in his heart, and he must pluck it out, or die.

When she looked at him so accusingly, he wanted to beat her, to humble her accursed pride. And yet she was so beautiful that the desire to hold her in his arms was stronger than every other emotion. What spell had she conjured that he was so bound to her that he cast aside his pride and wed her, knowing she was a faithless wanton? A hot, mindless wanting rose up in him, pushing all else to a distant corner of his brain. It was not anger that drove him now, but a demented desire that had taken possession of his senses so that he acted blindly without conscious thought. Reaching for her as she instinctively tried to avoid him, his fingers caught the silken material of her bodice, and it ripped as she jerked away from him, revealing the creamy swell of her breasts.

Perhaps it was her cry of alarm that sent him wild, or the sight of her naked flesh. He moved towards her like a man in a dream, swooping to catch her up in his arms as she protested angrily and tried to fight him, stopping her scream with a cruel kiss that took all and gave nothing. As he dumped her unceremoniously on the bed and began to strip away his own clothing, he saw defiance and temper glinting in her eyes, but she made no attempt to escape him.

'If you do this, I shall hate you!' she cried, and he laughed.

'You swore to hate me long ago, *querida!* It matters not to me now. You are my wife, and I shall not be denied.'

She lay still and unresisting as he undressed her, neither helping nor hindering his movements. Her eyes were sullen as he bent over her, and she turned her face to the pillow, trying to avoid his hungry lips. It was useless. He meant to have his way, and her resistance would simply inflame his passion, but he must take all he got of her. She would give him nothing!

Nick saw the smouldering anger in her eyes, smiling wryly. She was so defiant! But she would yield to him as she had yielded before. She might be all the things he had accused her of, but she could not deny her own nature. He had felt the response of her lips to his kisses too often to doubt that he could win her. When she was trembling and helpless in his arms, he would at last have the revenge he sought.

She had expected violence, but his slow, tantalising assault on her body was a torture beyond bearing. If he had raped her she could have accepted it with fortitude, hating him for his bestial behaviour; but rape would not have satisfied the deep need in him for revenge, she knew that now. It was not a swift, meaningless release of physical frustration that Nick wanted; it was her total surrender. Only the sound of her desperate cries as she begged him to possess her would satisfy the craving in him. And he was a master in the art of seduction!

Steeling herself against the unfair tactics he was using to bend her will to his, Magdalene closed her eyes, fighting the betrayal of her own body. She hated him and what he was doing to her, but oh, how her limbs melted beneath the sweet assault of his caresses! She clenched her teeth hard, holding back the cries that would reveal her weakness to him. Yet her body pulsated with a heady sensation that swept her on a tide of passion, carrying her beyond the limits of her control. His slow, sensuous kisses touched every part of her from her toes to the hairline of her brow, sending her senses whirling. She arched towards him wildly as his body covered hers at last, moaning softly as she thrashed beneath him and crying his name again and again as he established his mastery over her.

When it was finished, she lay with her eyes closed, the tears squeezing beneath her lashes as she felt a queer, choking pain in her breast. He had meant to humiliate her, to show her that she was powerless to resist him. She had fought him with all her strength, but he had won. And she hated him for it. Opening her eyes to find him smiling triumphantly down at her, she looked at him with disdain.

'Are you satisfied, sir?' she asked bitterly. 'You have won. I am your possession and you may do as you will with me, but though you may command my body, my heart shall never be yours.'

Nick drew away from her, the smile leaving his face. The victory was his; he had proved that she could not hold out against his love-making, but somehow his moment of triumph had left him empty. She had yielded to him, but she withheld her heart. As the pain twisted inside him, he realised too late what he had done. Carried away by bitterness, he had taken his revenge and lost that which he most desired. He could force her to yield whenever he chose, but if she did not love him, it was not enough.

Dressing, he felt the hard core of disappointment in his chest. Throughout all the months of pain and frustration, he had kept the hope alive in his heart that she would one day learn to love him as he loved her! He had loved her almost from the first, believing that she was the woman he had searched for all his life. His true soulmate. At times he had felt so close to her that it was as if they were one person, but that was long ago and he had destroyed whatever had been between them...

Magdalene sat up as he walked towards the door. 'Where are you going?' she asked, an odd fear clutching at her heart.

Nick turned to look at her, drinking in the beauty of her silky skin and the soft flush of her downy cheeks. The flame of her hair made him blink as if he were blinded by its glory. Gall gathered in his throat, choking him as he thought of the man who had stolen her love from him. At last he managed to speak, pain making him lash out as if to wound her.

'I am going to kill your lover,' he said, then went out. He heard her cry of anguish as he closed the door, and it cut the heart from him. He knew then that either he or Anton must die that night.

CHAPTER NINE

It had begun to rain; a cold drizzle that looked set to last the night. Nick felt it trickle down his neck, dampening the crisp starched ruff, and cursed. Already it was late, and the moon had hidden behind a heavy cloud, leaving only a sprinkling of stars to light the darkness. In the distance he could hear the watchman calling the hour – midnight – and still he had not found the man he sought, though he had searched a score of taverns Anton was known to frequent. A scowl passed across his face. If he did not know him better, he would have believed Barchester was in hiding. Damn the man! Must he search for him the whole night?

Trudging the dark streets, his temper had cooled somewhat, but he knew it was too late for him to relinquish his quest now: he had to find Anton and have it out with him. He should have done this long ago, instead of nursing his bitterness. Was he such a senseless boor that he could not ask the questions that must be answered without flying into a rage? This thing must be settled between them one way or the other, but if it

chanced that the only way to gain satisfaction was a duel, then so be it. Another
duel might provoke the Queen's wrath,
but... Hearing a sound behind him, Nick
stiffened, his instincts alerted. If he were not
mistaken, he was being followed. And by
more than one person.

Looking about him, he saw that he could
not be in a worse position. The street was
narrow and led to the river – a convenient
place in which to dispose of his body if the
men shadowing him had murder on their
minds. Remembering Elizabeth's warnings
of an unknown enemy, Nick cursed himself
for a careless fool. By going from one inn to
another enquiring for Anton, he had
advertised his whereabouts plainly, giving
anyone who had been waiting for such an
opportunity plenty of time to plot against
him. If he had an enemy, this was surely the
moment he would choose to strike!

At least he was armed. If there was to be a
fight, it might as well be now, he thought,
his fingers touching lightly on his sword-
hilt. He stopped walking and swung round
to face whatever lay behind him. Instantly
he saw that he was heavily outnumbered –
there were six of them, and they were almost
upon him. Their faces were masked, but
their clothes proclaimed them as quality.
Even as he drew his sword, he was dimly
aware that he had somehow fallen into a

trap, and that someone had hoped to provoke him into action of this kind – Allingham! The conversation he had overheard had been meant to reach his ears. Of course! He had been seen at the inn the night before, and was expected to return in search of his friends. Allingham and his cronies had probably thought that he would seek revenge immediately; they must almost have given up hope by the time they learned of his search for Anton. What a blind, jealous fool he had been! He was well served for his stupidity.

He had no idea why Allingham should want to kill him, but he knew that a cowardly attack in a dark alley was the method the decadent aristocrat would choose. He had not the courage to fight man to man!

The masked assassins had steadied their advance, realising that he was waiting for them. He saw them glance at one another warily as they approached him, and it confirmed his suspicions. These were not paid bullies, but vindictive braggarts bent on some petty revenge. He threw back his cloak over one shoulder, balancing his sword lightly as he prepared to defend himself. There might be six of them, but there was not a true man among them! His mouth curled with scorn as he waited for their attack, and saw the hesitation in them.

'Come, gentlemen,' he mocked. 'Why do

you wait? Surely the odds are even?'

They rushed at him then, stung to action by his scorn. His sword flashed out in a circle, holding them at bay like a pack of dogs before a maddened bull. He had lost none of his old daring: his sword met and parried each in turn, flicking from one to the other with a consummate skill that kept them hovering uncertainly, not daring to break ranks and risk a single-handed confrontation. But they were too many for one man. A blade slid up his to pierce his sleeve, bringing a sharp searing pain as it scored his flesh. He retaliated instantly, bringing his sword up with a lightning thrust that went under his opponent's guard, entering his side. He gave a scream of pain and staggered back, dropping his weapon as he stumbled to the side of the road and collapsed.

Nick's teeth gleamed whitely in the moonlight. All at once the clouds rolled back and he could see his attackers clearly. The fate of their companion had driven them to desperate action, and of one accord they pressed forward, as though hoping to finish the affair quickly. Nick fought back solidly, but he knew that the odds were against him. He could not continue at this furious pace for much longer, and one slip would have them on him...

He heard a shout from behind and then

the sound of running feet. If there were more of them, he would be overwhelmed by sheer numbers, but he dared not glance over his shoulder. One of his assailants was pressing him so furiously that he was forced to give ground temporarily. Parrying the wild thrusts, he regained the ascendancy, advancing step by step, forcing the other man to retreat. Then something strange happened. Two of the swordsmen gave a shout, turning to meet a new attack. It seemed that someone had come to his assistance. Now the situation was changing rapidly, and he was vaguely aware of someone fighting fiercely at his side, easing the pressure on him. Slashing at the opposing blade, Nick caught it with a deft twist of his wrist and sent it flying through the air. His sudden action shocked his opponent, who hesitated, looked over his shoulder at his friends and then decided to abandon the fight, fleeing down the street in apparent terror.

Nick smiled wryly, turning to seek a fresh challenge; but seeing the flight of their cowardly comrade, the others faltered, and then threw down their swords.

'I'll not die to save Allingham's skin,' one of them cried, ripping off his mask to reveal himself as one of those who had been drinking at the inn that morning. 'It was his idea, Treggaron. For months he has been plotting to kill you.'

Nick stared at him. 'I guessed he was behind it, but why should he want to murder me? We had scarcely met before this morning.'

'I can answer that. Allingham was terrified you would force a duel on him, so he planned to have you killed before you discovered his secret.'

Seconds before he spoke, Nick had seen and recognised the man who had come to his aid. He frowned, bewildered and confused by his own emotions. Silently he lifted his brow, waiting for Anton to continue.

'We always knew Chevron was not the leader of those devils who attacked Cathy. Don Rodrigo was drunk, and merely followed in the wake of the others. Before he died, he whispered a name to me – the name of the man who was the first to violate her...'

'Allingham!' Nick's face blenched with shock. 'Of course! Is he not related to Chevron through his sister's marriage?'

'Ay. We need look no further for our third man, Nick.'

'It's true,' the man who had removed his mask said. 'He confessed it in his cups one night. He was in fear and trembling for his life for months. I'll testify against him, if you'll absolve the rest of us of any blame for this night's work.'

'I'll deal with him myself!' Anton growled.

'No, Anton, let the law take its course now. We have proof of his guilt, and this man will testify – or answer to me!'

'You have my word on it, Treggaron. I was a fool to get involved in this affair. Allingham is scum, and I'll stand by him no longer.'

'Go in peace then – all of you. I'll seek no revenge for what has happened here tonight if you keep your promise. You have my assurance.'

The silent, shamed men replaced their swords, moving away to collect their injured companion and carry him with them. For a time the sound of their boots echoed eerily in the stillness of the night, then faded away. The two men left together in the semi-darkness looked at each other, their eyes meeting and holding.

'So Cathy is avenged at last,' Anton said. 'God be praised!'

'Amen.' Nick's eyes were thoughtful. 'Why did you come to my assistance?'

'I have been searching for you. I heard you were looking for me, and I found you by a process of elimination.'

'I had intended to challenge you to a duel! Allingham told me he saw you at the Craven Cock with Magdalene. I thought…'

'She has never been mine, Nick. I swear it on all I hold dear. I'll not deny I would have taken her from you if I could, but I thought you would be relieved to be free of an unwanted burden. You refused to see her. You acted as if you hated her. She was desperately unhappy, and I could not bear to see her suffer any more. She loves you, Nick. She always has.'

A muscle flicked in Treggaron's cheek, and he avoided the other man's eyes as the pain seared him. 'Perhaps that was true once.'

'It is true, Nick.'

'You do not know...' Nick's breath was ragged in his throat. What had he done? God, how blind he had been! She was innocent, and he had treated her worse than a whore. The agony racked him as he acknowledged all he had lost.

'I know that you would be a fool ever to let her go.' Anton laughed oddly. 'You thought I betrayed you, but I could have had her if I had offered her marriage. She would have come to me then because she thought you hated her. I pretended it would be a casual arrangement, thinking to give her time to recover from the wounds you had dealt her. If she had come to me, I should have married her in time...'

'Why did you not tell her so?' Nick stared at him, understanding dawning in his eyes. 'The Devil! You fool, Anton! Nay, it is I who have been a fool, I see it now. I know you too well, my friend. Can you forgive me?'

'I have never thought of you as other than my friend.' Anton grasped his hand and

328

smiled. 'Go home to your lovely wife, Nick. She was always yours.'

'You—You will visit us at the manor?'

'One day, perhaps. When Magdalene has your son at her breast, and your eyes do not spark with anger every time she smiles at another man.'

Nick nodded his head, knowing that it would be a long time before Anton accepted his invitation. The anger was gone, but there was still a wide chasm between them – a gap that might never be bridged. Only time would heal the hurt in both of them.

All night Magdalene had lain awake, watching the dawn break slowly while the pain settled into a hard lump in her breast. It had been a bitter bride-bed indeed! She felt bruised and torn emotionally, though her body was still tingling from her husband's caresses. She was nothing but a whore to him, to be used for his pleasure whenever he chose. And she could not deny him, for her betraying body responded to his every touch. Oh God, what was she to do? He would kill Anton and then come back to her. She wished that he would kill her, too. At least then she need never feel so wretched again. If it were not such a wicked sin, she would take her own life.

Tears slid silently down her cheeks. She would never forgive him for what he had done – never! He had humiliated her deliberately, making her aware of how weak she was where he was concerned. She should have been able to resist him. She should have found the strength to force him to leave her. As she rose at last to wash and dress in a travelling-gown of green silk, a hard determination settled over her fine features. He would not use her so again. She would die first!

She had been sitting staring out of the window for an hour or more when he came in. She knew instinctively it was he, though she did not turn her head. A little tremor ran along her spine as he spoke and she clenched her fists in her lap to stop them shaking.

'Magdalene...' Nick sounded odd, almost as though he could not breathe. 'I – I want to beg your pardon. Anton has told me ... I should have listened to you. I am sorry ... so very sorry...'

'You are sorry?' Slowly she rose to her feet and turned to face him, her eyes dull. 'It is too late for that now, Nick. I want ... nothing from you. You called me a whore, and I still married you. I married you because I loved you so much that I thought I could bear anything rather than lose you entirely! Tonight you killed that love.'

'No!' he cried, his features contorting with agony. 'Don't hate me, Magdalene. I love you. I was out of my mind ... mad with jealousy because I loved you!'

'You do not know the meaning of the word,' she said bitterly. 'For you it is enough to possess... Well, I am your wife. I shall care for your home as befits my station, but if you ever force me to yield to you again, I shall leave you. If I have to lie in the open fields, I shall do it. I would rather die than let you touch me again.'

He looked into her cold eyes and conceded defeat. She hated him. He had destroyed the love she had once been willing to give so freely. The taste of ashes was in his mouth, and he turned away, unable to face the bitter truth.

'We shall leave as soon as you are ready,' he said. 'I accept your terms, Magdalene. I shall never trouble you again...'

He went out, closing the door softly behind him, while she stared at it unmoving and unmoved. Somewhere inside her a woman was weeping, but the tears would not come. She had wept too much for him. Now there was only a terrible coldness inside her. She was so numb that she could not feel anything at all.

The air was heavy with the scents of summer. Nick breathed deeply of its heady perfume, his eyes narrowed and thoughtful as he surveyed the fields of bright gold

331

wheat that were slowly ripening to perfection. Soon it would be harvest-time, and then he would be forced to return to Court. The Queen had sent an impatient message, but he had pleaded the pressure of work on his estate. Once the mists of autumn began to shroud the land, however, he would have no more excuses. He must return to Court and leave Magdalene alone. He could not take her with him. They scarcely spoke these days, and she left her rooms only to walk in the gardens when she was sure he had left for the day. She was pale and quiet, even with the servants. No, he could not take her to Court as she was now. He was afraid ... but he would not face that fear. Her mood was unnatural, but she was in full possession of her senses. She was not ill: she simply hated him. Perhaps she would be happier if he left...

Yet, despite her coldness, he had seen something in her face now and then. An uncertainty, as though she were beginning to regret the barrier she had erected between them. That she had good cause for her anger he did not deny, nor did he feel any bitterness because of it. The knowledge that he had misjudged her weighed heavily on his conscience. He had built with his own hands the wall that stood between them, and he would willingly tear it down if she gave him any indication that it was what she wanted.

He was unfailingly courteous to her, smiling, though she never responded to his politeness. He was ready to go down on his knees and beg her pardon if she demanded it, knowing that her pride was hurt. Even if he had not quite killed her love, it must take time to reach her heart. Somehow he must be patient until that moment came. He could only hope that it would.

His wandering had brought him to the cove. The tang of salt water and the relentless crashing of the waves against the rocks brought a surge of nostalgia. Surely it was a lifetime ago that he had stolen Magdalene from under the noses of the Inquisition! He felt a sharp longing to be at sea again ... with her!

Something caught his eyes as he stared at the horizon. What were those dark shapes? So many of them that his blood ran cold, and he knew that the day England had long feared had come at last. Philip of Spain had sent his armada against them! He turned to yell at the villager permanently on watch at the top of the cliff, and saw that the beacon was already alight. Soon fires would be burning across the whole country, warning of the invasion.

His pulses racing with excitement, Nick began striding towards the house, his reflective mood dispersed by the promise of action against the enemy. The reconciliation with Magdalene would have to wait until he returned. At the moment he was needed elsewhere! England would have need of all her sons if she were to stave off the Spanish invasion.

'There is a gentleman to see you, Mrs Treggaron,' the housekeeper said, frowning slightly as she saw the pale cheeks of her mistress. 'I am sorry to disturb you, but he is most anxious to speak with you.'

'Then I shall come at once.'

Magdalene got to her feet, steadying herself as she felt a wave of dizziness. It had happened several times recently, and she had been hoping to feel better now that the morning sickness had passed. She smoothed her skirts, determined that no one should guess how ill she had been feeling, though she thought Mrs Penrith suspected her condition. Walking slowly downstairs, she wondered just how long she could keep her secret. In another month or so it must become apparent to everyone, and it was wrong to keep it from the one person who should be told, but she could not bring herself to do it.

Reaching the warm and sunny back parlour where she liked to sit whenever she could be sure of being alone, Magdalene saw her visitor standing by the window, and gasped in surprise.

'Anton!' she whispered. 'Why have you come? If Nick...'

'Nick invited me, Magdalene,' he said, his eyes noting her pale cheeks. 'I have come to join him. He will understand that I could not sail with anyone else now.'

'I do not understand you. Are you... Is Nick going on a voyage?'

'The Spanish armada has been sighted. I came as soon as I heard the news. Fortunately I was at home, and not more than half an hour's ride from here.'

'The– The armada?' The room seemed to spin round her and she grabbed at the table to prevent herself from falling. 'No! You must not...' She had to warn him of the danger.

'Are you ill?' Anton came towards her solicitously. 'You should not fear for Nick, Magdalene. No harm will come to him, I promise you.'

Magdalene shook her head. 'You do not understand...' Her words trailed away and a flicker of fear showed in her eyes as she heard heavy footsteps outside. 'Nick...'

Before Anton could reply, Nick flung open the door. Without hesitation, he strode towards his friend, extending his hand. Anton grinned and took it.

'I knew you would come, Anton.'

'How could I do otherwise?' Anton said. 'We shall sail together, as always.'

335

Magdalene sat down before her knees gave way, watching them with an odd expression. They seemed on the best of terms, as if there had never been any misunderstandings between them, and it annoyed her a little. She saw the excitement in their faces as they made plans to join the other English sea-captains, feeling excluded and slightly jealous. It was silly to feel this way, but she could not help herself. Then Nick turned to her with a smile that sent her heart leaping wildly.

'I fear we must leave you alone, Magdalene, but you must not be frightened. The men from the village are well armed, and they will protect you if there is cause. However, our army is prepared for invasion and I am sure that there will be nothing for you to worry about.'

'The Spanish dogs will never set foot on English soil,' Anton said confidently. 'We'll soon send them scurrying home with their tails between their legs!'

'I must go now,' Nick said, looking at his wife intently. 'Will you not kiss me goodbye?'

She nodded wordlessly, unable to find words to express what was in her heart. Standing stiff and straight, she allowed him to take her into his arms; but as his lips caressed hers tenderly, she melted against him, her arms sliding up round his neck. Tears were in her eyes as he released her, and he brushed them gently away with his thumb.

'I shall come back to you,' he promised. 'Until then, remember that I love you, Magdalene.'

She smiled tremulously, her throat choked with emotion, the silent tears running unchecked as she watched the two men stride away together.

'God bless you,' she whispered when they had gone. 'May the Lord protect and keep you both.' But, in her heart, she knew that only one of them would return.

It was on the nineteenth of July that the Spanish fleet was first sighted off the coast of Cornwall. At first, hardly anyone believed that the attack had come at last. For years, village folk along the coast had frightened naughty children with threats of the wicked Spaniards who would gobble them up if they misbehaved, but no one credited that King Philip would really dare to invade England.

Now the fires were burning across the land, and everywhere on the coast folk crowded to stare curiously at the great armada that threatened their security. The Spanish ships had huge towers and looked almost like floating castles; their looming presence a sight to chill the stoutest heart. Rumours abounded, flying from mouth to mouth as the hysteria mounted... The

English fleet had been destroyed and all was lost… The armada had turned back and the country was saved… In the midst of all the confusion it was said that Sir Francis Drake calmly finished a game of bowls – a tale that set them laughing in every tavern from London to Land's End!

The first victory was England's. The English ships were lighter and swifter than the clumsy Spanish galleons. They struck like lightning and were out of range before the enemy could manoeuvre into a firing position. For seven days a fierce battle raged about the island's shores and the Spanish vessels took a cruel battering, but by the twenty-eighth of July the armada had struggled across the channel and was anchored off Calais, hoping to recoup and take on their main army of fighting men, trained soldiers under the Duke of Parma's command. Under cover of night, the English sent fire-ships drifting among the galleons, causing panic and utter confusion. The Spanish ships were trapped, unable to move swiftly enough to avoid severe damage. It was a trick Sir Francis had used at Cadiz the previous year, but it seemed that the Spanish commanders had learned nothing.

Wounded, but not yet defeated, the Spanish fleet gathered its resources for the inevitable contest. Brave men on both sides lost their lives during the battle of Gravelines; at least sixty of them were English, but the Spaniards were slaughtered in their hundreds. Their ships were packed full of men who had been trained to fight on land; the swords they wore never left their scabbards, and the decks were stained with their blood as the sea turned crimson. All day they were raked with the cruel fire that killed and maimed, destroying the pride of Spain. Those vessels that managed to survive were driven up the coast as they sought an avenue of escape. Terrible storms met them in the North Sea, and they were driven into the rocks or simply broken up by the pounding waves that swamped their decks. Top-heavy in the water, they floundered helplessly, many to be lost without trace. Thirty thousand men had set sail from Spain, but fewer than a third of that number were ever to return.

England waited expectantly. At Tilbury, Elizabeth rode among her loyal troops on a fine grey horse. She wore a steel corselet over her gown to give her the appearance of a commander, and her presence heartened the men, who were constantly on the alert for the news that the Duke of Parma's men were advancing. The Queen spoke to them from her heart; words that stirred men's souls and would live on in their memory.

I have always so behaved myself that under God, I have placed my chiefest strength and goodwill in the loyal hearts and goodwill of my subjects; and therefore I am come amongst you, as you see, at this time not for my recreation and disport, but being resolved in the midst and the heat of battle, to live or die amongst you all; to lay down for God, my kingdom, and for my people, my honour and my blood, even in the dust. I know I have but the body of a weak and feeble woman; but I have the heart and stomach of a King, and a King of England too, and think foul scorn that Parma or Spain or any Prince of Europe should dare to invade the borders of my realm.

It was no wonder that they loved her and called her their 'Gloriana'. She gave the men pride in their country and their Queen, making their hearts stout and their courage high. If she were willing to lay down her life for them, then not a man among them could do less for her. Nor did she run back to the city after delivering her speech, as many would have done. She stayed near the camp until the triumphant news came and it was definite that there would not be an invasion. Her sea-captains – those pirates Spain had so often vilified – had done their duty, and her faith in them was vindicated. At last, when all was safe, Elizabeth returned to London so that the celebrations could begin.

Throughout the land church bells rang

out joyfully. Mothers kissed their children, and lovers embraced beneath a harvest moon. Village folk danced around the maypole, and the Morris Men played the fool and pranced for sheer delight. Farmers took their pitchforks from behind the kitchen doors, returning them to their rightful place in the barn. And at Treggaron Manor Magdalene waited for news with a fearful heart.

She had been expecting it, so when the letter came, she felt no surprise. Opening it with shaking fingers, she scanned the words written there, and gasped. This was not what she had seen in her vision that day on the beach with Anton – it was far, far worse. Nick had been seriously wounded and was lying at an inn at Portsmouth. He had asked for her, and the writer begged her to come at once. It was signed 'A. Barchester'.

Magdalene frowned over the letter, wondering at Anton's formality, but then it fluttered from her hand unheeded as she called for her women. There was no time to lose if Nick were ill. Their quarrel was forgotten in her anxiety. What did her pride matter now? She must go to him at once!

'You'll never go traipsing off to Portsmouth in your condition!' Mrs Penrith scolded. 'And you faint and dizzy as often as not.'

'I should have known you would notice,'

Magdalene said ruefully, 'but I must go to Nick. He is wounded, and he needs me. Do not be concerned; I am much better now. Besides, Hanna will come with me.'

The housekeeper shook her head, but it was plain that Magdalene would not be denied. 'If you are determined to go, then I shall come with you myself.'

'You will accompany me?' Magdalene was surprised. 'But you dislike travelling?'

'I could not rest easy in my mind if I let you go alone in your delicate situation, ma'am. Hanna has no knowledge of these things, and I shall be there to see that you do not tire yourself nursing the master.' Mrs Penrith set her mouth primly, and Magdalene saw that she had made up her mind.

'Then I shall be glad of your company.' She smiled at her trusted servant. 'In truth I have little knowledge of the healing arts, and I know your advice is sound.'

Mrs Penrith beamed at her, hurrying away to set the maids flying about their business. There was much to be done if the household were not to disintegrate in her absence!

Left to herself, Magdalene sipped a glass of cordial to steady her nerves. She was trying to keep calm for the sake of her unborn child. The physician she had summoned only the day before had told her that her condition was not unnatural, but warned her to take great care of herself for the next few weeks. He would not be best pleased with her for undertaking a journey at such a crucial time. But she had to go, even if it meant she risked her babe. She had to see Nick and tell him that she loved him. If he should die now, thinking that she hated him, she could not bear it...

It was dusk when they reached Portsmouth after a slow, tedious journey that had taken a day longer than necessary, due to Mrs Penrith's caution. She had lectured the coachman before they left the manor, insisting on a slow, steady pace that would not jolt her mistress too much. Magdalene had been impatient for their journey's end, fearing that they might arrive too late, but in her heart she was grateful for the older woman's concern. The child she carried was precious and it would break her heart to miscarry now, when it might be all she would ever have of Nick. Yet the delay set her nerves screaming, and she was fretful when the coachman admitted that he was not sure of the direction of the Queen's Head tavern. After some enquiries by their second groom, it was ascertained that the inn they sought was close by the harbour.

Magdalene was tired when she alighted from the coach and her head had begun to ache, but not wanting a fuss, she said nothing to her companion. Looking at the outside of the inn, she thought that it was of a rather unsavoury appearance and wondered at Anton for choosing it; but perhaps Nick's condition was so desperate that he had had no choice. The thought made her uneasy, and she hurried Mrs Penrith inside. A sour smell of stale wine made her wrinkle her nose, and she wondered again if it was the right place as the host came to greet them.

'What may I do for you, ladies?'

'I believe my husband may be here,' Magdalene said. 'I received a message to say that he was wounded and lay in one of your chambers...'

'You'll be Mrs Treggaron, then.' He sniffed loudly, wiping his hand across his nose. 'Who be that with you?'

'Mrs Penrith is my housekeeper.' Magdalene frowned. 'Pray be good enough to conduct me to my husband's chamber, sir.'

He looked at her craftily, his eyes narrowing. 'Be she coming with you?'

'Certainly I shall accompany my mistress,' Mrs Penrith snapped. 'Don't stand there gawping, man! Take us to Mr Treggaron.'

'As you wish.' The innkeeper's beady eyes gleamed with a secret satisfaction. 'If you'll follow me upstairs then, I'll take you to the gentleman.'

There was no light on the stairway, only the wavering flame from the chamberstick carried by their guide. He turned left at the

344

top, and they followed along a narrow passage until they reached a door at the end. Here the innkeeper stopped and knocked sharply.

'The lady you are expecting is here, sir – and her housekeeper with her.'

The door was opened, revealing a dark bedchamber lit only by a candle on a table by the bed. The hangings were tightly drawn around it and it was impossible to see if anyone was lying there. Magdalene stepped quickly inside, and her eyes strained towards the bed as she moved towards it. A sound startled her, and she glanced over her shoulder just as the door was slammed behind her. She heard Mrs Penrith's indignant cry as she was shut out; it was followed by a muffled scream and a thud, then silence. Seeing a shadowed figure by the door, Magdalene gave a gasp of fear. What was happening? That wasn't Anton... She caught her breath as the shadow moved towards her through the gloom, and she saw a face she remembered from the nightmares that had once haunted her.

'You!' she ejaculated, her blood running cold as she realised she had walked into a trap. 'I demand that you open that door and let me go at once!'

'So the years have not changed you, Doña Magdalene. You are as proud as ever.' The priest's soft voice sent a chill of horror through her. 'I am so happy that you decided to accept my invitation. I have waited for this day for a long, long time.'

Magdalene stared into her enemy's face and shivered as she saw the hatred in his eyes burning like fire. He had waited for his revenge on her all this time, and now she was his prisoner.

'Father Ludovic,' she said calmly, knowing that it was the light of madness in his eyes, 'you cannot hope to get away with this? Surely you know that my husband will come looking for me?'

His lips curled in a sneer. 'Your husband is in London, celebrating his victory with all the others. By the time he realises what has happened to you, you will be on board one of Don José's ships and bound for Spain. Once you have been delivered to the Inquisition, he can legally take possession of your estate, and I shall have my reward. But long before that I shall have taken my own, personal revenge…'

Magdalene looked into his eyes and the sickness rose up in her as she realised what he meant to do. Oh, dear God, no – not that! All at once the room was whirling around her and she felt the ground move beneath her feet. The blackness was closing fast as she crumpled into a heap at his feet.

While the whole of England celebrated the

magnificent victory, Elizabeth, its Queen, lay in her chamber weeping. The Earl of Leicester was dead, and she was inconsolable. Her beloved Robin was gone from her. No more would he be her 'eyes', and she had lost the one man she believed had truly loved her. She was distraught with grief and would see no one.

Nick left London before the news of Leicester's death reached the Queen. He was anxious to be at home again, and he had not felt inclined to join in the celebrations. There was a deep sadness in his heart, and he wanted to share his grief with the one person whom he felt would understand. England's victory had been glorious, but not without its price. *Treggaron Rose* had suffered some damage in the fierce fighting and the shattered main-mast had trapped three men beneath it as it fell. One of them was a man whose like he would not see again. Anton had died in his arms, and tears pricked Nick's eyes as the memory rode with him.

Sighing, Nick turned his horse towards the house, relieved to be at home at last. How good it would be to see Magdalene's lovely face again. He had thought of her constantly these past few days, and he knew that somehow he must mend the situation between them. Life was too short to waste in bitterness – he knew that now, to his cost. He had been taught a sharp lesson that he would not soon forget. He believed that his wife had begun to regret the coolness between them before he left, and that perhaps she still cared for him a little.

As he dismounted, a groom came to take his horse, and he saw a startled look in the man's eyes. His heart jerked and some inner instinct sensed trouble. Then Hanna came flying down the steps towards him. He moved to meet her, fear making his voice sharp.

'What is it, Hanna?' he asked urgently. 'Where is your mistress?'

'She has gone, sir.'

'Gone?' The pain struck deep into his heart. Surely she had not carried out her threat to leave him! 'Where has she gone?'

Hanna's eyes were dark with fear. 'There was a letter, sir. It– It said that you lay ill at the Queen's Head at Portsmouth, and my mistress left at once. Only the gardener told me afterwards that the messenger was a foreign gentleman, and I wondered…'

'She went to Portsmouth alone?' Nick said, fear making him clutch wildly at her arm. 'You let her go alone?'

'Mrs Penrith went with her, sir – because of her condition.'

'Her condition?' He stared at her. 'Is she ill?'

'She is with child, sir. I – I thought you knew?'

A muscle flicked in Nick's cheek. Magdalene was with child! She was carrying his child! It was no wonder that she had been acting so strangely these past weeks. She was carrying his child, and she was in danger. The letter was a trick of some kind – and it could have come from only one of two persons. In either case, it meant that his wife's life was at risk!

'Get me a packet of food and a flask, girl, and tell the groom to saddle me a fresh horse. I leave for Portsmouth without delay!'

'Will you take me with you, sir? If my mistress is in danger...'

'I cannot stop for you,' he muttered. 'Every minute is precious if I am to save her. Now do as I tell you. She will have need of you when I bring her home.'

Hanna fled, and Nick strode into the house.

CHAPTER TEN

Magdalene's head was aching, and her eyes hurt when she opened them to find herself staring at a candle flame. She was lying on a bed in a dark room and someone was bending over her. She gave a cry of alarm and shrank back as she saw who it was.

'If you touch me, I shall scream!'

'Your screams would do you little good!' the priest sneered. 'The landlord has been well paid, and your woman has been bound and gagged. We shall take her with us and dispose of her when we are at sea.'

'You are evil!' Magdalene whispered. 'She has done you no harm. Why must you kill her, too?'

'Because she has seen and heard too much. Your husband must believe you have run away with your lover. You will write a letter, telling him that you are well and that you do not wish to see him again.'

'No! No, I shall never do that.' Magdalene looked at him defiantly. 'Even if you put to sea, Nick will find you. He will come after me and he will kill you.'

'You are so sure of your power over him, witch? Yet your spells can be broken.'

'I do not need spells ... that is all your superstition.' She twisted her mouth in scorn. 'My husband will follow me because he loves me. He is a true and natural man – not a fanatic eaten up by lust...'

Even as she flung the words at him, she knew that they were true. Nick had sometimes been cruel to her, but it was because of misunderstandings between them. The nature of their love was such that it could never have run smoothly. They would always quarrel because they were both passionate and hot-tempered, but despite all their quarrels their love was too strong to be destroyed – ever. And perhaps she had in part been to blame for the rift between them on their wedding night. Nick had tried to apologise, but in her indignation she had refused to listen to him. Yet he had never really harmed her. She had called him a murderer, but he had saved her life more than once. She had said that she hated him and would laugh to see him dead, but after all he had suffered, he had showered her with gifts. He had seen her with Anton, and she knew he believed that she had betrayed him, but still he had married her. Only when he was driven to desperate action by his jealousy had he sought revenge – and, even then, he had been gentle with her. It was only her pride that had suffered at his hands.

'Your pride will be your undoing yet, witch!'

The fanatical look in her enemy's eyes warned her, and Magdalene rolled away as he grabbed at her, scrambling from the far side of the bed, and making a dash for the door. She struggled with the key and felt it turn at last, but it had taken her too long. He grasped her from behind, jerking her away from the door. She lashed out at him with her nails, gouging a deep line across his cheek. He thrust her from him with a curse, and she stumbled, almost falling.

'Witch! Mark me with your talons, will you? You shall pay dearly for your defiance, I promise you.'

His eyes glittered insanely. He was breathing hard, his mouth slack as a trickle of saliva ran down his chin, and he giggled like an idiot. Revulsion flooded through Magdalene, making the vomit rise in her throat. She backed away from him cautiously, her eyes seeking a way of escape. A weapon – she needed a weapon of some kind. Then she saw the pistol lying with a pair of saddlebags, and hope flared in her. She would kill him rather than submit to his foul lust!

Somehow he must have guessed what was in her mind. As she made a dart towards the pistol, he lunged at her and caught her, wrestling with her as she tried desperately to reach the pistol. He forced her away from it by reason of his superior strength, and she felt the bed at the crease of her knees. Giving a scream, she tried to fight him off, but he pressed her back, and then she was falling and he lay on top of her. The sour smell of him was choking her as she twisted her head wildly, trying to avoid his greedy mouth. His hands were scrabbling at her bodice, pawing at her breasts as his weight kept her pinioned to the bed, crushed beneath him.

'I have you now,' he muttered feverishly. 'You were always so proud – so haughty – as you dismissed me from your presence, as though I were less than the dust beneath your feet. I could not sleep for thinking of you … wanting you…'

'You disgust me!' Magdalene hissed. 'You had no right to think of me with lust. I was betrothed to another.'

He laughed: a high-pitched sound that made her shudder. He was surely mad! She had thought him merely a fanatical member of the Inquisition, but he was insane.

'That fool!' he cried scornfully, his eyes gleeful like a child who has been caught in an act of mischief. 'He thought to dismiss me – me! He threatened to report me to my superiors when he found me in bed with that slut of a servant wench. She was willing enough before he came, but she ran to him with tears and tales of cruelty … he was going to send me away in disgrace, and I knew I had to kill him.'

'You killed Don Sebastian?' Magdalene gasped, recoiling in horror. 'You are a murderer: a disgrace to your calling. A devil!'

She twisted wildly beneath him, arching and tossing as she fought to rid herself of his weight. His knee was forcing her legs apart and she felt him lift himself to rearrange his clothing. As she screamed again, the door burst open and he jerked with surprise. He turned his head and glanced over his shoulder, a cry of alarm escaping his lips as he saw the man standing on the threshold. For a moment he stared in sheer disbelief, then he rolled hastily away from Magdalene, falling to the floor in an unsightly huddle. Before he could rise, the cold-eyed avenger was towering over him.

'I'll kill you for this!' Nick said between clenched teeth. 'If you've harmed her...'

'He has not,' Magdalene choked, emotion stinging her throat. 'You came just in time.'

The priest had risen. His face was deathly pale and his fat body was quivering with fear. He looked at Nick, his eyes glittering in the candlelight.

'She– She made me do it,' he babbled, all control gone as he saw the look in Nick's eyes and knew himself doomed. 'She is a witch! She cast a spell over me – I became her creature. I killed the Don because she

355

had taken possession of me...'

'Serpent! From the first, I saw the lust in your eyes when you looked at her. She is no witch, but you are the spawn of the Devil, and it is to him you will return this night.'

Desperation drove the priest to an act of madness. He suddenly grabbed the pistol Magdalene had tried to reach earlier and pointed it at Nick, his hand shaking so much that he could scarcely hold it steady.

'Stay away from me,' he wavered. 'If you come any nearer, I shall kill you!'

'No!'

Magdalene had rolled over to sit on the edge of the bed when she realised what had happened. She was behind him and she acted instinctively, launching herself at his back and pushing him with all her strength. He staggered, steadied himself and turned, bringing the butt of the pistol down on the side of her head. She gave a little cry of pain, sinking to her knees before collapsing. The last thing she saw was Nick's face before the darkness claimed her.

Magdalene's head moved on the pillow and she whimpered with pain. A cool hand stroked the damp hair back from her forehead, easing the ache at her temples. Her eyelids fluttered and then she opened her eyes, looking up into Nick's face. As memory stirred in her, she clutched at his arm, her eyes dilating with fear, but he only smiled and bent to brush her lips gently with his own.

'Try to sleep, my darling. You are quite safe now.'

'W-What happened to-to...'

'He will never harm you again, Magdalene. He is with his master in hell.'

'He was mad.' She shivered. 'I was afraid he would kill you! It was a foolish thing to do, wasn't it?'

'It was a brave act, my love. Don't talk about it any more. You must rest. You have our child to think about now.'

She smiled sleepily, not wondering how he knew, but content that it should be so. 'You will not leave me?' she said, needing to have him close even while she slept.

'I shall stay with you always,' he promised, stroking her glorious hair as it spread out on the pillow. 'Here by your side – if you wish it?'

She nodded shyly, and he lay down on the bed beside her, his body close to hers but not touching her. She let her eyes dwell on his beloved features and sighed. How good it felt to have him near – and how often she had longed for him in the lonely nights at Treggaron Manor!

'We are not at home?'

'No. I brought you to a decent inn, and Mrs Penrith tended you herself. When I found her, she was near out of her mind with worry over you, though unhurt herself.' He smiled and touched her cheek. 'We shall go home when you are well enough to travel.'

'Tomorrow,' Magdalene said, and nestled against him. 'I shall be well enough by then.'

In the morning her head was still sore, but the throbbing ache had gone. Nick could deny her nothing. She wanted to go home, and home they went. For a week she was fussed over by her husband, Mrs Penrith and her maid. They fluttered round her anxiously, never allowing her to do so much as rescue a fallen kerchief, and in the end she could bear no more of it.

'I am quite well,' she announced one sunny morning. 'I am going for a walk, and if anyone tells me I must not, I shall scream!'

Nick grinned as he saw the sparkle in her eyes. 'I should not dream of forbidding you, madam! May I come with you if I promise not to say one word?'

She laughed, her annoyance evaporating as she saw the caressing look in his eyes and felt the familiar melting sensation inside her. 'I should be glad of your company, sir. Providing you do not fuss over me!'

'You have my word on it! I may even set you to milking in the dairy.'

She smiled at his jest, shaking her head at

him in mock reproof. This was the man she
had fallen in love with so long ago – and she
was so glad to have found him again. She
was happier than she had ever been, and she
knew that only the moment when she held
his son in her arms would give her more
pleasure than she felt now.

It was too warm for her to need a wrap of
any kind, though Mrs Penrith hovered with
a lace scarf just in case. Nick shook his head
waving her away and winking at Magdalene
as he gallantly offered her his arm.

'Shall we go?'

Magdalene laid her hand on his arm, but
once they had left the house, he grinned and
slipped it round her waist, holding her close
to him as he bent his head to kiss her.

'Are you truly well, my love?'

'I feel wonderful,' she said, laughing up at
him. 'The dizzy spells have gone at last. But
why do you ask?'

'I have been summoned to present myself
at Court. Her Majesty has been coaxed
from her chamber – actually, Burghley had
the door broken down – and she wishes to
see me. It seems that I am to be honoured
with a knighthood for my services to the
Crown.'

'Then you must go,' Magdalene said at
once. 'I shall miss you, of course, but you
will come back to me soon?'

'Will you come with me? The journey

would be uncomfortable for you, but we could travel very slowly.'

'I am well enough to undertake the journey now. The child will not be born for months. We both know when it was conceived.' An odd look flickered in her eyes, and his arm tightened about her.

'Can you ever forgive me for what happened that night? Can you forget that our child was conceived in anger?'

'It was my fault as much as yours, Nick. It matters only that your child is in my womb – I was not thinking of the babe...'

'What then?' He looked down into her anxious eyes and smiled. 'What foolish notion is in your head now, my love?'

'It is not a foolish notion!' She pulled a face at him. 'Are you sure you want me to come to Court with you? You– You will not be jealous if a man looks at me too often?'

'I shall be mad with jealousy if you smile at him too warmly,' Nick replied honestly. 'I cannot change my nature, Magdalene. But I shall not suspect you of having an affair with every man you speak to. I have learned to trust you. You see, I know you love me now. I was a fool ever to doubt you.'

'Oh, Nick,' she whispered, reaching up to plant a kiss on his lips and laughing. 'We were both fools! I should have known you cared for me long ago.'

'I worship you,' he said, holding her close

to his heart so that they were as one. 'You are the woman I have searched for all my life. My heart – my soul – the very breath I take...'

She sighed contentedly as he kissed her, then looked up, a hint of mischief in her eyes. 'I am quite well now, Nick. Could– Could you not come to my room tonight?'

His eyes glowed with blue fire. 'Are you sure it's what you want?' he asked. 'On our wedding night, I behaved no better than those devils who attacked Cathy. I can never forgive myself...'

'You must.' She soothed him with a kiss. A great tenderness filled her heart and she knew that her love for this man went beyond passion. She would love him to the end of their days, and her love would never waver no matter what the future had in store for them. 'You must forgive yourself, for I shall not allow any shadows from the past to cloud our lives. I love you, Nick, with my heart, my soul and my body...'

He gathered her to him, his lips saying more than words could ever convey. Then he held her away from him, gazing down into her face. 'Before he died, Anton told me that you thought I was haunted by my love for Cathy when we first met. It was not so, Magdalene. I was haunted by the cruel fate that had robbed her of life. She was young and sweet – and I loved her as a sister. I think that she once had hopes of a stronger relationship between us, but I never felt more for her than a brother's true affection. You see, I had been father, mother and brother to her when she was left with no family. I was haunted because I thought I had failed her.'

Magdalene nodded, knowing that he spoke the truth. 'I myself had begun to think it was something like that. You gave me her rooms because they were the best in the house.'

'I was ashamed that I had so little to offer you on board my ship. I wanted to shower you with gifts, to lay the world at your feet, but I was afraid of frightening you. There was something in your eyes when we met that told me you had suffered.'

'I had lost both my parents, and I loved them,' she said. 'The man I remember was not the monster you knew, Nick. Even though I know the truth now, I shall always think of him as he was with me.'

'And I would not have it otherwise. His death lies between us.'

'No.' She touched her fingers to his lips. 'There are no shadows hanging over us, my beloved husband. The past, with all its pain and tragedies, has gone. Let it lie. We have the future before us. Our child will be the completion of our happiness.'

'Yes. I have made up my mind that I will

give up the sea and stay at home. Now that I am to be Sir Nicholas, I think I should buy more land and perhaps build a bigger house. What say you, Lady Treggaron?'

'What, will you not take me adventuring with you again?' She pouted at him mischievously, and then she laughed. 'Oh, I can see there will be no bearing with you now! You will be so fine and full of airs. I must tell Mrs Penrith that she must curtsy to you every time she addresses you.'

'Wretch! You will do nothing of the sort. I care not for titles – and you know it.'

'Indeed?' She arched her brow at him. 'For myself, I have a hankering to be Lady Treggaron. Yes, it has a grand sound to it. I think I shall come to Court with you, sir – if only for the pleasure of hearing myself addressed so by all those ladies who ignored me the first time. And I shall wear my burgundy gown – though I fear the seams will need to be let out a trifle – and the pendant you gave me.'

'More than a trifle,' Nick retorted. 'Lady Treggaron, you are growing fat...'

She gave a little scream of indignation and he caught her to him, his eyes alight with laughter as he looked down at her. 'It means only that I have more of you to love,' he teased, nibbling at her earlobe. 'Must I wait until tonight, my darling? Could you not tell Mrs Penrith you wished to rest – and then I could sneak into your rooms when no one was looking?'

'Sir, I do not know if you realise that what you are saying is immoral? It is scarcely noon!' She glanced up at him, and he caught his breath as he saw the look in her eyes. 'Yet I think, perhaps, I might take a little rest...'

The publishers hope that this book has given you enjoyable reading. Large Print Books are especially designed to be as easy to see and hold as possible. If you wish a complete list of our books please ask at your local library or write directly to:

Magna Large Print Books
Magna House, Long Preston,
Skipton, North Yorkshire.
BD23 4ND